THE FALLEN VISCOUNT

NOTORIOUS NIGHTINGALES
BOOK THREE

WENDY VELLA

This is a work of fiction. Any resemblance to actual persons, living or dead, business establishments, events or locales is entirely coincidental. All rights reserved. Except for use in a review, the reproduction or use of this work in any part is forbidden without the express written permission of the author.

The Fallen Viscount is published by Wendy Vella

Copyright © 2024 Vella Ink

Sign up to Wendy's newsletter: wendyvella.com/subscribe

WENDY'S BOOKS

The Notorious Nightingales
The Disgraced Debutante
An Imperfect Gentleman
The Fallen Viscount

The Raven & Sinclair Series
Sensing Danger
Seeing Danger
Touched By Danger
Scent Of Danger
Vision Of Danger
Tempting Danger
Seductive Danger
Guarding Danger
Courting Danger
Defending Danger
Detecting Danger

The Deville Brothers Series
Seduced By A Devil

Rescued By A Devil
Protected By A Devil
Surrender To A Devil
Unmasked By A Devil
The Devil's Deception

The Langley Sisters Series
Lady In Disguise
Lady In Demand
Lady In Distress
The Lady Plays Her Ace
The Lady Seals Her Fate
The Lady's Dangerous Love
The Lady's Forbidden Love

Regency Rakes Series
Duchess By Chance
Rescued By A Viscount
Tempting Miss Allender

The Lords Of Night Street Series
Lord Gallant
Lord Valiant
Lord Valorous
Lord Noble

Stand-Alone Titles
The Reluctant Countess
Christmas Wishes
Mistletoe And The Marquess
Rescued By A Rake

*This book is for my dad who was one of the best men I knew.
You taught me how to be the best version of myself because that was how you lived your life.
A true gentleman and hero.
Love and miss you always dad.*

*Any man can be a father, but it takes someone special to be a dad.
-Anne Geddes*

CHAPTER ONE

Leopold Nightingale, bearer of the disgraced title of Viscount Seddon, listened to the clip-clop of hooves as he and Ram rode through the rapidly darkening London streets.

Once, he would have been preparing for an evening out in society. Some ball or function where his chief aim would have been to ensure he looked his best and people knew it.

Leo was often disgusted with memories of the man he'd been... and angry. He felt like he was always angry. He just rarely let anyone see what lay beneath the controlled facade he outwardly portrayed.

"I thought the Butcher was a bit off his stride this evening," Ramsey said.

"It's the first time he's been knocked out in fifty fights, I believe," Leo added.

When Ramsey Hellion had knocked on the front door of his family's home, Leo had been enjoying a rare moment of solitude, as his aunt and uncle had taken everyone out to the park. He had said, politely, that he had no wish to go to a boxing match. Ram had then debated with him, which he excelled at, until Leo had yielded simply to shut him up.

"I fear, after the beatings he has taken in his lifetime, he will not be a happy old man when the day he retires eventually comes," Ram said.

"I know how long I take to recover from a fist in the face," Leo said.

"When did you last receive a fist to the face?"

"Not that long ago, actually."

They were silent as they navigated around a large, lumbering landau. Leo glanced in the window, and a woman caught his eye. He drew back slightly, which had Ram obscuring his view. It was possible she walked in society and they'd once known each other. Leo had no wish to become reacquainted. The reaction was pity or disdain. He liked neither, so he avoided those from his old life whenever possible.

"Do you plan to hide forever from both your title and the world you were raised to live in, Leo?" Ram said.

The words nearly unseated him, but squeezing his thighs into the saddle, Leo stayed upright.

"I beg your pardon," he said in his most haughty Viscount Seddon voice. The title may be as useless as the man he'd inherited it from, but occasionally it came in handy.

"You heard."

"I have no wish to continue this discussion."

Leo had been raised a nobleman. He'd loved his life, because it had allowed him to do as he wished. As the heir, he'd been a spoiled and small-minded fool. He'd cared little about anyone but himself. All that had changed with his father's death and the shame and disgrace that followed.

The Nightingales had been plunged into turmoil. If it weren't for their father's youngest brother and wife, Leo wasn't sure where they would have ended up. He liked to think he was strong enough to have cared for his siblings, but it wasn't as if he'd been equipped to cope with what life had thrown at them. His uncle and aunt had stepped in and taught the Nightingale siblings to be a family, and he would be forever thankful for that.

Ram snorted. "My cousin is the haughtiest bastard I know, even if your sister has softened him ever so slightly. Your pompous tone does nothing to deter me, Leo."

Ram was cousin to Leo's brother-in-law, Gray. Leo usually enjoyed his company, as the man was funny, intelligent, and as yet unwed, like him.

"I left because my father's actions made it impossible to stay." His tone was icy.

"That was years ago, Leo. Will you let him keep you from what you once loved?"

The vision slid into his head so fast, it unseated him, and he slid sideways. Ram's hand shot out and steadied him.

"I'm sorry. I didn't mean to upset you. It's just my way of saying what I'm thinking. Both a curse and a blessing, so my mother tells me, but it does cut through all the chatter around an issue," Ram said.

"I—ah…."

"Leo? What's wrong?" Ram's words were urgent now.

"I have to go." He looked around him. "That way." He pointed to a narrow lane to his left.

"To avoid me?"

"No."

"All right, then. Why?"

"I need to find something, Ram. You go home."

"No."

"Pardon?"

"No. I am not leaving you in your current shocked state to ride about darkened streets alone," Ram said calmly.

"I am more than capable of looking after myself," Leo

said. He then briefly closed his eyes and pictured the single gold cuff link.

Why did he need to find it now, tonight?

"Yes, I know you are, and that you Nightingales are all well-schooled by your uncle on how to defend yourselves. However, I am not going anywhere."

"Please leave," Leo said, wondering what was driving him to seek the cuff link his grandfather had given him. He couldn't even remember when he'd lost it.

"You Nightingales have many gifts, but you are not alone in that, you know," Ram said as Leo started his horse moving again.

"What the hell does that mean?"

Left, the voice inside his head said. Suddenly the lethargy that had been dogging his footsteps for days fled, and in its place was the hum of expectation. *Why?*

"It means I am not a wet-behind-the-ears weakling," Ram said. "I am more than able to protect myself in a dangerous situation. I don't just have a handsome face and sharp wit, you know."

"Imagine my surprise," Leo said, wondering what he was about to step into. "But I don't think I'll need your protection, thank you."

"I was raised in India, as you know, Leo," Ram continued, drawing Leo's attention back to him. "My parents put me in the care of their staff—Kavya and her husband, Ishaan. They were wonderful people who taught me a great deal. Part of my education at their hands was learning to fight. So have no fear that I will not aid you should it come to that."

Leo looked at Ram. He was a man who did not seem bothered by much and was most often laughing. Leo's sisters Frederica and Matilda said he was handsome, and they had made him promise that one day he would wed one of them.

However, perhaps there was a great deal more to him they had yet to see.

"Now, where is it we must go?"

"Left," Leo said. "We go that way." He pointed to a street.

"Why?"

"I just need to."

"It is to do with this gift you all have. Or, more importantly, the one you deny?"

"I don't deny it," Leo lied.

"Of course you do. Ellen said you refuse to acknowledge it, and then suddenly you'll appear with something that has been lost for some time, or you'll say things like 'We need to go there and find this.'"

"Shut up, Ram." Leo rode his horse down the narrow lane and then turned right at the end.

"What are we looking for, Leo?"

"A cuff link."

He could feel Ram's eyes on the side of his face. "You are joking, surely? How is it possible to find something so small?"

He blew out a loud breath. How the hell did he answer that? "Any chance you can just shut up?"

"No chance at all," Ram said. "I like to think of it as one of my finest qualities."

"Persistence?"

"Annoyance," Ram said.

Leo let the voice inside his head direct him down narrow roads, where danger could lurk in crevices.

"Be alert, Ram."

"Aye."

Leo wasn't sure how far they'd traveled, but as yet, they had not reached where he was supposed to go... which was foolish, as he was the one guiding himself. Even thinking those thoughts made him sound like a fool.

"We are heading to the Thames, Leo."

"I can see that, Ram."

"South Bank," Ram added, "near Vauxhall Gardens."

"I can see that too." He could feel the tension inside him climb as the water appeared before him. His throat felt tight, and his body was so tense, his back ached.

"Is that the Duke of Allender's yacht?"

"How would I know what his yacht is like?" Leo asked, his eyes scanning the area before him.

He felt twitchy as the crowds grew. This was a haunt of the wealthy. Men and women wandering about to be seen. Some heading to the gardens, as he once would have been.

"Are we any closer to your location?" Ram asked, raising his hat. "Good evening, Lady Pickle. How lovely you look."

The lady tittered at him. Her eyes then landed on Leo, and the smile fell from her lips. Leo nodded and rode on.

What am I doing?

"When did you lose this cuff link, Leo?"

"Many years ago." The urgency was almost choking him now. Leo kept his eyes forward, searching for… what? Would he simply find the cuff link on the road before him? *Why now?*

Moving closer to the water, he dismounted, watching as a small rowboat approached.

"Hold my horse, Ram."

"Pardon?"

Leo threw the reins at him.

"What's going on?" Ram asked.

"Oh, it is you, Mr. Hellion," a woman gushed. "I had so hoped to see you this evening."

"Miss Tattling, my night is now complete with your arrival."

Ignoring the flirting going on behind him, Leo made his way to the edge of the bank and looked at the rowboat's occupants. Beside the oarsman, there were three others on board. Two women and a man. He recognized the man, as he was the only one facing Leo. Lord Charles Bancroft.

"Lord Seddon? I say, it is you." A voice to his left queried.

Leo was already tense, but having someone from his past approach made him more so. He turned from the rowboat. "Mr. Anderson." He bowed.

"Wonderful to have you back among us, my lord." The man looked genuine, but you could never really tell. Leo nodded, bowed again, and walked away from him without a word to where the boat would reach the bank.

Taking the steps down to the small platform, he heard the voices behind him. His name was being thrown about like leaves in the wind now. He'd just done what he loathed: shown his face willingly in society.

The boat bumped into the dock, and the oarsman climbed out, as did Lord Bancroft. He turned to help one woman out. Leo stood back, watching. His cuff link was close, but why did he need to find it now? As that thought entered his head, he watched the other woman stand. She then looked his way and stumbled. Seconds later, she was tumbling into the water.

"Cyn!" the other woman screamed.

Leo tore off his jacket and jumped in. He could swim; his uncle had taught him that also.

"Hurry!" the woman cried. "Charles!"

"I can't swim, damn it!" Bancroft said the words as he climbed back into the boat and grabbed an oar.

Leo saw the woman surface a few feet in front of him, her hands slapping the water to keep herself above it, but she sank again. Leo dived and grabbed a handful of her clothing. Tugging hard, he pulled her into his body, and then, wrapping a hand around her waist, he kicked his legs and took them to the surface.

"Stop struggling. I have you now."

She was gasping for air, her arms still thrashing.

"You are all right," Leo soothed.

He made his way to where hands waited to pull her up. Leo pushed her from behind, and soon she was in the arms of the woman who had been in the boat with her.

"Give me your hand, sir." Leo looked up into the face of Lord Bancroft.

"Lord Seddon?"

"My God, Leo!" Ram arrived at a run, dropping to his knees beside Bancroft. He then helped pull Leo onto the platform.

"I am all right, Ram," he said when he'd regained his feet. "Just wet."

"Thank you, Seddon." Bancroft held out his hand. "She would have drowned had you not saved her, as I cannot swim."

He shook the hand and then looked at the woman. She had her back to him, but Leo desperately needed to see her face. He moved closer to where she stood with the other lady.

"Are you all right?" The expectation inside Leo rose as she turned to face him, and then he realized why. He was looking into the eyes of the woman he'd once vowed to marry.

CHAPTER TWO

"*H*yacinth?"

She gave him a curt nod, her topaz eyes cold.

"Are you all right?" Leo asked, because he didn't know what else to say. This woman should have been his wife. Would have been, if not for his father's actions.

"I-I am. Thank you, my lord." She was shivering now.

"We must get you dry, Cyn," the woman who had been in the boat said. Leo didn't recognize her, but he had been out of society for years. "Good evening to you, sir, and thank you for saving my friend."

"Here, wrap my coat around her," Lord Bancroft said, shrugging out of it.

The woman fed Hyacinth's arms into the sleeves as she continued to glare at Leo, who had just saved her.

"Wh-why are you here?" she asked. "You n-never frequent such places." Her teeth were chattering. The woman was now behind her, running her hands up and down Hyacinth's arms.

How did she know what he did or didn't do?

"I needed to find something," Leo said, unsettled. His head

was all over the place, and he couldn't seem to make sense of his thoughts. *Hyacinth was standing before him.*

"Do you have my cuff link?" he blurted when nothing else came to mind.

Leo was the Nightingale who was coolheaded in every situation. He was far from that now.

"I beg your pardon?" She spat the words at him.

"My cuff link. Do you have it?"

Someone gasped. Someone else groaned—he thought maybe it was Ram. But Leo never moved his eyes from the beautiful woman before him.

She wore no bonnet, and her long dark blond hair was half down and half up now. The collars of Lord Bancroft's jacket were up. She looked far from the elegant society miss she had once been. Her face was pale, but the years since he'd seen her had only enhanced her beauty. The once darling of the ton had grown into a stunning woman. Even if she was wet as a drowned rodent.

He watched as she forced a soggy gloved hand into her pocket and pulled out something. She then slapped it into the sodden shirt over his chest.

"Thank you for saving me, and I hope never to see your face again, Lord Seddon."

"I beg your pardon?" His words came out in a growl.

"It seems you are excellent at locating things," Ram said, looking at the cuff link Leo now held in his palm and clearly sensing the tension between Hyacinth and him. "Good evening, Lady Lowell," Ram added, bowing before her. "If I may suggest you make haste to get warm before you catch a chill."

"Who is Lady Lowell?" Leo demanded, shooting his friend a look before returning to Hyacinth.

"Me," she said, her tone cold, face expressionless. She then sneezed twice, which suggested she was indeed going to catch a chill.

A memory slid into Leo's head as he looked at her. *"I sneeze when I'm nervous sometimes. It's embarrassing, but I fear there is little I can do about it."*

"You are married?" Why was it such a shock that she could have children and share another man's bed? *After all, you walked away from her.*

Leo had not once considered she would marry someone else, but then he'd barely thought of her at all, if he was honest. *Which said what about him and the feelings he'd once had for her?*

"Did you expect me not to?" Her tone was haughty. "To sit about the place pining in the hopes you would change your mind, my lord?"

Her tone was mocking now. It was a shock, considering the woman she'd once been. It seemed not only he had changed.

"Speak up below. We can't hear!"

Looking at the bank behind them, Leo saw people were now lined up, listening to them. One of them had called out those words, and others were listening with rapt attention.

"You really should get out of those wet clothes, my lady," Ram said, clearly eager to get Leo away from her. "And lower your voice," he whispered.

"Yes, Cyn," the woman at her side said. She was now glaring at Leo. "Come along, or you will catch a chill as Mr. Hellion has said."

Hyacinth's eyes moved from Leo to Ram.

"What odd company you keep, Mr. Hellion." She then sent him a glare filled with anger. A sneeze had her eyes closing briefly.

"You married the Earl of Lowell?" Leo asked, not wanting her to leave, even though he knew they both should.

She nodded. "My husband was a good man."

Was. She was a widow now. He remembered her husband. A somber man at least thirty years her senior. *Had her family forced her to wed him?*

"I say, is that Seddon?" someone above them asked.

"Hard to say, as he is quite sodden and has no doubt changed in the years since his family's disgrace."

"Yes, it is Seddon. I'm sure of it."

"And to think I nearly didn't come tonight. I would have missed all the excitement."

"This is not a sideshow!" the lady with Hyacinth called back. "Go about your business!"

No one moved. Leo would have known that without looking to check. Gossip was part of the foundation that society was built on. He refocused on Hyacinth.

"Why did you have my cuff link in your pocket?" Leo asked.

"To remind me, I will never be something for a man to discard with ease ever again." Her chin lifted.

"I beg your pardon?"

"Cyn, we really must go," Lord Bancroft, who had been standing silently listening, intervened. "We are drawing attention, and you will end up ill if we do not get you warm."

She ignored him and continued glaring at Leo. "Has age caused your hearing to fail you, my lord?"

This Hyacinth was very different from the woman he'd once known. She never would have spoken to him this way. She'd always adored Leo and hung on his every word. Not once had she mocked him.

"There is nothing wrong with my hearing," he snapped.

"Let me explain it in words you will understand, my lord." She leaned in closer; her lips were now turning blue with cold. "I kept it to remind me that most men care little about women. That one day, they will be there for you, and the next, gone without a word, discarding you like a tatty old shoe."

"I did what needed to be done," Leo gritted out.

She snorted in his face. Hyacinth, the epitome of elegance and poise, just snorted. She then turned her back on him.

"I could offer you nothing. It was all gone," Leo added under his breath.

She spun back, hearing his words. Her eyes narrowed into angry slits. There was definitely emotion now. Before he could stop her, she'd shoved him hard, sending him back into Ram, who steadied him.

"You should have sent me a note, anything. But you left me without a word."

"And said what?" He moved closer once more, no longer cold. Now he felt the heat of anger.

"I really don't think this is the place—"

"You knew what was going on. The gossip would have reached you," Leo cut off Lord Bancroft's words.

Hyacinth jabbed him in the chest with a pointy finger.

"Oh, now they are really going to have something to discuss over their crumpets," Ram muttered.

"I had a right to be told from you, Lord Seddon. I had a right as your future wife to know that you would no longer marry me."

"Cyn, I really think—"

"I had nothing to offer you," Leo said, cutting off the woman who had spoken. "And when your family heard the circumstances, they would never have allowed us to marry. That should have explained everything to you," he said, sounding every inch the lord he was.

"Had you lost the ability to write? Did I mean so little to you that—"

"I lost everything," he cut her off.

Her face softened briefly before resuming its stony mask.

"I know, and I'm sorry for that. But you did not give me the choice to support you. Did not allow me to choose—"

He snorted. "What? To walk away from all that you had loved to live with an outcast in shame away from your family? I would not have asked that of you. You had the right to continue to live the life you loved," Leo said.

"How magnanimous of you," she mocked him.

Everything ceased to exist around them. There was just Hyacinth and his anger.

"Don't you dare mock me." This time, it was he who leaned into her, finger pointing, eyes blazing, the demons inside him roaring to be let out. "I did what I believed was right for my family and you."

"And I had no say in the matter?"

"I doubt your life changed a great deal. Balls, parties, and pretty things." The words were insulting and beneath him, but he spoke them anyway.

She inhaled a sharp breath at that, almost as if he'd slapped her. He watched her fingers curl into fists. "I should have been given a choice to support you or not!"

"Clearly it did not take you long to get over your feelings of neglect on my part if you married Lowell."

He heard Ram groan and then saw the hand coming. He took the slap to his cheek, because perhaps he had deserved that.

"You, sir, are a brainless idiot, and I no longer wish to be in your company. If you see me again, then I suggest you go the other way. As you can be assured, I will do exactly that!"

She then left with Lord Bancroft and the other lady at her side. Leo looked above them and saw the bank was lined with people watching. They would be gossip fodder for society over the breakfast table tomorrow morning.

"That went well," Ram said.

"Shut up."

"Let's go." Ram nudged him forward, and Leo went, because now he was no longer arguing with Hyacinth, he was cold again. Gripping the cuff link hard, he felt the edge of the small gold disk dig into his palm. He needed the small bite of pain to ground him.

Climbing the stairs behind her, he heard the voices whispering. Some were asking after her; others were speculating over what had just happened.

"It is Seddon," a woman gasped. "The cheek of the man!"

"Lady Lowell, you have my apologies that you had to suffer in such a way, but what can you expect from someone such as a Nightingale? For him to have spoken to you in that manner, it is not to be borne. Allow me to escort you to your carriage."

Leo stiffened as he looked at the owner of that voice. Baron Ellington stared back at him, his eyes filled with hate. The man had been a friend of Alex's once but turned his back on the Nightingales along with many.

"Ellington," Ram said, striding forward. "If you speak ill of my friend again, I will break your nose and likely take out a few of your front teeth."

"Ram," Leo cautioned, looking at the interested spectators who were taking everything in.

They had indeed put on a show, and Leo had just done what he'd vowed to never do. Made himself gossip fodder for London's wealthy and elite. He'd lost control and now loathed himself for it, because that was what his father used to do. He'd throw tantrums, and then they all had to walk around him as if on broken glass.

"That such a man is among us again," Ellington said, refusing to back down, "is—"

"Ellington, Lord Seddon just threw himself into the water to save Lady Lowell. I did not see you doing the same," an elderly woman said, stomping forward. Leo tried to place her in his memory and thought maybe she was a duchess, but the name wouldn't come to his waterlogged thoughts. "I've always found that those who crow the loudest are the most cowardly."

Baron Ellington opened and closed his mouth several times, looking like a codfish.

"Well done, Seddon," she said with a gracious nod.

"B-but he should not be among us! His father—"

The woman who Leo guessed was about eighty or older spun with surprising agility, considering she was stoop shouldered and walked with a cane, to glare at the woman who has spoken. "I have never been one to believe a child should pay for his father's sins. Were that the case, Lady Albright, then surely you and your brother would be called light-skirts, as your father was quite free with his favors."

"Well!" the woman gasped, clutching her heaving bosom.

The old lady turned back to face Leo. "Pay these idiots no mind. Every society has a few, but for the most, we have a good bunch, which you will see if you rejoin us." Beside her was a large shaggy- and gray-haired dog. He made a rumbling sound deep in his throat.

"Thank you." Leo managed a curt nod.

"He is a coward, like his father!" Ellington yelled.

Leo stepped toward Ellington with Ram at his side.

"Allow me," his friend said and punched the baron in the nose. There was a definite crack, and then the man was falling onto his ass. The elderly lady and her dog moved closer and peered down at him.

"You, sir, are a fool, and considering the rumors about you, I would suggest you are not one to cast about insults. Now be gone, as I have no wish to look upon your face any longer. You are making me nauseous."

"He hit me!" Baron Ellington cried.

"You're lucky someone else hasn't done so already,"

someone muttered. Leo couldn't see who, as his teeth were now chattering loudly. He looked for Hyacinth, but she had disappeared into the crowds of people.

"Don't let the fools keep you from living the life you were born for any longer, Lord Seddon," the duchess then said, returning to him. One gnarled hand patted his cheek. She then stomped away, clicking her fingers to the dog. "Come along, Walter."

"Well," someone said. "The Duchess of Yardly is not one to take a backward step when a forward one is needed, but I have never seen her behave quite like that."

"Come, Leo," Ram said, gripping his shoulder. "We need to get you dry, and then you have some explaining to do."

Leo walked away, squelching, leaving his name on everyone's lips, and wondered if tomorrow was too soon to leave the continent.

I just saw Hyacinth, and she was married.

CHAPTER THREE

Cyn's heart had yet to slow to its normal rhythm as the carriage carried them home. She was wrapped in two blankets and holding Charles's whisky flask.

"Sip it slowly. It would not do to arrive home to Meg and Simon tippled," Charles said from the seat across from her.

She took another mouthful, a smaller one, and let the alcohol burn its way down her throat. Cyn was warming up now, and the reality of what had just happened was sinking in.

She'd looked to the platform and seen Leo. That had made her stumble, and she'd fallen into the water. He'd rescued her.

"I don't remember him that well, but he is certainly a handsome man," Lady Letitia Bancroft said from the seat beside her husband.

They had become friends when Kenneth had introduced them. He and Charles were business partners. Letitia and Charles Bancroft had been the ones she'd turned to after he'd passed for support. They had been there for Cyn, Simon, and Meg ever since. She would be forever grateful to them.

"I don't think Cyn wants to discuss Lord Seddon, my sweet," Charles said.

"It will be hard not to, as his name will be on everyone's lips and coupled with hers after the display they just put on," Letitia added. "So, she may as well get used to it by talking to us."

Cyn closed her eyes on a moan.

She had just seen Leo, the man she should have married and had once worshipped. Well, that had soon passed along with her belief that life would be exactly as she and her family had planned it to be.

Because you were a naïve fool.

"You do not speak of him or that time, but I know you were to wed him, because you told me. Also, that his family was ruined after his father took his life," Letitia said.

"I really don't want to talk about this," Cyn said.

"Well, we now know he walked away from you without a word," her friend continued.

Elegantly dressed as always, with her flaming red hair pulled up on top of her head in a froth of curls, Letitia Bancroft was Cyn's best friend in society and loved the man at her side to distraction. He carried his title well but was the opposite in every way of his exotic wife. Usually in subdued colors, Charles was tall, thin, with brown eyes and hair, and the least flamboyant person Cyn knew.

"And that you kept his cuff link. It's all very odd that he tracked you down to get it back now, so many years later," Letitia said.

"I kept it to remind me what a fool I'd been," Cyn said, which was only partially the truth. She'd just never gotten around to throwing it away. Clearly, if tonight told her anything, it was that she should have.

"How diligent you were to that task, seeing as you were carrying it with you tonight," Letitia said, her tone mocking.

"She has just been tossed into ice-cold water and met the man who broke her heart. I think we can be a bit nicer to her, don't you, my love?" Charles, always the peacemaker, said.

"He was very handsome," Letitia continued, undaunted. "But also has much anger smoldering inside him."

Cyn had seen a flash of that anger, and then he'd been the cool lord once more—very different, as she was, to the people they'd been. "Once, he was never angry. Usually laughing or mocking. Society had loved him."

"And you have not seen him since he left?" Charles asked.

Cyn shook her head.

"We have, of course, met his aunt and uncle the few times they attend social events. Lovely couple and clearly not worried about the gossip surrounding their name," Letitia added. "I can't believe he never contacted you, Cyn. That's extremely shoddy behavior, even considering that the average society gent has terrible manners."

"No, please, I cannot take any more flattery," Charles drawled.

"Not you, my love. You are the epitome of a gentleman," Letitia said.

"I am relieved."

Cyn had once been a naïve fool who believed Leo cared for her, and that he would never simply walk away from her without a backward glance. She was no longer that gullible fool, but a widow who ran her family's household and businesses alone.

"It was shoddy behavior, but then his father had just taken his life," she said, able now to admit with the hindsight of age and distance that what Leo and his family suffered must have been horrendous. She'd reacted to seeing him tonight like the young innocent fool she'd once been. It had been the shock, Cyn told herself. If ever they met again, she would be in control.

"It must have been devastating for you when he simply disappeared," Charles said.

She hadn't wanted to believe it was over. That her happiness had been dashed, and Cyn would not live out her silly, innocent dreams of a happily-ever-after with Leo. So, she'd gone to his house and stood outside the front door, only to be turned away. She'd written to him, but he had not replied. It took her six months to stop grieving the man she'd loved. Then her future husband had approached her with his proposal for her future, and she'd moved on with her life.

"Well, I'm quite sure that after tonight, he will have no wish to see you again either," Letitia said. "But now I want to know how it went tonight with your efforts to gain more funding for the agency."

"Wonderful," Cyn said, happy to change the subject. "Lady Tilbury was most impressed and wants to come and visit the Phoenix Agency to see if she wishes to donate to the worthy cause of aiding women into gainful employment."

"Of course, you forgot to mention that most of those women are ladies of the night," Letitia added.

"I doubt she would feel so charitable if I did," Cyn said.

"And you hide it by stating that the Phoenix Agency is simply for all women seeking work," Charles said. "Kenneth would be very proud of you."

"He would be," Cyn said. Her husband had been a cool, emotionless man, and he only unbent slightly at home with his children. Fair-minded if a little gruff, Kenneth had taught her to survive in a world she was not equipped to without the protection of a husband. He had also championed the disadvantaged members of society. He'd once told her that it was not their fault they had not been born having their every need met. Before he'd died, he'd told her to continue on with what he'd started, and she was more than happy to oblige.

Theirs had not been a marriage formed in love. But she'd

learned a great deal about life and how to contain her emotions from her late husband.

"Be careful where you tread there, Cyn. Not everyone will be pleased with what you do at the agency. There are those who control the ladies of the night you aid and have no wish to relinquish that," Charles said. "I am always here should you need me."

"Thank you, but I will have a care," Cyn said.

"I'm sorry seeing Lord Seddon upset you, Cyn." Letitia squeezed her hand. "And there will be gossip, but we will face it together."

"Morning callers." Cyn sighed. "I think I will have many over the next few days."

"Very possibly. Send word if they get too much for you. I am excellent at clearing a room," Letitia said with a wicked smile.

It was the tiredness that had tears filling her eyes as she said goodbye to her friends. That and the fact she'd seen Leo again. The man had always been far too handsome, and although she'd hoped otherwise, it seemed he was now even more so. Why could he not have lost his hair or put on an excessive amount of weight? Cyn had wanted to see him again and feel nothing. That had not been the case. Not that it mattered. He did not walk in society, and she did, so they would not have to face each other again.

Cyn was part of society because it was important for her children's future. One day they would walk in society too, and likely marry someone from that world, so she kept up appearances and stayed visible as their father would have wished.

Stepping inside the Lowell town house, she was greeted with a loud shriek.

"Mother!" Meg came running down the stairs, all arms and legs, like a colt. "Good Lord, you are all wet."

"I had a wee accident when the boat brought us back to the bank from the Duke of Allender's yacht. Why are you not in bed?" She kissed her daughter's cheek. Tall like Kenneth, she had dark hair and blue eyes, and she was, according to her elder brother, who was coming down the stairs behind her in a more sedate manner, excessively annoying.

"Because she is trying to wheedle hot chocolate and toast with lashings of butter out of Mrs. Mayberry," Simon said, arriving next. "You need to dry off and get warm, Mother."

Looking at her sixteen-year-old stepson was like looking at a younger version of the man she'd married. He was steady natured and calm usually, unless his sister got under his skin.

When their father had approached her with his proposal, she had said yes, and she'd never regretted marriage to her late husband once. She loved her son and daughter, and they had changed her life for the better at a time when she'd thought nothing ever would. Yes, sometimes she longed to be held by a man like she was special to him, as Charles did Letitia, but for the most part, she was happy.

"Yes, I will change, and then we will meet for hot chocolate and buttered toast in the small parlor," Cyn said.

"You do know that I am sixteen, don't you, Mother?" Simon said. "I could drink tea," he mocked her. "And I would like to hear the full story of how you fell into the water."

"Such a great age," Cyn said. "However, hot chocolate is better for all of us before bed, and I promise there is nothing more to the story than my clumsiness."

The huge town house that they rattled about in was a home for the three of them, and it had been their sanctuary in the months after they'd lost Kenneth.

Lord Kenneth Lowell had been an astute man who nurtured the dwindled inheritance his father had failed to into a fortune. Their marriage had been another business contract to him. He'd taught his young wife everything he knew because his heart had been failing him, and he was determined his children would be left in good hands… her hands.

So, Cyn had pushed aside memories of Leo and the burning love her innocent heart had felt for him and learned to be a countess who could control a fortune until her son was of an age to do so.

"Good evening," their butler said, appearing just as they prepared to climb the stairs. "You are all wet, my lady."

"Good evening, Hadleigh, and yes, I can see that and am about to go to my room and change. We will take hot chocolate and toast in the small west parlor, if you please."

"The fire is already lit, my lady, so I will bring the toasting forks."

"Lashings of hot chocolate too, Hadders," Meg said.

"And jam, Hadders. Plenty of jam," Simon added.

"Of course, I didn't know you could eat toast without jam, my lord. I will send Prue to you at once, my lady." Hadleigh was not overly tall, of large build, and known for his wicked sense of humor. Kenneth had told Cyn, when she'd entered his household as a terrified young woman, that he was a font of knowledge should she need anything. That had proved correct through the trying times after her husband had passed.

She liked to think a great deal had changed since then. There was spontaneous laughter and the occasional speck of dust. Kenneth had been a stickler for cleanliness and loathed loud noises.

"Meet me in the parlor." Cyn waved her children off. They ran up the stairs.

"I shall inform the cook to make lashings of hot chocolate, my lady."

"Thank you, Hadleigh."

Cyn felt weary and cold as she climbed the stairs, her eyes

going to the portrait of the man who had given a heartbroken young girl hope.

"I hope you are proud of what we have become without you, Kenneth." The portrait of her late husband hung above the stairs and was an excellent portrayal of the man she'd married.

In life, he had been more like a stern father to her, and he'd educated her on how to survive without him when the time came. He'd been the most intelligent man she'd known, and while he was not demonstrative to those he loved, Cyn would always be honored that it was her he'd chosen to care for his children.

She picked up her sodden skirts and ran up the stairs.

"You are a woman of great intellect, Cyn. A woman who does not need a man to find her way in this world." Kenneth's words always slid into her mind when she needed them. And tonight, after seeing Leo, she needed to remember them.

The house was decorated with touches of old and new. Some rooms she'd kept the same, as Kenneth had loved them. Others she'd put her mark on with the help of the children. The result was a home they all loved and felt comfortable in. This was their sanctuary.

Her room was large, with a desk she often sat at to write letters and a sofa to read on while her bare feet warmed before the fire. They all often sprawled out in here.

"My lady!" Prue, her maid, said, hurrying into the room behind her. "What has happened? Hadleigh said you are all wet."

"I was clumsy, Prue, and fell into the Thames, but as you see, I am unhurt."

Prunella Bromley was large, dependable, and lacking a sense of humor. Kenneth had employed her to watch over both Cyn and his children because she was a large, formidable presence.

Stripping off her sodden clothes, Cyn changed into her nightdress and dressing gown and then slipped her feet into slippers. Warm now, she left her room and found her children seated on the floor, arguing over toppings for the toast that they were charring in the flames.

"Here, Mother. Come and sit before the fire after your impromptu swim, and I shall pour your hot chocolate, as Simon is intent only on filling his belly," Meg said.

"Harsh but true."

"Was it a lovely night before you had your swim?" Meg asked.

"You could have drowned, Mother," Simon said soberly. "Falling in the water wearing all those clothes—"

"Someone jumped into the water and saved me. All is well, Simon, don't fret."

"Did you enjoy your night until you fell into the water?" Meg asked again.

"Most of it," she said. "Now tell me what you two got up to."

This was a tradition in the Lowell household, and the first night she'd partaken, they had still all been dressed in their day clothes, as Kenneth was not one for informality. But they had toasted crumpets or bread and drunk hot chocolate.

She had relaxed more of Kenneth's strict rules since he had passed, doing this in their nightwear being one. But for the most, she adhered to his wishes when raising his children.

"Who did you speak to tonight, Mother?" Meg asked.

"I met someone from my past, actually," she said.

"Who?" Meg said, handing her a steaming cup of hot chocolate.

"Lord Seddon, and many years ago, we were to marry."

"What happened?" Meg asked.

"You'll burn that," Cyn said, stalling for time as she pointed at the charred edges of the bread.

"Just how I like it." Simon smirked.

"I met Lord Seddon at my first ball, actually. I think he danced with me because he felt sorry for me, as I was shy, and it was my first season." She felt the smile tug at the corners of her mouth at the memory. Cyn had taken one look at Leo and tumbled headlong in love.

"So, he wasn't a bad man, then?" Simon asked.

"No, not bad. A spoiled nobleman, yes, but not bad. Like many in society, he was raised to believe he was better than most."

"Like Simon." Meg smirked.

They sat across from her, backs resting on the sofa, shoulders touching, watching her closely. She saw the similarities between them. Their noses and eye shape—so many little things you never noticed until they were close.

"I am not spoiled. I am lordly," he said in a snooty tone that had Cyn and Meg giggling.

"I'm pleased you married Father and not Lord Seddon, but why didn't you?" Simon said.

"Because his father was ruined in the eyes of society, and the family disgraced. One day, he was in my life, and then the next, not," Cyn said.

"And you loved him, so you were very upset," Meg said softly.

"I was, but that soon changed when your father asked me to marry him, and I got to be a mother to you two," she said, smiling.

In fact, she'd wondered if the pain of Leo leaving her would ever pass, because at the time, she'd taken to her room and wept as if the great gaping chasm in her heart would never heal. Then she'd grown up and realized that, in fact, she did not need a man who did not want her.

And tonight she met that man again.

CHAPTER FOUR

"Thank you for that punch to Ellington's nose, Ram. I'm sorry it came to that but not sorry I heard a crack," Leo said as they rode toward his home.

"You are most welcome. Ellington is a parasite."

"N-no arguments here," Leo said, then snapped his teeth together to stop them from chattering.

"What with the plunge into the Thames and slap from Lady Lowell, if I may suggest a nip of brandy to help you sleep when you reach your house," Ram said. "You must be chilled to the bone by now."

"Thank you, but I am well," Leo lied, still reeling from seeing Hyacinth and the humiliation of society watching him behave as he had tonight. He'd done what he'd vowed never to do again: given society another reason to have his name on their lips.

Leo wanted to crawl into his bed and stay there. But he knew it would be worse for her, because unlike him, Hyacinth would have to face the titters and whispers that would result from their argument tonight.

"So, you and Lady Lowell were once betrothed?" Ram asked.

"I have no wish to discuss this further, Ram."

"But you will, seeing as I will simply ask one of your siblings if you don't tell me."

Leo sighed.

"Come on. Spill, Leo."

"We had an understanding. I had just not proposed as yet when my father took his life."

"And you walked away from her without a word?"

"I'm sure you heard everything that passed between us, Ram, just as those standing above us did." Leo shivered as a blast of cold air whipped through his damp clothes. Gritting his teeth, he refused to show how much he was suffering.

What had happened to her? There was a fire in Hyacinth that had not been there before. She'd challenged him, and that had never happened all those years ago. Yes, they had not seen each other for years, but she was not the innocent he'd once known. Leo would stake his life on that.

"When did she wed?" The words sounded like a demand, but in that moment, he didn't have politeness in him. There was a tightness inside his chest, which was due to seeing her, and a chill in his bones from the icy wind buffeting his wet clothes to his body.

"She was married when I returned from India," Ram said calmly. "I first met her at a musical. She was seated in the last row, clearly wishing she was any place but there, forced to listen to the hideous warble of the woman singing. There was a seat beside her. I took it."

When his friend fell silent, Leo only just stopped himself from demanding Ram tell him what they talked about.

"I doubt she remembers the occasion, but I do, as I had just entered society," Ram continued. "She told me that there was every hope that our ears would never be the same after

THE FALLEN VISCOUNT

Miss Alderslade's performance, and that next time, we should plug our ears with something."

He could imagine her saying that. She'd had a sense of humor when he'd coaxed it from her.

"We then talked about her children, Leo," Ram added.

"Pardon?"

"She has two.... Well, they are Lord Lowell and his first wife's, but Lady Lowell called them hers."

He'd been reeling that she married someone else, which he had no right to do, but to know she now had custody of two children also… he didn't know what to think.

Furthermore, he had no right to think anything, if he was honest. She was a stranger to him now, as he was to her.

"Your aunt and uncle surely know her," Ram continued. "They walk in society occasionally, even though you others are too scared to."

"We are not too s-scared," Leo snapped.

"For pity's sake," Ram snapped, pulling his arms from the sleeves of his jacket. He then threw it at Leo.

He was now so cold, he did not argue and wrapped it around him, nearly moaning at the warmth.

"When will you return to society, then?" Ram looked at him. "Enough time has passed, surely, and with your family's support, it will be easier. Words no longer have the power to harm any of you with so much love and happiness now in your lives."

"I don't want to," Leo snapped. "And after the exhibition I just performed, I'm fairly sure my name will be on everyone's lips for some time."

Ram started clucking like a chicken, but as punching him would likely hurt Leo more, he simply said, "I'm bloody freezing, so shut up, because I can think only of the warmth that I have waiting for me at Crabbett Close."

"Gray too. There is nothing stopping him and Ellen from

entering society," Ram added as if Leo had not just spoken. He thought about moving into a gallop, but the streets were busy, and Ram would simply do the same.

"Are you quite done with the lecture?" Leo glared at him.

"No, but that will do for now. Back to Lady Lowell. She is very popular with both men and women. Her beauty, of course, plays a part in that," Ram added.

Leo was surprised he felt the lance of jealousy considering his body was a block of ice, but he did, and it was not welcome. He had no right to feel anything for Hyacinth now. Because he'd believed it the best action to take for her, he'd walked away from her without looking back. Clearly, she believed otherwise.

You left me without a word.

There had been hurt in those words. But he'd done the right thing… hadn't he?

"She rarely dances with a man more than once and is most often chatting with people," Ram said. "I danced with her last week, actually. It was the most entertaining conversation I'd had with anyone in a society ballroom since I arrived in London. We discussed the plight of women struggling to survive while earning money on the streets. It's clearly something she is passionate about."

"How did such a subject come up?" Leo asked instead of the other fifteen questions he had. "Surely ladies of the night are not a subject for a woman like Lady Lowell?"

"Don't be a snob, Leo. Many, both men and women, care about the plight of such people."

"I'm not a sn-snob," he hissed. "I understand and help where I can. But I didn't think she would."

"Because clearly you know her so well," Ram mocked.

"If you keep poking at me, I will not be r-responsible for my actions," Leo said with a growl.

Ram snorted. "You would fall off your horse if you lunged at me. Right now, I should imagine several of your body parts have stopped working, as they are frozen."

He wasn't wrong.

"I have heard some of the good deeds she has done."

"What good deeds?" Leo demanded. The Hyacinth he'd once known had been nothing more than her family and society expected her to be. A young lady he'd seen as someone who would make him a suitable wife.

If Leo was honest—and only with himself—he'd not thought his love for Hyacinth a deep and sonnet-worthy passion. He'd thought about her fleetingly, of course, in the years since he left society, but there had only been a small regret. He would have married her as was expected and no doubt grown to love her more, and they would have muddled along together.

But it would not have been a love like Alex, Ellen, and Uncle Bram had. It would have been like his parents' marriage. Soulless.

Hyacinth had been one of the diamonds in her first season, and he had wanted her because many others did. Because he'd been a shallow, self-indulgent fool.

"Lady Lowell is on many charitable boards," Ram continued, oblivious, thankfully, to Leo's thoughts.

"Really?" He tried to reconcile himself with the girl he'd once known doing such things. She'd giggled a lot, which had annoyed him, and agreed with his every word while rarely venturing anything into the conversation or having an opinion.

"Really. She's well respected in society."

Leo exhaled in relief as they turned into Crabbett Close. He was going to move out as soon as he found suitable lodgings, but right now, he was glad there would be light and love in his home when he reached it. Plus, warm clothes and food, which he desperately needed.

"And why are you coming to my uncle's house, when yours is that way?" Leo pointed to his right.

"Your family has a far superior supper tray that I can swoon over, plus I need to explain why I brought you home looking like a landed trout."

"There is that." Leo sneezed.

"So, I had not heard even a whisper that you and Lady Lowell were once betrothed, which is odd. Even Ellen has not told me, and I will have a serious talk with her about that."

"My sister is loyal to me."

"Yes, you bloody Nightingales are fiercely protective of one another. It is the trait I loathe most about you."

"J-jealously is a weakness," Leo taunted.

"How is it you fence with your peers but will not enter society?" Ram said with a relentlessness Leo hadn't realized he had until now.

They walked down the street, which circled at the end and had a large body of grass in the center, where all manner of odd things took place. The houses were of different shapes and sizes. Some butted up to the next, others standing alone.

"That's different, and we face a few snide comments there as well." Leo thought he was now in mortal danger of having a finger lopped off as he began to lose feeling in his extremities.

"I had no idea that your sensibilities were so easily hurt, Leo. I'd thought you had the hide of an elephant before today. You always seem to not give a damn about what people think of you. It seems you have had me fooled."

He shot Ram a look. There was no smirk on his face, and his eyes were steady as they stared back at Leo.

"You need to step back into your life, my friend. Lucky for you, I am just the man to help you."

"Not bloody likely," Leo muttered. He never wanted to face those that had turned on his family again.

CHAPTER FIVE

"Well now, it's a lovely evening for a ride."

"Hello, Mr. Greedy," Leo said, nodding his head as they drew level with the elderly man who'd called out to them. He was in his small front garden. "You'll pardon me for not stopping to chat, as I'm chilled through."

"He fell in the Thames saving a woman, Mr. Greedy," Ram said, which had Leo glaring at him again.

"Did he now? Well, I'll bring a tonic along shortly. It will warm up that chest and stave off infection. Well done on your heroic actions, my lord."

Mr. Greedy was a healer and cared for most of the residents in Crabbett Close.

"Pulling weeds at this hour, Mr. Greedy?" Ram asked.

"Aye, they come out nice and easy when the sun's not holding them in the earth." The man wore a cap pulled low and, like many of the elderly residents in the street, a woolen scarf wrapped several times around his neck. London was experiencing warm weather at the moment, so Mr. Greedy should be sweltering under all those layers. But winter or summer, he dressed the same.

THE FALLEN VISCOUNT

"I'll bring something for what ails your head also, my lord," Mr. Greedy added.

"I-I—"

"Get along with you now, and change your clothes at once." He waved a hand at Leo as he tried to speak. "Tell Bud to heat some water for your bath, and I'll bring your tonics."

The elderly man then moved with surprising speed out of his garden and to the front door.

"The residents in this street," Ram said, shaking his head. "There are no words."

"A-amen," Leo said as they rode the short distance to number 11. It was a large three-story redbrick home their aunt and uncle had brought them to when they returned to London. The siblings had not left it for at least a week when they arrived, but slowly, the Crabbett Close residents had lured them out the front door.

Leo dismounted and then yelped as his numb booted feet hit the ground.

"What?" Ram asked.

"My feet are numb."

"Being heroic always comes at a cost," Ram said, joining him.

Inhaling a deep breath, Leo released it slowly.

"And what are you doing now?"

"Bracing myself for the cutting words from Mungo when he sees the state of me. Then the worry from Aunt Ivy, and Uncle Bram's demand to know what happened in detail. I sometimes feel like I'm still in short pants."

"How wonderful to be so loved," Ram said.

Leo's smile was small because his lips wouldn't go any wider. "It is." Looking up at the brick facade, he knew that inside these walls was support. Laughter and hugs. Something the Nightingales had gained late in life but now embraced. Light filled several windows on all floors, and his family would be spread throughout.

Home, he thought. Right then, he needed that.

Leo walked to the front door and opened it. Stepping inside, he saw their newest staff member, Benjamin, coming down the stairs. Mungo terrified the young man, and the household he'd entered was mayhem, but for all that, he was standing up to the challenge.

"Lord Seddon, are you all right? You are wet!"

"Yes, I just ran into a bit of trouble. Could you take our horses to the stables, please, Benjamin?"

"At once." The boy rushed outside, all eagerness.

Leo put his cane into the stand by the door. He then hung Ram's jacket, and after taking his cuff link from the pocket, he attempted to peel his off his frozen body.

"You'll not stomp those wet feet through the house!"

"He's wet and cold, Mungo. Lay off," Ram said. "Get hot water for a bath."

Mungo stopped before Leo and stared at him. "Who did this to you?"

Brusque, rude, and downright belligerent most of the time, Mungo was huge. He had bright blue eyes and brows like hedgerows he used to great effect, like now. They were drawn together and glaring at Leo and Ram.

"No one. I fell in the Thames."

"There's more to it, and we'll have the tale, but for now, get up to your room. I'll bring you water for washing," the Scottish behemoth said.

"I hope there is apple cake, Mungo," Ram said.

Mungo and Uncle Bram had traveled the world together, and when Leo's uncle returned to London, his friend had accompanied him and fallen into the role of his right-hand man. He'd stayed when he'd married Aunt Ivy and then taken on their nieces and nephews. For all he blustered and roared,

Leo knew he cared for all the Nightingales as if they were his own.

"Do you not have a home also, then?" Mungo said to Ram as Leo started for the stairs.

"Well now, you'll be pleased to know that Bram has offered me Alex's old room, and I've a mind to take it, seeing as the food in this household far exceeds mine."

"Over my dead body," Mungo muttered. He then turned to look at Leo. "Up the stairs with you and change before you get sick and we have to go to the trouble of tending you. I'll tell Bud tea is needed."

"I can't walk any faster," Leo muttered, attempting to get his legs moving. The stairs suddenly seemed a Herculean effort.

"Mr. Greedy will arrive shortly with his supplies and asked that water be heated, Mungo. Seeing as your nature is so sunny, perhaps you could ask Bud to do that," Ram said.

Mungo snarled, muttering something about smooth-talking Sassenachs, and stalked away.

"It's a wonder you're not all terrified of that man."

"We are luckily on his good side," Leo called back down.

"He has a good side?"

Leo didn't answer because he was using all his strength to reach his room. Once there, he stripped his clothes from his frozen body and dragged on his dressing gown. He liked order, so his room didn't have clothes lying about on the floor like his other siblings'. His books sat neatly on shelves also, in order of when he'd purchased them. Where Gray alphabetized his, Leo was possibly the only person he knew that ranked his books from the date they became his.

He was sure his bones creaked as he sat on the bed to tug off his boots.

The door opened after one hard knock, and Mungo

walked in carrying two large cans of water. He poured them into a basin.

"Thank you."

Mungo stopped before Leo, then bent to tug off his boots, nearly yanking him off the bed. Once that was done, he stomped back out and slammed the door behind him.

He had absolutely nothing to laugh about, but it was there inside him. Getting to his feet, Leo went to the water and washed his entire body thoroughly twice, scrubbing hard with the cloth as if to erase the night he'd just endured.

He'd made a spectacle of himself.

"And this is why I do not walk in society," Leo said to the empty room.

When he felt almost normal again, he pulled on clean clothes and left to face his family and the inevitable inquisition, as there was no hope Ram would have kept his mouth shut.

The Nightingale home was usually full of noise and color. Most often there was something lying about in a hallway for someone to trip over. It was nothing like their childhood house, which had been immaculate and all about appearances. Leo bent when he saw the corner of a boot sticking out beneath a side table.

The family dog appearing at the top of the stairs followed a loud woof. Large, white with black patches, he fit right into the household because he was exuberant and occasionally forgot his manners.

"Mungo has been looking for this," he said, waving the boot at the dog. "Good boy, you keep up the torment." He then placed it on the floor.

"Come along, Chester. We may as well do this together," he said to the dog after ruffling his large ears.

Feeling much better going down than he had coming up, he made his way to the parlor his family was in. He found his aunt and uncle seated together as they usually were. With them was Theodore, his younger brother, who, at eighteen, was showing all the signs of growing up to be identical to Leo. The rest of the family were all in their beds, so at least he was saved from that. Tomorrow would be soon enough to listen to the excited chatter and endless questions from the younger Nightingales.

"Ram told me you jumped in the water to save Lady Lowell, Leo. Are you all right?" Uncle Bram got out of his seat. Nightingale men were big, and he was no exception. The younger brother to the late Lord Seddon, his uncle was nothing like the man who had ruined his family.

Steady, intelligent, and fiercely loyal, he had taken on his nieces and nephews without hesitation. He loved them as if they were his own, as did his wife, the small woman who had also risen.

"Hello, darling, I hear you've had a trying evening," she said, moving in to hug him hard, not letting him go until she was ready. He inhaled her scent and felt everything settle inside him.

"I am well, don't fuss."

"He had an urge to find something," Ram said, now seated before the fire with a cup in one hand and a crumpet slathered with jam in the other.

Leo's mouth watered. He was suddenly starving.

"What?" Theo asked.

"It matters not what." Leo dropped onto the rug before the fire. He then stretched out his hands and warmed them. The heat was bliss. "Why did neither of you tell me about her? That she'd wed and was raising two children?" He looked at his aunt and uncle. They were both frowning down at him, clearly worried.

"You never asked, so we thought you didn't want to know because the memory was too painful," Uncle Bram said.

"You have shut everything from your past away, Leo," Aunt Ivy added. "We respected that, even while we did not believe it healthy for you."

Before Leo could reply to that, Mungo came in holding a mug with steam coming out of it.

"Mr. Greedy wants you to drink this, as you clearly have a weak constitution, and he's afeared you'll end up with a chest inflammation. There's also something in there for your head, although I have no idea what, as there is not much in there," he said in his deep burr.

Leo regained his feet and took the mug. "Your generosity humbles me." Mungo's reply was a grunt. "I found your boot by the table in the hallway upstairs. There are only a couple of teeth marks on it."

Chester climbed onto his hind legs and placed the two front ones on Mungo's chest.

The large Scotsman did not intimidate the dog.

"Get down, you nasty beastie," Mungo said. But his hand was on the top of Chester's head, stroking it as he spoke. Theirs was a love-hate relationship.

"Back to you, Leo," Theo said, also eating a crumpet now.

Leo moved to take the last one before anyone else could.

"I remember Hyacinth. We met her in the park once, and she seemed nice. Giggly and looked at you in a nauseating way but was a great deal of fun," Theo added.

"She was enamored by your elder brother," Bram said.

"Well, it's fair to say she's not enamored with him now," Ram said. "In fact, if my memory serves, which it usually does, she said she had no wish to see you again."

She had said that and meant it. Leo was still grappling with the fact that the vision he'd always carried of Hyacinth would now be changed forever. That now she was a woman and no longer the sweet girl he'd once known. Why he found that far more intriguing, he had no idea.

CHAPTER SIX

Leo had kept himself busy in the five days since saving Hyacinth in the Thames, but he'd not managed to put the entire incident out of his head, like he normally could. Usually, he locked it into the box deep in the recesses of his brain and never thought of it again, which could explain the anger that usually simmered inside him.

Leo was no fool. He knew that suppressing the past and the emotions connected with that time was not good for him, and that the darkness that came upon him suddenly was likely due to that. But it was the only way he knew how to deal with what happened to him and his family.

Hyacinth seemed to have slipped into his head and was intent on staying there. He could see her standing before him, wet, cold, and angry. He could see her beautiful topaz eyes glaring at him.

"Stop brooding, Leo, for pity's sake," Ellen snapped.

"I am not brooding. I am wondering why I am in this carriage with you two and not going to this appointment alone, as I'd first thought," Leo said to the two siblings seated across from him—his brother Alex and sister Ellen. "And I'll add a second point to that. Why are you both not home with your beloveds?"

They'd arrived at 11 Crabbett Close and told him they were accompanying him to inspect the property the Nightingales were looking at leasing. There had been no dissuading them.

"Because Gray is working, and Harriet is at the orphanage this morning," Ellen said. "And we were bored."

She had once been a darling of society along with Hyacinth. Blond haired and blue-eyed, even he, if pushed, could admit that she was beautiful. She was now very different from who she'd once been. Also like Hyacinth, he thought. Ellen had fallen in love with Grayson Fletcher, a detective from Scotland Yard, who had also turned his back on society, but it had been his choice alone to do so.

"All likely true, now tell me the real reason you are accompanying me when I am perfectly capable of inspecting the property alone," Leo said.

"If we are to run our businesses from the place, then I want to like it," Ellen said. She wouldn't look at him, which was a sure sign she was not being truthful. Elegant as always, she looked the same, no matter the time or day—unlike his younger sisters, who couldn't get through an hour without tearing a shoe ribbon or piece of clothing.

"You're not telling me the truth, are you, Ellen?" Leo asked.

"Oh, for pity's sake," Alex snapped, joining the conversation. "Of course she's not telling you the truth. Clearly we were called in to ferret out what is really going on with you, seeing as you are even more somber than you normally are."

Leo stared at his brother while he grappled with the fact his family thought he was not himself. He'd not realized his moods had been any different.

"Subtle as always, Alex," Ellen snapped.

Alexander Nightingale. The easygoing sibling, who was not as well-built as Leo but tall with dark hair and eyes. He was the brother who women in society had once swooned over. He could talk to anyone and often did. Recently he'd wed the love of his life, Harriet. He was also Leo's best friend.

"We are never subtle with each other," Alex said. "Leo, we are here as something of a family intervention. Apparently, since you threw yourself heroically into the Thames to save Hyacinth, you have been maudlin, but you will not talk about it. Uncle Bram thought a day out with your two favorite people would change that." Alex smirked. "I still can't believe Hyacinth blistered your ears about what occurred all those years ago. I mean—"

"Yes, thank you, Alex. I know what happened, as I was there," Leo snapped. "Ram did not need to go into quite that much detail, and I do not want an intervention. There is nothing wrong with me."

"Oh, but Ram did need to go into detail, and yes, you need the sage and wise counsel of your two siblings," Alex said. "I wish I had been there for you, brother," he added, all laughter now gone.

"I'm all right, Alex."

"You know I am always there for you if you wish to go anywhere. You are not alone, Leo."

Ellen sniffed, then rummaged about in her reticule for a handkerchief. Sighing, Leo handed her his.

"Just because we are married does not mean we are not part of your life. It saddens me you think you cannot come to us—"

"That is not the case," Leo interrupted Alex, even as he knew it was. He'd left his siblings alone to live their lives with their loved ones. It seemed he'd been wrong about that.

"We are worried for you," Ellen said.

"We are," Alex agreed soberly. "There is a darkness inside you, Leo. Both Ellen and I have seen it."

"No, there isn't," he denied. How had they seen... known what he was battling? "There is nothing wrong with me," he lied. In fact, he'd felt the darkness closing in on him lately. Love surrounded him, and yet he could find no joy in it or, for that matter, anything.

What do I want in my life that I don't already have? It was a question he'd struggled to find the answer to.

"You are not happy," Alex said. "You try to hide it, but those of us that know you well have seen it for a while now."

"I am not reentering society, if that is where you're leading. I told Ram this and our aunt and uncle."

"We would not expect that of you, and furthermore, when we do, it will be all together," Ellen said.

"When?"

She waved his words away.

"I am fine and have no wish to discuss this further," Leo said, looking out the window. "If you do not cease this line of conversation, I will leave the carriage and continue on foot alone."

"Is that a threat? Because if it is, I'm not sure why you think it would work, seeing as this family has absolutely no idea of personal boundaries," Ellen said.

"Amen," Alex agreed. "I'm sorry you saw Hyacinth and it brought back the pain—"

"Alex," Leo growled out a warning.

"You hide your feelings from us, Leo. But we feel it," Alex said. "Both Ellen and I."

"How—"

"We believe it is linked to what we are... what all of us are," Ellen said, giving him a steady look.

"I'm well," Leo said again. "I promise."

THE FALLEN VISCOUNT

"No, you are not. You need a wife," Ellen said. "I spoke with Gray about this, and he agrees with me—"

"I beg your pardon?" Leo cut her off.

"You heard. You need someone in your life to love, Leo, like Alex and me."

He looked at his siblings, who simply returned his glare with calm expressions.

"Just because you are married does not mean I have to be. Not everyone is cut from the same cloth and wishes to live their lives dictated to by their spouses."

"I won't tell Harriet you said that, as I know you are simply reacting like a cornered rodent," Alex said.

"Gray would simply laugh," Ellen added.

His siblings were never easy to insult.

"For now, we will discuss it no more, but only because we are to get out shortly and attempt to be civilized, and you look like that sour-faced Mr. Crockett," Alex said.

"Is he the man who sells those delicious macarons?"

Alex nodded to Ellen. "The only reason he has any patronage is because they are such tasty morsels. He told me yesterday that I had shortchanged him." Alex looked incredulous. "I demanded he recount what was in his palm and then get eyeglasses."

"What flavor did you have?" Ellen asked Alex, as if a minute ago they weren't making their eldest brother extremely uncomfortable with a personal dissection of his life.

"Cherry." Alex made a humming sound low in his throat, and Leo felt his mouth water. Even annoyed and unsettled and ready to toss both siblings from the carriage, he could still lust after one of Mr. Crockett's cherry macarons.

"But we digress," Alex said.

"As this conversation is over—"

"One part of the conversation is over," Alex continued,

ignoring Leo. "But I would like to read you an article from the *Trumpeter*." He produced a newspaper from his inside pocket. It was folded into a rectangle. He then cleared his throat and began.

"Lord Seddon, with no thought to his own safety, plunged into the Thames to save Lady Lowell from certain death. Witnesses said it was an act of incredible heroism."

"Tell me you're making this up?" Leo demanded.

Alex smiled at him before continuing, "Lord Seddon is well respected along with his family by many, and it is wonderful to see him dipping his toe, both figuratively and metaphorically, back into the waters of society. The insult that followed from Baron Ellington was both unjust and unacceptable. It was dealt with by Mr. Ramsey Hellion, who beat Lord Seddon to the chase, and Ellington's nose was dealt a blow that will see him with a large, throbbing snout for many days to come. The Duchess of Yardly and Walter also did not stand for Ellington's behavior and was heard to comment on the baron's nature in a disparaging manner and then state loudly that his presence made her nauseous. Well said, Duchess! We applaud you. Walter barked loudly at Ellington."

Ellen started giggling, and Alex snorted as he stuffed the paper back into his pocket.

"It's a brilliant piece. Cam wrote it, of course," Alex added.

Cambridge Sinclair, one of the notorious Sinclairs, owned two newspapers in London, which was odd, as he walked in society. Yet like the rest of his family, he cared little what anyone thought of him, which was possibly why everyone put up with him.

Leo wasn't sure how he felt about the article. On one hand, he loathed being gossip fodder, but on the other, Cam had said he and his family were respected.

"It's a wonderful piece, Leo," Ellen said.

"I know it is, but I have no wish for any of our names to be gossiped about ever again."

"It is written in our favor. Stop being so serious," Alex said. "But enough for now. We will look at this property you wish for us to inspect."

Leo was happy to put the entire incident aside, although he wasn't sure the memory of Hyacinth would allow him to do that.

"We have the orphanage, the investments, and I have lately been looking into other avenues for us to expand our business ventures," Leo said. "We also need to employ someone to oversee all of this, and the office will be where they work from."

With help from friends, the Nightingales had become business savvy and started increasing their financial coffers with several interests. Leo had to say he enjoyed that side of things, and he found he had a knack for numbers. It was one way he kept himself busy, because too much time to think was never a good thing.

"We are here," Ellen said, interrupting his thoughts as Mungo pulled the carriage to a halt.

Leo got down first and then helped his sister. Alex followed. After their father's disgrace, it had been the three of them who had been hit the hardest by what happened, as they had walked in society. Because of that, they were a great deal closer than they had once been.

"I'll return in an hour," Mungo said.

"Most gracious." Alex looked up at him.

"Be off with you, gowk."

"Mungo just called you a simpleton, Alex."

"He's not far wrong." Leo smirked. Insulting his siblings was something he'd missed. Clearly, he needed to spend more time with them.

CHAPTER SEVEN

"*A*Mrs. Abbot and Lady Mullins have called to see you, my lady," Hadleigh said, appearing in the doorway of Cyn's office.

"Already? When is this going to stop?" she muttered, rising. "Can you not send them away, Hadleigh, stating I have a disease that has me lying feverish and near death?"

"I fear not, my lady, as they were most insistent that they have brought you a tonic for your chest, which is surely paining you due to your brief plunge into the Thames."

"Send Prue to deal with them," Cyn said, sounding testy to her own ears.

"She is gone from the house with the children, my lady. They have gone to the park along with Mr. Dildersdale. He is taking Miss Meg to paint leaves. Lord Lowell has a book, as he stated quite clearly that he is too old for such things."

"I would have accompanied them had they asked." Cyn sighed, and of course, she could not send her maid to deal with two of society's notorious gossips. "Their adventure sounds a great deal more exciting than mine is about to be. Make more tea, please, Hadleigh, and bring plenty of milk.

We will prepare their cups lukewarm so they can drink it fast. And if there are any cakes left from two days ago that could be stale, bring those too."

Hadleigh bowed. "I will see to it at once," her unflappable butler said.

"They can wait," Cyn muttered, picking up the letter that had arrived this morning from Mary, who lived and worked at the Phoenix Agency she had started after Kenneth's death.

Last night a woman was found beaten and left for dead in Whitechapel. It's my belief she was one of their women, and she is the fourth in two months. When next you visit the agency, we should discuss this matter, my lady. I've attempted to find out where she is, but it is difficult, as no one will speak out against these men.

Cyn felt the familiar anger she experienced every time word came to her of a lady being hurt because of the life she was forced to live.

Rising, Cyn pushed aside the anger roiling around inside her. She'd go to the agency as soon as she'd dealt with her morning callers and speak to Mary. Hurrying to her room, she tidied her appearance and then made her way back down to the parlor Hadleigh would have put the guests in.

Exhaling at the door, she then pushed it open and entered.

"My dearest Lady Lowell." Mrs. Abbot rose and rushed to Cyn, with Lady Mullins on her heels. "How is it you are from your bed after such a terrifying ordeal just days ago?"

Her callers had spoken in much the same way over the last few days. All sympathizing insincerely over her harrowing experience and then attempting to coax her to tell them everything that was spoken between her and Lord Seddon.

"I have quite recovered, I assure you, but thank you for calling to check on me," Cyn said, waving them back to their seats. A loud meow preceded the family cat entering the room in the same way she did most things—with speed. The furry black beast then yowled loudly at her for no reason, as she did often, and wandered to where the ladies sat.

"No, Berry!" Cyn ordered. "The ladies have no wish for you to put hair over them."

Lady Mullins flapped her hands about, shooing the feline away. Berry stretched, digging her claws into the carpets, and after a yawn that suggested they bored her, she wandered to the windowsill to sit in the sun and clean herself.

"Excuse my cat's manners," Cyn said as Berry licked loudly.

"Quite all right," Mrs. Abbot said insincerely.

"We came, as it is our duty as your dearest friends to do so," Lady Mullins said, bringing the conversation back to the reason they had called.

They weren't her friends, and she rarely spoke to them at society functions, but she kept that thought to herself.

"You are too kind."

"To have run into Lord Seddon in such a way... why, it must have been distressing for you, considering," Lady Mullins cooed.

And so it begins.

The more she thought about that night, the more ashamed she'd become. Yes, Leo should have at least sent her a note, and at the time, he'd left her distraught and hurt because her future had supposedly been set as Lady Seddon. But not once had she considered how he and his family were suffering, as she'd been too consumed with her own grief.

"It was, of course, quite a to-do after you'd left," Mrs. Abbot said. "Baron Ellington was most vocal about seeing Lord Seddon again and—"

"I have heard what happened, thank you," Cyn interrupted. She could only be so polite and had no wish to hear how Leo was insulted. Although she did like the part about the duchess stepping in to defend him.

"The Duchess of Raven and Lady Raine," Hadleigh said from the doorway.

Mrs. Abbott actually gasped, and Lady Mullins clutched her chest at the exalted company entering the room.

Both women were stunning with their dark locks and beautiful faces. Both had figures anyone would die for. The duchess had threads of silver now shot through her hair, which of course looked wonderful.

Cyn had overheard a group of women talking about her one evening and stating how unfair it was that those of Sinclair blood tended to age so well. She had to agree.

The duchess wore a deep red, and Lady Raine, emerald.

"Hello," the duchess said, coming to where Cyn now stood. "We heard you had been inundated with nosey morning callers and thought we'd join them."

"Exactly," Lady Raine said. "Can't abide gossips, personally, but what can you do in society? We're surrounded by them. Isn't that right, ladies?" she said to the two women who were still seated, open-mouthed. They both nodded.

"How are you?" The duchess gripped her hands.

She wasn't terribly close to many people. Letitia and Charles obviously, but after Leo had left, many had gossiped and pitied her. The duchess had not been one, and Lady Raine had not been in society.

"I am well, thank you, Duchess."

"I knew you would be. You're not someone who falls about the place like many. Now where is the tea?"

As if on cue, the door opened, and in walked Hadleigh with a laden tea tray. He lowered it to the table before the still silent Lady Mullins and Mrs. Abbot.

"I shall pour. Thank you, Hadleigh," Cyn said.

The butler left, closing the door behind him.

"It is a shame my brother Cambridge and the Duchess of Yardly are not present. We could have a literary saloon," the duchess said.

Cyn shuddered at the thought. Thus far, she'd avoided the infamous occasions by running the other way if she saw a group forming with the duchess in it.

"Lady Mullins, how is your husband's delicate condition?" Lady Raine asked, making the other woman choke on air.

Cyn busied herself pouring the tea while Lady Raine and the duchess proceeded to fire questions at the two women, who had just been doing exactly that to her. In that moment, she could have hugged them both.

"Mr. Bramstone Nightingale and Mrs. Ivy Nightingale," Hadleigh said from the doorway seconds later.

Dear Lord. Why had Leo's aunt and uncle called upon her?

"How wonderful to see you," the duchess said, rising. "We are having quite the tea party."

"And as Lady Mullins and Mrs. Abbot were just about to leave, there are enough seats for you both," Lady Raine said, giving the women a hard look.

"Oh... well, of course," Mrs. Abbot said, looking like she could think of nothing worse than leaving. But when you were in the company of two powerful, high-ranking women of nobility, you did not offend them.

"I hope your nephew has fared well, Mr. Nightingale," Lady Mullins said as she passed him on her way to the door.

"How incredibly kind of you to ask," Mrs. Nightingale said with a sweet smile that did not reach her eyes or her lips. "He is quite well and showing no ill effects, I assure you. We, of course, heard a few rumors that when he dived heroically into the Thames, some members of society were not polite to him. I know, of course, you ladies were not counted among those?"

The two women gobbled like turkeys briefly and then

stammered out that of course they were not and would never do so.

"Excellent. Good day to you both." Ivy Nightingale then followed the two women to the door and shut it with a decisive snap behind them.

"Good riddance," the duchess said, dropping onto the sofa like Simon sometimes did, as if his limbs had given up working. "Can't abide those two gossip-mongering biddies." Berry took that moment to wander over and leap into her lap. "Well now, you are sweet," she said, uncaring that the animal was covering her in black fur.

"But they are simply two of many that walk among us," Lady Raine added.

"Yes, society is full of idiots," Ivy Nightingale agreed.

"We will not stay long, Lady Lowell," Bramstone said with a gentle smile. "We simply wished to enquire as to your health after falling into the Thames, my lady."

Cyn saw Leo in him. In his size and the shape of his eyes. Her eyes went to Ivy Nightingale. Where her husband was tall and broad shouldered, she was slender.

She knew little about Leo's family—only the gossip she had overheard. But she knew that the Nightingale siblings had left London with their aunt and uncle.

"I am well, thank you," Cyn said. "And your nephew? He is well also?" She had to ask. It would be rude if she didn't. But everyone in this room knew what lay between her and Leo. That was never in doubt, even as they were too polite to mention it.

"He is, thank you," Bramstone said. "My nephew has learned resilience, my lady, and, for the most part, can handle a great deal."

For the most part. What did that mean?

"It was a terrible time for you all," the duchess said, and there was only sincerity in her words.

Cyn did not want to give a damn about the man who had broken her heart, even if she had today realized she needed to forgive him and move on. But she could be curious about what had become of him, seeing as she noticed he was a vastly different person from the man she'd once known.

"Leo suffered, as they all did" was all Bramstone added.

"I can only imagine. Society is both wonderful and horrible," Lady Raine said, "and seeing as I was once a piano teacher who did not know she was, in fact, French nobility, I have had firsthand knowledge of just how malicious some of its members can be."

"And we are much happier for your entrance into our lives," Bramstone said graciously.

"Will you take tea?" Cyn asked them.

"We won't, thank you," Ivy said. "And we can see you are in excellent health, so we will bid you good day, as the children will create havoc if we do not return home soon and take them out."

"How many children do you have?" Cyn asked.

"Charlotte is ours, and then we have our nieces and nephews that we think of as ours too, and of course, Anna," Bramstone said, smiling down at his wife with so much love.

She'd never had that. Kenneth had cared for her and treated her well, but he had not loved her. Cyn knew there would be no grand passion in her future.

"Essie told me about Anna," Lady Raine said. "It is a wonderful thing you have done taking her into your lives."

The Nightingales smiled. "It is us who are blessed. She has brought us so much joy, and everyone loves her."

She wanted to ask who Anna was, as she knew all the Nightingale siblings' names, and she was not one of them.

"Good day to you all," Mrs. Nightingale said. "I hope we can meet again soon," she added, her eyes on Cyn.

"Well, that was wonderful," the duchess said after they

THE FALLEN VISCOUNT

had left. "They live in Crabbett Close, which is quite an amazing little street. The locals are colorful, and the entire place is like this little pocket of unusual in London. We have attended two weddings there now, and we are hopeful we will be invited to more."

"Crabbett Close is where the Nightingales live?" Cyn asked. "I've heard of it, because Simon and Meg have been there. I believe they go to the park and meet with friends."

"I wonder if they have met the younger Nightingales," Lady Raine mused.

Both women looked at Cyn then.

"What?"

"What happened between you and Lord Seddon did so many years ago, Cyn. You have both moved on, and perhaps this could be a way of showing society that," the duchess said.

"He doesn't walk in society."

"But if he wanted to, it would be less awkward if you and he were at least nodding acquaintances. Especially after what happened when he pulled you from the Thames."

Could they be? Considering the grudge she'd harbored against him for years, the idea seemed a foreign concept to her.

"My husband said that we need the Nightingale family—all of them—back in society to raise the intelligence level of the ton," Lady Raine said. "Perhaps you could help with that?"

"I don't think so." Cyn bent to pick up Berry because she felt the need to hold the soft, heavy weight in her arms.

"He's no longer the spoiled man he was, as you are no longer the young lady you were," the duchess said. "And now that we have given you our sage advice and scared away your noisy morning callers, we shall leave also. But not until I hand you this, which was my real reason for calling. It was simply a bonus that we could scare away Lady Mullins and

Mrs. Abbot." She handed over a thick plain white card embossed with gold.

"It is an invitation to my husband's charity ball. I expect you there."

"Of course."

"And this year our violinist cannot make it, so you will have to play," the duchess added. "And do not tell me you can't, because Kenneth may not have been an exuberant fellow, but he often talked about you playing that instrument."

Cyn sneezed at the thought.

CHAPTER EIGHT

"Good day to you, Lord Seddon," a loud voice boomed to the Nightingale siblings when they approached the town house that they were considering taking a lease on. The man coming toward them was short and wide. His moustache was impressively waxed, and his clothes stated he was a man of means, which Leo was sure was the intention.

"Mr. Taylor, I presume?" Leo said, holding out his hand. "This is my brother, Mr. Nightingale, and sister, Mrs. Fletcher."

"Wonderful," he said, bobbing his head. "Wonderful indeed," he added with another head bob. "And it is a lovely day to view property. I always say looking at a new investment when the sun is shining is the only way," he added. "As you will have noted upon approach, there is not one house that is not up to the high standards set by the residents of the street. Riffraff will not be tolerated."

"Riffraff?" The word had come out of Ellen's mouth coated in ice.

"From a class far beneath yours, Mrs. Fletcher," Mr.

Taylor said, beaming as if he'd said something complimentary. The look on Ellen's face told Leo that was indeed far from the truth.

"Because we were lucky enough to have been born into wealth in no way makes us better than those that were not," his sister snapped.

Leo looked at Alex, and they exchanged a silent communication to stand back and let Ellen say her piece.

"Of course it does," Mr. Taylor said, still smiling.

"Mr. Taylor." Ellen raised a finger to wave at the man. "Shame on you for believing yourself better than those that have had to fight for their very survival through no fault of their own."

"As a woman, I'm sure you feel—"

"I would not continue this conversation, sir," Leo snapped, no longer willing to remain silent if the man was about to insult Ellen. "My sister is far more intelligent than either of her brothers... for that matter, most of the members of our family. Be very careful how you speak to her, Mr. Taylor, or this appointment will be over before it has begun."

The man paled. "Apologies, no insult intended," he said nervously.

"Shall we take a look inside?" Alex asked, his tone clipped as well. "Perhaps you can keep your opinions strictly to details about the house going forward."

"Wonderful idea," Mr. Taylor said quickly.

Leo looked at the buildings on either side of the one they were about to enter. Both were all white with black iron railings running along the front. They went below the street level and above it two stories.

"We have many people interested in leasing the property, you understand," Mr. Taylor said, getting into his sales pitch. "I've put everyone on hold just because I knew you were coming today." He beamed at them again, although there was a nervous edge to the man now as he bobbed his head.

"Of course you did, and we are extremely grateful," Alex said, doing what he did best, lying while smiling. He was the Nightingale most likely to stop an argument and could manipulate most people into giving him what he wanted before they realized it.

Leo looked to the small brass plaque above the door of the property to his right. He read the words *The Phoenix Agency*.

"What is the Phoenix Agency, Mr. Taylor?" Leo asked.

The man coughed and then cleared his throat. "Ah, well, as to that, my lord, it is an agency."

"I can see that. But what kind of agency." Leo kept his eyes on the man as he asked the question. His discomfort had just increased, and it was not from Ellen's earlier words.

"Well"—his head bobbed—"I believe it helps place young ladies into positions," the man said quickly.

"Something that many agencies across London do, sir. Why does this particular one make you uncomfortable?" Leo asked in a polite tone. His brother and sister remained silent, happy for him to ask the questions.

Nightingales had learned to back one another's intuition many years ago.

"Uncomfortable? What?" His laugh was more a high-pitched squeal. "Not at all. They are wonderful people and doing an excellent job for those who need to find employment."

"How long has this building we are about to enter not had tenants?" Alex asked suddenly.

Mr. Taylor was now sweating. The Nightingales often had that effect on people.

"Ah, well, things are taking some time to—"

"How long, sir?"

"A year."

"Because?" Leo asked.

"I have no idea." The man was busy riffling through a ring of keys he'd just pulled from his pocket. "W-would you like to see the property?"

Leo took pity on him, and after a final glance at the Phoenix Agency, he followed his siblings down the stairs inside the property.

The ground floor offered two rooms, with a door outside to a small garden. The first floor had three more, and the second, a further four. It was tidy and spacious, and for what his siblings felt they needed in their family, it would be perfect, except for the niggling doubt he had about the Phoenix Agency. He could see no reason why someone had not taken on this property.

"I'm going next door to see what that agency is about before we make any decisions," he whispered into Ellen's ear. "I expect you to hound the man until he gives us the lease at a vastly reduced rate after his misconception that you are a brainless female, which if I'm honest…" She smacked his arm.

"I can do that," Ellen whispered with an impish grin. "I will have him eating out of my pathetic female hands in no time."

"I have no doubt."

Leo excused himself and walked back outside. He then took the few steps to reach the next property and was soon knocking on the front door. When that failed to get a response, he tried again. Since no one answered, he was just about to return to his siblings, but then Leo heard a voice coming from inside.

Trying the brass handle, it turned, and he entered. If this was a brothel or some other place of ill repute, he wanted to know, as his family would not be leasing the property next door.

Inside the entranceway were olive-green walls and a red oriental carpet. He counted three doors off the long hallway. As he approached, a man appeared through one of the doors.

"Good day to you, sir," he said, moving to the reception desk. He had a wide mouth and large brown eyes all set in a long angular face that oddly worked. His hair was bright red and curly.

"Good day. I knocked, but no one answered," Leo said.

"All are welcome here at the Phoenix Agency. However, we only find placements for women, I'm afraid. Therefore, you must have come to the wrong address."

"This was my intended location. I am looking at leasing the property next door and wanted to enquire as to the nature of the Phoenix Agency." To Leo, it seemed a simple enough question. However, the smile fell from the man's lips, and his eyes narrowed.

"Nature?" The word came out a great deal cooler than his tone had previously been.

"Nature," Leo repeated. The word hung in the air between them, but he did not back down.

"We are an agency, sir," the man snapped.

"Yes, but what is the agency for?"

The man straightened his shoulders, which gave him at least three inches over Leo, who was well over six feet himself.

"For?" the man asked.

He had not thought the question a difficult one; clearly it was.

"Look," he tried again. "I just want to know who our neighbors will be. I am not asking you to introduce me to everyone who works here or show me your accounting," Leo snapped.

A loud bang reached them from somewhere below.

"We are having alteration work done," the man said. "We are an agency for placing women into work, sir. I hope you don't find that too offensive. Now, if you will excuse me, I must see if I am needed."

Leo blinked. Had he just been dismissed? He watched the man he'd offended by asking a simple question stalk away from him and back through the door he'd recently exited.

"All I asked was what was the nature of this business," Leo muttered, looking at the now-closed door. Clearly the man was sensitive.

Another loud bang was followed by a muffled yelp of pain.

It wasn't that he didn't believe the man about what went on here, but then would he have said what they were using the premises for if their intentions were nefarious?

Leo had come to his suspicious nature late in life, but it had stood him in good stead many times. Something was niggling at him like a loose eyelash.

He looked around the space but saw little else except the desk. Leo thought briefly about going behind it to see what he could find and then thought again. Not the best way to treat your neighbors, if indeed they decided to take the lease on the property next door.

He heard raised voices. Surely someone was in need of his assistance? Those voices sounded panicked. He was now duty bound to investigate.

Opening the door, he walked into a room where coats hung on hooks. Beyond that, another door stood open and led outside. As there was no sign of the man in here, he surmised he'd left. Following, Leo took the stairs down.

The garden was small and held a few plants. A wooden fence separated this area from the house next door the

Nightingales were inspecting. The other side of the garden had a wall with stairs up to the street level.

"I told you to wait for me, Cyn! Now you have hurt yourself." That was the voice of the man Leo had just met, and it was coming from inside.

"It is nothing but a scratch," a woman said. *Do I know that voice?*

"That is more than a scratch."

"Don't fuss, Lewis. Did we just have a visitor?"

"Indeed, we did. A man who wanted to know the nature of our agency, as he is looking at the property next door. He had a snooty, arrogant way about him."

So, on short acquaintance, I come across snooty and arrogant, Leo thought. That was harsh considering they'd spoken no more than a few words to each other. Although his family was always stating he had a resting scowl that could scare most people away.

"Excellent, just the sort of neighbors we need, considering our clients," the woman said. He knew that voice, just not who it belonged to.

Moving through the door, he stepped inside and was met with a room full of discarded household items ranging from an ugly sofa the color of moldy apples to several uncomfortable-looking chairs. Circling around the ugliest vase he'd ever seen, he saw a door that must lead to another room. Reaching it, Leo looked inside.

The room was cluttered like the one he'd just walked through, but it was the two people standing in the corner with their backs to him that caught and held his attention. The prickle of awareness had him clearing his throat.

The woman turned so fast, she stumbled; the man who had spoken to Leo steadied her. Hyacinth's eyes then locked on him.

CHAPTER NINE

"What are you doing here, Lord Seddon?" Cyn demanded, fighting the urge to sneeze. Leo was in the Phoenix Agency; it was almost too hard to believe. Dear Lord, surely he was not the man Lewis said was looking at leasing the property next door?

"Stand still, Cyn," Lewis snapped as he attempted to wrap his handkerchief around the wound on her palm. "You are bleeding." Her friend then shot Leo a look, which she was sure would be a glare. "And you, sir, are on private property."

"Exactly," Cyn said. "I suggest you leave," she said, battling to subdue the rapid beat of her heart at seeing him again. *Be nice, Cyn,* she reminded herself. *He has suffered far more than you, plus you are now an adult and can behave as such.* "Please," she added, which had his brows drawing together in a frown.

"What is going on, Hyacinth?"

"Lady Lowell," Cyn said. "And what do you mean what is going on?" She congratulated herself on the polite tone. She could do this. Talk to him like she did to other acquaintances in society most evenings.

"Of course, forgive me, I am used to calling you

THE FALLEN VISCOUNT

Hyacinth." He bowed slightly, keeping his eyes on her the entire time.

"Ouch!" Cyn hissed as Lewis pushed down on the cut she'd received from a nail sticking out.

"It needs to be tight to stop the bleeding," her friend said.

"Can I be of assistance?"

"I am well, thank you, my lord. Lewis will fuss and—"

"I do not fuss," Lewis scoffed. "You have a cut, and I have no wish for you to track blood through the agency."

"It is a mere scratch. Don't be dramatic, Lewis."

"It may need a stitch, Cyn. Perhaps you should see a doctor," Lewis said.

"Listen to your friend," Leo said.

Cyn shot him a look. Now he was not dripping wet and hunched from the cold, he appeared bigger. Broad shoulders in the immaculately cut black jacket. His face was harder too, his cheekbones more pronounced. Why had he not grown a wart on the end of his nose, or at least a mole that had long hairs sticking out of it? But no, there he stood, handsome and far too disturbing.

"Do you own the Phoenix Agency, my lady?"

She didn't hide that the building was owned by her... or more importantly, the Lowell family, and yet she rarely discussed what was the true purpose of the premises.

"Yes, Lord Seddon, I do." Was he like so many of her peers, who believed a woman should be painting badly and stitching useless things no one would ever need?

"And I believe you help women seek employment?" he asked. In one large, gloved hand, he held a hat, tapping it slowly against his thigh. The other held a cane, as many noblemen did these days.

"Let me see your cut. Having younger siblings, I am quite handy in a medical situation." He lowered his hat and cane to a cabinet inside the door and then moved closer.

"Lewis is more than capable of tending it, my lord. Thank you," she added, reminding herself that manners were important even when you were off-balance.

"Let me see," he demanded. Hyacinth did not respond to demands anymore.

"I have said that is not necessary," she said with a snap to her voice now.

"You're definitely not the woman I remember," he said. "That lady had far prettier manners."

"She is long gone."

"Is your husband to blame for that?" The words were spoken softly.

She whirled on him, anger surging to life. Lewis let her go as she faced Leo. "My husband was a good, honorable man. I will not allow you to say otherwise, Lord Seddon."

Those brown eyes studied her. "Forgive me, I did not mean to suggest he wasn't."

"I'm not sure what the words 'is your husband to blame for that' meant if not an insult." She was not someone who lost control, and yet seeing him here, at her agency, was doing that to her.

He exhaled slowly. "Forgive me. It was wrong to speak about the late Lord Lowell that way. I always found him a good man."

She nodded.

"I had thought never to see you again," he said softly.

"At least you have learned to swim since we last met," Cyn said in the same tone, attempting to ease the tension between them. They were both clearly still uncomfortable being in each other's company.

He snorted. "Indeed, at least I can be of some use to someone."

Which meant what?

Lewis cleared his throat, and Cyn knew that, for a brief

moment, she'd forgotten he was there, because Leo was standing before her. It had always been like that with him. He could make her forget to eat; such had been the love she'd had for this man once. Not now, however. She was not that silly fool anymore.

"There is brandy upstairs, Cyn. We can wash it with that," Lewis said.

"Oh, very well."

"Your storage room is full," Leo said as Lewis led the way around him and back out the door, with Cyn following.

"Hold it up so it doesn't bleed through the bandage and all over you and the agency floors, please," Lewis ordered her as they walked out of the room and then to the gardens.

Cyn was aware of Leo on her heels and fought the urge to look over her shoulder at him.

"Don't trip, Cyn."

"Yes, thank you, I am quite capable of walking up the stairs with an elevated hand," she said to Lewis.

Cyn had met Lewis the day she'd been standing on the street looking up at the plaque being attached above the front door. He had asked her what the Phoenix Agency was, and she'd found herself talking to him about it and her plans for the women she wanted to help. Before she'd known what she was about, Cyn had hired him to help her run it. Not once had she regretted that.

Lewis was kind when kindness was needed and strong when required also. The women loved him for his forthright manner, and Cyn counted him as a friend.

They entered the upstairs, and she thought Leo would walk out the front door and leave. He didn't and followed her into the small parlor Lewis waved her to.

"I am quite all right, my lord. You may leave."

"Hello!"

"In here, Ellen," Leo called, his eyes on Cyn. "Come and say hello to an old friend."

Every muscle in Cyn's body clenched as she heard the footsteps. She then sneezed. *Damn.* Ellen Nightingale had once been a friend, and it was through her that she'd first been introduced to Leo.

Her eyes went from him to the door, and then two people walked through it—Alexander and Ellen Nightingale.

Smaller than her brothers and slender with lovely blond curls, Ellen had been the epitome of a debutante, just like Cyn had been. They'd been drawn together from the start, and possibly that was because they'd been popular, but she had also liked Ellen's humor, when she let it out. They'd often giggled over ridiculous things.

When the Nightingales' life had imploded, Cyn had not only lost the man she loved but a friend too.

"Hyacinth?" Ellen stopped beside Leo. "Is it really you?"

She nodded. Ellen then took a tentative step closer, holding out a hand to Cyn.

"It is lovely to see you again. Leo told me what happened the other night, and I'm so pleased he was there to help you when you fell into the water."

"Yes, I was very grateful." Her voice sounded odd, like a rusty door hinge.

"You look different. Older, which is silly, because of course you are, but still so beautiful," Ellen said.

"As are you," she managed to get out around the tightness in her throat.

"I am married to Detective Grayson Fletcher," Ellen added.

She'd missed her friend. Not with the bone-deep ache of missing the man she loved—*thought* she'd loved, but Cyn had pined for Ellen also.

Ellen moved closer and then grabbed her in a hug, wrapping her arms around Cyn and squeezing. "I've missed you."

"Well now, this is a surprise," she heard Alexander Nightingale say. "Imagine Lady Lowell being here, in the building next door to the one we plan to purchase."

"Alex," she heard Leo growl.

Cyn backed out of the embrace, and Ellen's arms fell away, as did her smile.

"Hello," Alexander said, moving forward next. She remembered he was usually smiling or flirting with young ladies when they'd been in society together. "Lovely to see you again, my lady."

She curtsied and then turned to face Lewis, whose eyes were wide, enquiring, and flitting around the people now in the room. He'd have plenty of questions later.

"This is Mr. Crowe," she said, waving her good hand his way.

They greeted him.

"Do you have the makings for tea here?" Alexander asked.

"We do," Lewis said before she could deny it. "I will make some."

Drat. How was she to get rid of these people now? Being near them made her remember the connection they'd once shared. They made her feel off-balance.

"Mary will return shortly," she said, giving Lewis a hard look. "We have an appointment also arriving soon."

"Plenty of time, as we usually take tea at this hour, and if she returns, she can join us," Lewis said calmly, which had Cyn wanting to snap her teeth together. *We've never had a set teatime. What's his game?*

"I will just pop out to that tea shop we passed on the corner and see what I can find for us to eat," Alexander said. "We shall have a tea party."

"They have wonderful iced buns there," Lewis said, clearly unaware that these were, in fact, the last three people she would like to take tea with. Cyn shot Leo a look; he was looking at her with the same guarded expression.

"Do they really? Well now, that seals it," Alexander said. "We have to secure the lease on the property next door. I will be back shortly, Lewis, so go and brew that tea."

Cyn looked from Ellen to Leo and could not find a thing to say after the two men had left. She excelled at social chitchat in the evening, but it had all deserted her.

"I'm sorry for what happened." Ellen broke the silence first.

"There is no need. I understand why you left London." Her words sounded cool and composed. Kenneth had taught her that too. He'd schooled her on hiding her emotions along with money management and being a great deal stronger than she'd been when he married her. "We have all grown up, and there is no need to speak of that time."

"But I'm truly sorry we left you without a word, Hy—Lady Lowell," Ellen said.

Cyn kept her eyes on Ellen; it was easier than dealing with her brother. She hated how aware she still was of him. He was nothing to her now but an acquaintance and hopefully someone she rarely saw going forward.

Don't take the lease on the property next door.

"It matters not, really. Please don't give it another thought."

"I understand you have two children," Ellen added.

"I do. They were my late husband's children and are wonderful." They were her life, in short. She had never loved anyone quite like she did Simon and Meg. Perhaps the only time she'd loved someone as fiercely was when she'd loved the man in this room.

"She has hurt her hand, Ellen," Leo said. "But won't let me look at it."

"It is fine, as I told you." She glared at Leo. He simply raised a dark brow.

"Let me see, Hyacinth."

"There is no need to fuss, Mrs. Fletcher. I will pour some brandy on it." Cyn backed away as the Nightingale siblings approached. "We keep some in the cabinet there for clients," she added, babbling. She was usually controlled, but not now, today, with these two close.

A large hand reached over her shoulder as Cyn opened the cabinet and grabbed the brandy decanter.

"You will let us look at your hand, my lady." Leo said the words into her ear, and she refused to shiver. Instead, she sneezed.

"Do you still sneeze when you are nervous?" Ellen asked. "Or are you reacting to something? Mungo, he lives with us, reacts to lavender."

"Yes, it is the dust in the air," Cyn lied.

"Let me see your injury. It may fester if it is not treated and need to be lopped off." Ellen grabbed her hand before she could stop her and began to unwind the bandage Lewis had applied. She then tsked. "This needs cleaning, my lady."

"It will not fester." She tried to tug her hand free, but Ellen held on.

"Here." A large hand held out a square of white linen.

"Pour some of the brandy on it, Leo," Ellen ordered. "Then we will place it under the bandage and rewrap it. It will do for now, but when you get home, have it cleaned, and I'm sure someone in your household has ointment."

Cyn tensed when Leo placed the pad on the wound, but as his fingers didn't touch her skin, she relaxed slightly, then hissed out a breath as the alcohol stung. Ellen efficiently rewound the bandage.

"Thank you."

"You are welcome." Ellen smiled.

Dressed in pale sage green, her old friend was the epitome of elegance and beauty. Beside her brother, they looked as prosperous, titled people should look. But they weren't that anymore. They could be prosperous—she wouldn't know—and they were titled, but they no longer walked in society.

"I'm back!"

Leo's eyes rolled, and Ellen laughed as Alexander's voice reached them. Family and love, she thought. She'd always envied them that. Her parents were old and spent their time in the country, and her older sister lived away from London now, settled not far with her husband and four children. There were ten years between her and Penelope. Cyn tried to see them a few times a year, but she could not always make it work.

Alexander Nightingale burst into the room with his arms full. "They had apricotines—I must tell Ram. In fact, it all looked delicious, so we will be returning often after we take the lease on the place next door."

"If we take the lease," Leo added.

"Tea," Lewis said, entering behind him.

"Why are you looking at leasing the building next door?" Cyn asked, because maybe she could dissuade them. She moved to a chair across the table from where Leo and Ellen stood.

"To run our businesses from," Alex said when no one else spoke. "We are no longer the indolent noblemen you once knew, my lady."

"I'm sure there are a great many things different about all of us from the people we were," Leo said.

She had to agree with that. Leo was somber, and even

Ellen seemed different. Alex, she was sure, had changed, even as he seemed the same.

Should she tell them about the Phoenix Agency's clientele? That would surely change their mind about taking the property next door, and that had to be a good thing.

CHAPTER TEN

*H*yacinth had always been beautiful, and now she was dry, even more so. The shy innocence he'd once seen in her was now gone, and in its place was a silent, composed woman. Her topaz eyes were cool and wary, but he'd seen the flare of emotion briefly when Ellen had walked into the agency. It had gone in seconds, but Leo was sure there had been longing.

He knew Ellen and Hyacinth had been friends, because that's how he'd met her. His sister, like him, had walked away from her. He'd never given thought to how she'd suffer when they left. He thought she'd just move on after mourning what she'd lost briefly, but her anger the night he'd saved her from the Thames suggested otherwise.

Leo realized the depth of his love for Hyacinth had been as deep as he'd been capable of then, which was not very deep at all. Shame washed through him. He'd left and thought only of himself and his family's suffering, not hers.

"Seeing as your hand is sore, Cyn, I will pour," Lewis said.

Alex placed his package on the table.

"Surely you can find a plate for that," Ellen snapped.

Heaving a weary sigh, Alex regained his feet and went to hunt out a plate with Lewis directing him.

"So, my lady, what is it you do here?" Ellen asked.

"We are an agency that helps young ladies seek gainful employment," Lewis said when Hyacinth didn't answer straightaway. "Not a brothel like Lord Seddon insinuated when he first arrived."

"I did no such thing," Leo protested. He hadn't said it, even if he'd thought it.

"I beg your pardon?" That got a reaction out of Hyacinth. Her lovely eyes fired to life. "How dare you think such a thing."

"I did not say you ran a brothel."

"But you thought it," Lewis said.

"I concede I wasn't sure what it was you were doing here," Leo said. "But seeing as the man who showed us next door said they were struggling to lease the property we looked at, I did wonder why, considering the location is desirable."

"He is the untrusting Nightingale," Alex said around a mouthful of food as he reentered the room.

"Can you not swallow before you speak?" Leo snapped.

His brother ignored him and took another bite of bun.

"And while I know that even saying the word *brothel* makes you uneasy, my lord," Cyn said in a frosty tone, "let me assure you it is not the desired choice of occupation for many who are forced into that line of work."

"I'm sure," Ellen soothed.

"A woman's lot in life is not to be scoffed at," Hyacinth added.

"I did not scoff," Leo said, trying to remain calm.

"You really must meet my wife," Alex said. "You two would get on swimmingly is my guess. She's a wonderful woman with a fiery independence and is part of the suffragette movement."

Leo heard the love and pride his brother had for Harriet.

"Hello!" Another voice could be heard outside.

"I'll go," Lewis said, rising.

"It is I, Mr. Williams!"

Leo was watching Hyacinth, so he saw her stiffen. Clearly, whoever Mr. Williams was, she was not pleased to see him.

"Where are your children today, Lady Lowell?" Alex asked, still eating. "I remember Lord Lowell. He was a good man, so I'm sure any progeny of his would be the same."

Her expression softened. It was a slow thing; her lovely mouth eased out of its line, and the edges tilted upward. The cold expression in her eyes softened too.

"They are well, thank you, and yes, the very best of children."

"What are their names?" Alex asked, slowly drawing her out, which he was good at. He could get anyone to tell him anything.

Leo often envied the ability Alex had to be comfortable around others. He could walk into any situation or meet anyone for the first time, and he was relaxed. Leo had never been that way and often came across arrogant, especially when he was in a situation that unsettled him.

"Simon is sixteen and Margaret is twelve."

"Great ages. Is your son to attend a school?" Alex asked.

Leo saw the uncertainty on Hyacinth's face, but before she could answer, Lewis returned.

"I'm afraid he is waiting until you have time to see him," he said to Hyacinth. "Apparently Mr. Williams must speak to you directly, and I cannot pass on the message."

She wasn't happy about that either.

"Then we will leave you," Leo said, shooting his family a look they understood meant it was time to go. Alex rose and bowed.

"Good day," Hyacinth said, sounding relieved at their

departure. At least she was more civil with him today than she had been after he'd saved her from drowning.

"Take care of your hand, my lady," Leo said, bowing before her.

"Yes, I will, thank you," she added.

"Goodbye, my lady," Alex said, elbowing Leo out of the way. "It was lovely to see you again."

"Yes, it was," Ellen said, nudging Leo even farther to the side so she could stand in front of Hyacinth. "I hope we meet again soon, especially if we take the lease next door."

Leo watched Hyacinth hesitate, and instead of answering, she said, "Goodbye, Mrs. Fletcher."

"Good day, my lady." Leo took his sister's arm and waved Alex before them, and then after a final look at the woman who should have been his wife, he left the room.

They walked out to the entrance area and found a man standing there dressed in a black suit.

"Good day." He frowned at them, clearly wondering why they were here. "Are you in need of the Phoenix Agency's services?" Mr. Williams asked.

"I'm not sure what business that is of yours, sir," Leo said in his best viscount voice. Clearly Hyacinth had not been happy about the prospect of seeing this man.

"I am a close friend of Lady Lowell's. As a widow, it is important she has someone watching over her interests," the man said in a pompous tone.

"She has plenty of people watching over her," Lewis said in a hard voice from the door, where he was holding it open for the Nightingales.

Mr. Williams blustered but said nothing further.

"Good day," Leo and his siblings said to Lewis as they left the building.

As Mungo had just pulled up, they all climbed into the carriage. Leo took the seat beside his sister.

"That went well," Alex said, always the one to speak first in any situation.

"She hates us, I'm sure of it," Ellen said. "I never thought the day would come that Hyacinth would hate anyone, as I did not believe she had that in her, but it seems I was wrong."

"Don't be dramatic. She does not hate us," Alex scoffed. "She was polite and yet distant, and why wouldn't she be. You are now strangers, Ellen, as is Leo. She once loved him desperately, and then he left, and that, too, has to leave a scar, along with likely everything else that has happened in her life. Her husband was old enough to be her father, after all. That cannot have been a desired match."

"Her family must have forced her to wed him," Ellen said.

"You have no idea what happened, so there is no need to speculate," Leo said, but he agreed. Hyacinth had likely been forced to wed Lowell, and he hated that that was probably due to him.

"She's exceedingly pretty," Alex said.

"And you're married," Leo snapped.

"Don't get testy with me. You know I need to vocalize everything," Alex said.

"It's your most irritating trait."

"Surely not. There must be others." Alex smirked.

"She was polite yet cold," Ellen said. "Angry no doubt because we both left her without a word."

"There was little time to send out goodbye letters, sister," Leo said. "We were under a cloud of disgrace. Our father had just killed himself, and we were facing ruin—I think we had other things to worry about."

Ellen turned watery eyes on him. "But even though she had family, they were not close, Leo. We were to be the family she had always wished for."

"What?"

"You never knew what her life was like, but I did. She

THE FALLEN VISCOUNT

wanted so badly to marry you, the man she loved and adored, and that I would become her sister only added to that."

He stared at Ellen. He hadn't known Hyacinth was lonely.

"She didn't talk to you like she did to me. Hyacinth was raised in a strict family. Yes, they loved her, but her life was spent being seen and not heard. She was younger than her sister by ten years, and they had not expected to have another child, but then there was Hyacinth. They had little time for her."

His chest felt tight suddenly as he remembered back to the times he'd spent with her. He'd known she was devoted to him and accepted that as his due back then. Arrogant sod that he was. He was Lord Seddon; therefore, he should be worshipped by the woman he had chosen to wed.

"We had no choice," Leo whispered, but they heard.

"We thought we had no choice, but perhaps we closed ourselves off to what we left behind?" Alex said. "The devastation and shock stopped us from seeing that there were those that had been our friends and more. Those that deserved at least a note from us."

Hyacinth had waited for them at every social occasion. Leo would arrive with his family, and she'd find him; it would never be the other way around. She was always doing things for him. Getting him a drink at a ball or bringing him sweets if he took her driving. The memories he'd locked away were leaking out, filtering information through his head.

I have this for you. I know you have wanted to read it for some time.

He'd called at her house to take tea, and she'd arrived with a book in her hands, and it had been the exact title he'd talked of only two nights before.

"She deserved more from both of us," Ellen said softly.

He'd not asked Hyacinth questions about herself. Not

asked what her favorite color was or food. Leo had talked about himself. Closing his eyes, he felt shame wash over him again.

"She is a different woman from the quiet, shy one I remember," Alex said.

"Very," Ellen agreed. "That Hyacinth we just left bears no resemblance to the woman I once knew."

His siblings talked, and Leo thought about that time in his life that he could only term as hell. He'd believed that keeping his family safe was to be his only concern, and then when his uncle and aunt arrived and loaded up the entire family and took them to the country, all he could think was relief. Leo was leaving London and the hell that awaited them if they dared to step outside their front door.

I never gave her a second thought.

"I had a vision while we were in there," Ellen said.

"Are you all right?" He hadn't noticed because Hyacinth had held all his attention.

"I'm well." Ellen waved away his concern. "It doesn't always make me feel unsteady. I saw Hyacinth standing in a room, staring out the window, and she was weeping. No noise was coming from her, but that she was devastated was clear to me. And then I saw her standing with a child on either side of her at a grave. Her husband's grave."

It hurt to hear those words. He didn't like to think of Hyacinth in pain, and yet he'd inflicted that and more on her.

"And now I should likely tell you who visited me while we were in the Phoenix Agency," Alex said solemnly. "I did not say anything, as I am sure she is not ready for that."

His brother was never solemn, so the hair on the back of Leo's neck rose.

"Who?" Ellen demanded.

"Her husband was there," Alex said. "He kept showing me the triquetra."

Leo frowned.

"You remember, Leo, that was the Celtic symbol that the Baddon Boys gang had tattooed on them when Gray was investigating George Nicholson's murder."

"Why would the late Lord Lowell be showing you that?" Leo asked.

"I have no idea," Alex said. "He is also showing me a bird, but it's up high, like on the side of a building or in a window or sign. The words he is filling my head with are *trouble*, *bird*, and *triquetra*. He feels a bit frantic, which is nothing like the Lord Lowell I remember, even though I did not have a great deal to do with him. Good Lord," Alex whispered seconds later.

"What?" Ellen demanded.

"Now, you'll not judge me—"

"Just tell us," Leo snapped.

"The Avis Men's Club that is basically a gambling establishment for those that are barred from more reputable ones—"

"You were barred—"

"We are not talking about me," Alex cut Leo off. "Avis is on the same street as a brothel called the Bird of Paradise."

"Avis is bird in Latin," Leo said.

Alex clicked his fingers. "By Jove, you are correct. The bird Lowell is showing me is the bird of paradise Uncle Bram told us about. You remember, he has that book with a picture in it from his travels."

"Is the brothel near the Baddon Boys' club also owned by them?" Ellen asked.

"I've never asked, but my guess is yes if Lowell is showing me these things. I'm just not sure where Hyacinth fits into all this, and why he is showing it to us, other than he wants us to look out for her."

"Do you remember when Gray did some investigating

into the Baddon Boys when all that business with him being kidnapped went down," Leo asked. His siblings nodded. "Did he tell you that he'd found out that the Baddon Boys are actually quite wealthy and own a lot of real estate and businesses?"

"Yes, that's right." Ellen clicked her fingers.

"The Phoenix is also a bird. It could be that you are seeing, Alex," Leo added.

"No, I'm sure it's the bird of paradise," Alex said.

"Do you think perhaps the Phoenix Agency is a front for something else?" Ellen asked soberly.

"Hyacinth would never do anything illegal," Leo said. "It's not in her nature, and I doubt she has changed that much, especially considering Lowell was well respected and she is raising his children." He knew this deep in his soul.

"Agreed. Then why is Lowell showing Alex these things if there is no connection to Hyacinth?" Ellen asked.

That he didn't know, but he would make it his mission to find out, because he'd wronged her, and perhaps helping her would put that right for both of them.

CHAPTER ELEVEN

"What can I do for you, Mr. Williams?" Hyacinth said, walking out to the entranceway five minutes after the Nightingales had left.

"You have hurt your hand. Can I help you, Lady Lowell?"

"No, it is fine, but thank you."

"I have come to see if you would take a drive with me in my new curricle, my lady. There is to be a fete nearby. I thought you would like to attend."

Mr. Williams was the son of a wealthy merchant who owned many properties and businesses in London. His father had married the daughter of a baron, and now the entire family walked in society. She'd met him four months ago and been avoiding him ever since. He had made it no secret that he wanted a titled wife and had decided on Hyacinth. She could think of nothing worse, but as yet had not dissuaded him.

Kenneth had ensured they were cared for financially, and she needed no man to look after her or her children. If sometimes she wanted to experience what Letitia and Charles had with a deep, longing ache inside, it soon passed. Her thoughts went to Leo, and she pushed them away. There was nothing to gain from going there.

"Come now, you must have some joy in your life, surely?" Mr. Williams said.

He was a good-looking man, she supposed. Women certainly thought so, and that was another reason she had no idea why he'd settled on her as someone he wished to pursue. There were plenty that would love Mr. Williams's attentions, but not Hyacinth.

He was always dressed immaculately and smiled a lot, flattering with ease. The man was harmless, if annoying. What he would never be was her husband.

"I have commitments with my children, sir."

"I suppose they could come."

"How gracious," she said with feigned pleasure. "However, I will have to decline. Good day to you, Mr. Williams. I must get back to work."

He scoffed. "You have no need of work, my dear lady. Let me take you out for tea. A woman such as you deserves to be pampered and spoiled, not work." His smile irritated her.

"No, thank you. I have just had tea with friends." Cyn wasn't sure why she'd said that, but it had come out. Perhaps old habits die hard.

"Friends? I don't think I have met them before."

"I did not realize you had to know all my friends, Mr. Williams." Hyacinth knew Lewis sat at his desk listening to every word they spoke. He was there should she require him to escort this man out.

"No, indeed, you'll excuse my presumption. But everything about you intrigues me, my lady."

She had tried to dampen his interest but failed. Perhaps she should be more direct in her approach. "Let me speak plainly, Mr. Williams."

"Of course, I want that between us," he said, his tone condescending.

"I am not looking to marry anyone ever again. I am a widow and will stay that way. My children are my only concern, and I'm sorry if you believed otherwise. Please expect nothing more from me than what we are—acquaintances."

His smile fell, and Cyn realized she had never spoken to him in such a direct manner before. Clearly, it was overdue.

"No woman wishes to live her days without a companion, surely, my lady."

"I do."

"If you will just allow me the chance, I can change your mind," he said, taking her hand before she could stop him. Hyacinth snatched it back. "I am not one to give up."

"Please do. There are plenty of more worthy recipients for your attentions. I suggest you seek out one of them. Good day to you, Mr. Williams. Please do not return."

"I am, of course, desolate," he said, looking like a mournful puppy.

Hyacinth heard Lewis mutter something, but she couldn't make out what. He then got out of his chair and walked to the door, opening it for the now-forlorn Mr. Williams to walk through.

"Well, that was a morning," Lewis said after he'd closed it.

"I'm exhausted," Hyacinth said.

"Do you want to talk about the dark, handsome lord and his family?" Lewis asked.

"No."

"But?"

"But nothing. They are from my past. I have no wish to discuss them."

"But I have a feeling they will call upon you again, especially if they take the lease next door."

"We will not see a lot of each other," Hyacinth said, hoping it was true. She was not sure she could take too much exposure to the Nightingales. It made her remember what once she'd longed for.

"Oh, I think you could be wrong there."

As the door behind them opened once more, the conversation, thankfully, finished.

"Good day," Hyacinth said to the young lady who stepped inside. She could tell at once the woman was nervous, and the look in her eyes was defiant. A dark, ugly bruise ran the length of her chin, her dress was deep red, and she wore no bonnet or gloves.

"How may we at the Phoenix Agency help you?" Cyn asked calmly.

"My friend Trixie said you would help me."

"Are you speaking of Trixie Leigh?"

The woman nodded at Cyn's question. She remembered Trixie well. Lewis had found her lying in a doorway one evening as he returned home from visiting friends. She'd run away from the place she worked as a prostitute and was living on the streets.

"What is your name?" Cyn asked.

"Leona Brown."

"Well, Leona, if you want our help, then we need to ask a few questions," Cyn said.

Only a select few knew the Phoenix Agency was for women such as Leona, and Cyn was determined to keep it that way. To keep it as a safe house of sorts for those who had nowhere else to run.

"Are you also a prostitute, Miss Brown?" Lewis asked.

One thing Cyn and Lewis had realized in their dealings with women who'd had hard lives was they did not want platitudes or lies about how things would be all right from now on. They wanted straight talking, and it had taken Cyn time to understand this. Lewis, however, was a master at it.

"I am. I work for him, but I won't anymore." She rubbed her arm. "Like Trixie, I want to get away."

Cyn thought she knew who she spoke of. Trixie had told her a few things, but so far, they had not been given a name.

"Him?"

"I only know him as the Wolf."

"You are one of the Baddon Boys' ladies?" Cyn asked next, having heard of the Wolf. "Do you work at the Bird of Paradise?"

Leona nodded. "They're a mean bunch, some of them."

"Well then, let's see what we can do to help you. Tea, please, Lewis," Cyn said. Leading Leona into the parlor the Nightingales had recently vacated, she waved her into a chair.

Cyn had started the Phoenix Agency six months after her husband's death, but she'd told Kenneth that this was something she'd wanted to do... well, not quite an agency for prostitutes and women who had fallen on hard times, but an agency to help women find work. Her late husband had told her about this building.

When she'd come here to inspect it, she'd met her first client. Miss Mary Coulter. The woman had been huddled around the rear of her property, sleeping, when Cyn arrived. She'd also run away from the brothel she had worked in. Cyn had told her she could sleep inside, and she'd never left.

"Do you have a place to sleep, Leona?" Cyn asked.

"I can't go back there, seeing as I spoke up and said I don't want to do it no more. No one leaves unless they wish it from the Bird of Paradise. I'm right fearful after what he's done to Clara when she tried to get away. She's hiding somewhere, but I couldn't find her."

"The Wolf?" Cyn asked.

"Yes, but it's never him who does the dirty work but one of the Baddon Boys gang. He's a mean one, and he'll have me roughed up or killed if he finds me."

"Then we will make sure he does not get near you again," Cyn said firmly, and that was all it took to crack the hard veneer of Leona Brown. Tears leaked from her eyes.

"And Clara. You have no idea where she is or what condition she is in?" Cyn asked gently.

"I-I don't know. He hurt her, and some others hid her somewhere. They wouldn't tell me where."

Often these women had taught themselves how to lock away feelings. But with a glimmer of hope, the facade frequently crumbled, and the cascade of tears falling down Leona's cheeks told her that was the case here.

"There now, Leona. It will be hard work, but if you are willing, we will make sure from this day forth that things are different for you."

"Tea," Lewis said, returning.

"Lovely," Cyn said. Her friend then set about pouring cups and handing them out, taking the seat beside Cyn after.

Lewis could be silent as a mouse when required. Like Cyn, he had sat through many interviews just like this one. He also knew that being a man, he was seen as a threat to these women.

"Upstairs, we have rooms you are welcome to stay in until you no longer need them," Cyn said. "But we insist you tell no one our address or that you are staying here."

Leona nodded. "I have no family, and my friends are at the Bird of Paradise, but I won't go back there." She looked down at her hands. "I need to tell you something, my lady."

"Of course," Cyn said.

"They're growing suspicious, my lady, so I'll understand if you want me to find other lodgings."

"Pardon?" Cyn wasn't sure why, but suddenly the hair on the back of her neck was standing.

"After Trixie, then you helped Cathy—"

"Cathy Miller was not one of the Baddon Boys' women," Cyn said.

"But she was known to them, and she was in Luther's stable, and he's a friend of the Wolf."

"How do you know this?"

Leona shrugged. "I hear stuff. It's amazing what a man will tell you when he's got his pants down. I didn't hear your name outright, but they said a high-class nob was interfering with the women, and she may have to be stopped."

Dear God.

"Hello."

Cyn looked to the door and watched Mary walk in while she grappled with what Leona had said. Was it true? Did they know her identity? Or was it like she said, they knew she was nobility? What of Meg and Simon? Were they in danger?

"Come in, Mary," Lewis said.

She pushed aside the thoughts for now; she'd think more about it later. Cyn focused on the woman who had just arrived.

No longer the frightened lady she'd found that day, Mary looked happy and confident. Her blond hair was pinned in a neat bun, and she wore a simple blue day dress. She had helped the Phoenix Agency become what it was today.

"Mary, this is Leona. She needs our help."

"Well then, she's in just the right place," Mary said.

"She needs a bed for a while, Mary," Lewis said, his eyes softening as he looked at her.

Cyn could not confirm it absolutely, but she thought perhaps he was in love with Mary. However, she had such a mistrust of men, and Cyn wasn't sure that devotion would ever be reciprocated. She hoped it was, as they were two of her most favorite people.

"Excellent, I will enjoy the company." Mary was the only woman who stayed at the Agency full-time. She was here to look after the other women who visited for however long they needed to.

"Leona told me about a woman called Clara, who was mistreated after she tried to leave the Bird of Paradise, Mary. It could be the same woman you referred to in that note," Cyn said.

"Then we must try to find her."

Cyn agreed. If there was a woman out there alone, hurting and scared, they would need to find her.

When Mary had taken Leona up the stairs to look after her, Cyn sat and sipped her tea, thinking about what Leona said.

"Do you believe we are in danger here, Lewis?"

"No one has approached us before, but I think considering what Leona said, we must take care."

"Do you think I should have someone watch the place to be safe?" Cyn asked.

"I could sleep downstairs if you are worried. Once we clear it out, that is."

"Of course, I would need to discuss it with Mary, but I would feel happier with you here until I know there is no danger, Lewis."

He got that smile on his face he always got when Mary's name was mentioned but simply nodded.

"Will you tell me about Lord Seddon now, Cyn?"

"He is someone I once thought would be my husband. But before that could happen, his father took his own life and left behind enormous debts. The family was ruined in the eyes of society and fled London."

"Society is a fool," Lewis said, disgusted.

"Indeed, it is," Cyn agreed. "I wonder how we can find the woman, Clara, that Leona is worried about."

"I will ask a few of the lads who drop by for food occasionally if they have heard anything," Lewis said.

"Excellent. I will have Mrs. Varney bake some more cakes and biscuits for them."

"And you never saw Lord Seddon again until now?" Lewis circled back to Leo.

"He was the one who pulled me out of the Thames a few days ago."

"Good Lord."

"And that is the end of the story."

"Oh, I doubt that, but for now, I am appeased. I knew there was something between you, as he could not keep his eyes off you."

Her heart absolutely did not flutter over Lewis's words. "I don't think so. Now"—Cyn rose—"we have work to do and cleaning out the downstairs so you can move in there for a while is the first task."

Lewis groaned but rose to join her. "Is your hand up to doing more work?"

"It is fine now. The bleeding has stopped. I shall put something on it when I go home shortly," Cyn said, walking out of the parlor.

"I have a nice pie for Miss Mary's supper, and I'll get about cleaning the downstairs rooms shortly," the woman who was bustling in through the rear door with her arms full said.

"Thank you, Mrs. Varney. How is your daughter?" Cyn asked. Beside her, Lewis shuddered.

Mrs. Varney had been working for them since they opened, and she occasionally brought her daughter to help. Tabitha tended toward flirtatious behavior and terrified Lewis.

"Well now, she's still not wed, for all the trying she does," the woman said, lowering her things to a table. She then took off her favorite bonnet covered in flowers and hung it on a hook.

"We are going downstairs to clean out. If you need us, Mrs. Varney, just call," Cyn said.

"If you need some help, I've a few friends who are able. You just let me know."

"I will, thank you, Mrs. Varney."

"Did you love him?" Lewis said as they left by the rear door once more.

"Lewis, I am not discussing Lord Seddon any more with you."

"Just answer that question, and I will ask you no more."

Cyn sighed. "I did. Very much. In fact, for a while, I wondered if I'd love anyone else, and then I grew up."

CHAPTER TWELVE

"I have received an invitation to the Duke of Raven's charity ball."

Leo, who had been feeding Chester beneath the table, looked at his uncle as he spoke.

"Excellent. I am sure you will enjoy it."

He'd spent the last week thinking about Hyacinth and telling himself he did not need to see her again. What was once between them, young and innocent that it was, could be no longer. He needed to forget about her.

"It will be a wonderful occasion. The duke always puts on an enjoyable evening and for such an excellent cause," Aunt Ivy said.

"I'm going this year," Theo said.

He was the mischievous Nightingale and spent much of his energy tormenting his sisters. Even heading toward the "advanced age"—Theo's words—of nearly twenty, he could still behave like a ten-year-old.

"I wish I could go," Matilda said from across the table. She had brown hair, but her eyes were blue, and she was the second-to-youngest Nightingale and usually had an opinion on everything.

"I'm sorry, darling, you, Fred, and Anna are too young, but I thought everyone else could attend this year," Uncle Bram said with his eyes on Leo.

"I don't go to society events," Leo said while his little sisters debated how unfair it was, as surely they would enjoy a ball the most.

"But this is a charity event, and as the duke has been kind enough to come here to our weddings and shown his friendship to you all when you needed it, I think it is the right thing to do," Uncle Bram said.

"It is unfair," Frederica, also known as Fred at her insistence, was the Nightingale most likely to have her nose in a book. She was taller than her sisters and had brown hair that curled in every direction and sat below Theo in the Nightingale ladder.

"And yet you won't be, as you are too young," Theo said with a smirk.

"There is no need to lord it over your sister, Theo," Anna, the last person at the table, said.

She'd been an orphan, and with Harriet's help, Anna had come to live with them after being injured and no one caring for her. The little girl fit into the family with ease, considering the hell she'd been raised in.

"You're too young also," Theo said.

"I'm sure I'm not invited, as my blood is not as blue as yours," she said.

"You are part of this family. Therefore, where we go, you go," Theo snapped back.

"Well said, brother," Leo added, smiling at her.

"However, not to this, as you are too young." Theo had to have the last word.

Anna poked out her tongue.

"That will do," Aunt Ivy said.

"I don't want to go to the Raven ball, Uncle."

"You saw some members of society the evening you saved Lady Lowell and survived, Leo."

"Ram punched someone who insulted me," Leo said, trying to stay calm. He was the rational and controlled Nightingale sibling, for the most part. But lately he'd felt himself changing. The veneer he'd carefully cultivated was cracking.

"Not someone. Ellington, who could not be considered civilized by anyone's definition. He is a leech and of no consequence, and I will be having a chat with him when next we meet," Uncle Bram said with that look he got when anyone came at someone he loved.

"I can look after myself, Uncle Bram. You do not need to do so."

"It has become a habit I doubt I will ever lose."

"I agree," Aunt Ivy said. "It is time, Leo."

"For what?"

"To dip your toes back into society. Even the Duchess of Yardly agrees," Uncle Bram said. "You attend the theatre and ride about London. While I know you try to avoid eye contact, I've seen you acknowledging some people when it is unavoidable."

"Slightly different from attending a social function, Uncle," Leo said, feeling cornered.

"People know you are here, Leo. There is really no reason not to attend the duke's ball. Many who are not members of London society do. Businessmen and others. It is the perfect occasion. I have asked your siblings, and they are considering it," Uncle Bram said, ignoring him.

"We are," Alex said, wandering in with Harriet. "But right now, we have a more pressing discussion."

"What?"

"Who wants to go to the Pickersons' tea shop and visit the street fair?" Alex said. "It's new, and Ramsey told me it has the best Florentine tartlets he'd ever tasted."

All hands were raised by those under the age of twenty. Leo thought seriously about getting on his horse and fleeing the continent again. Things felt as though they were spiraling out of his control. He liked control.

"I've heard about Pickersons' and had planned on going," Harriet said. "I've never tried a Florentine tartlet either."

"What, never?" Alex shot his wife an astonished look.

"No, Alex, my family did not eat them, and we rarely frequented tea shops."

"Well, my darling, that is all about to change." Alex kissed her on the cheek.

Leo loved his sister-in-law, and not just because she'd made Alex happy. She was kind, sweet natured, and had settled into their family with ease. Harriet also didn't judge people, which could not be said of some members of her family.

Born in America, the Shaws had come to England to join the upper echelons of London society. Her mother was a social-climbing dragon, and Leo was glad Harriet was now part of their family and not the one she'd been born into.

"Hello, we are here!" Ellen walked in with Gray.

"I thought you worked for a living?" Leo said.

"I worked late last night, so today I am spending the day with my family," the detective said with a besotted smile.

"Lord, save us," Leo muttered. "You are a hard-nosed detective, man, behave like one."

Chester, who had been seated beside Anna, barked loudly. He was inches from her chair because she was always slipping the dog food like Leo. She'd told Theo she'd never had a pet, so no one scolded her off for doing so, even though the rest of the family was not allowed.

"Right," Uncle Bram said, rising.

"Cakes!" Lottie shrieked, getting off her mother's lap and sprinting around the table, yelling. Leo caught her as she reached him. Standing, he threw her up in the air before putting her back on her feet.

"But first, there is a small matter of the man about to knock on our door, who we are to interview for the position of clerk," Uncle Bram said.

"Who would ever have thought that the spoiled, indolent Nightingales needed a clerk?" Alex mocked.

"Some of you are still indolent," Leo said, catching Lottie and repeating the process of tossing her into the air when she reached him again.

"Out front and dressed in one hour," Uncle Bram instructed.

"Do you need the presence of another intelligent adult, Bram?" Gray asked.

"No, thank you, Gray. I have it in hand," Uncle Bram said as Leo and Alex threw insults at the detective.

"We have no wish to listen to you interrogating the poor man, my love, as I know you will," Ellen said. "Besides, we are to leave soon. You can help Aunty Ivy get this lot ready."

Bram then kissed his wife, and Alex did the same. Ellen kissed Gray's cheek, and Leo told himself he didn't care that no one was in need of a kiss from him.

"I'm not going to the duke's charity ball," Leo said as they left the parlor.

"We'll see," Uncle Bram said.

"There is nothing to see."

"Be quiet, Leo. We will discuss it later, as I'm sure you have no wish for our future employee to enter and see you scowling," Alex said.

"He's getting more and more like Mungo," Ellen taunted him.

"You can be quiet too." Leo glared at his sister as they entered the office.

They spent a few minutes discussing what they would ask the man who would be here shortly, and when the knock sounded on the door a few minutes later, they were ready for the interview.

"Mr. Murphy," Mungo said, opening the door and waving a man inside. His scowl seemed more fierce than usual. "He's Irish," Mungo added, glaring at Uncle Bram.

"So I hear from Mr. Huntington, who recommended Mr. Murphy," Uncle Bram said, smiling at his old friend. "Thank you, Mungo. Now in or out of the door. Either way, I'd like it closed."

"In," Mungo snapped. He then shut it with a decisive click and leaned on the wall, folding his large arms.

Leo looked at his siblings, who appeared bemused as they rose to greet the man.

"Good day to you all," Mr. Murphy said. He had sparkling blue eyes and thick black hair that had not an ounce of curl, and Leo thought Mr. Murphy had attempted to flatten it with something and failed, as bits were sticking upward. He wore a neat black suit, white shirt, and necktie. On one lapel was pinned a four-leaf clover.

Mungo's lips curled as he noted it.

"I am Mr. Oscar Murphy," he said in a singsong voice that the younger Nightingale sisters were going to love. "And I am here to apply for the position of clerk."

Mungo harrumphed.

"Perhaps you can make us some tea, Mungo," Uncle Bram said.

Mungo stomped out with a final frown at Mr. Murphy.

"He seems an accommodating sort," Mr. Murphy said when Mungo left, and it was so ridiculous, they all laughed.

THE FALLEN VISCOUNT

"But have no fear that I am intimidated by him. I have five brothers and two sisters, and I am the youngest, you see."

Leo couldn't imagine what that was like.

"Five brothers," Ellen whispered. "How on earth do you cope? I have three and it's a trial."

Leo and Alex scoffed.

"What is it you did for Maxwell Huntington?" Uncle Bram asked, bringing the conversation back to the reason Mr. Murphy was here.

"His man of affairs, who happens to be my brother, was ill and laid low for a while."

"Oh no, I hope he has recovered?" Ellen asked.

"He has and is back to his annoying full health," Mr. Murphy said, which was exactly what a Nightingale would say. "I took up his duties until he could do so again."

"A very astute businessman, Mr. Huntington," Uncle Bram said.

"Very much so, as are most of his family members," Mr. Murphy said.

They talked, and Oscar Murphy answered the questions with confidence and intelligence. Leo liked him more and more as the interview drew to a close.

"Well then, when can you start?" Uncle Bram said after looking at Leo, Alex, and Ellen, who all nodded.

"I am honored," Mr. Murphy said. "And immediately if that is your wish. I have references," he added.

"No need." Leo waved them away. "Mr. Huntington is an excellent reference."

"Do you have lodgings here in London?" Alex asked.

"I am at present renting a room in Mr. Perceval's boarding house. A very shoddy establishment, so now I have secured a position, I will find another," Mr. Murphy said.

"There is a top floor in the building we are leasing to run

our business from. You are welcome to it, should you wish," Uncle Bram said. "I'm sure we can find something to furnish it with as well."

Until that moment, nothing had thrown Mr. Murphy, but he was speechless.

"You are under no obligation to take it, sir," Ellen rushed to add.

"I would like that above all things," Oscar Murphy said quickly. "To have a place that I don't need to share will be wonderful!"

"Well then," Leo said. "We will write down the address and meet you there in the morning. You can look, and we will work out what you need. Then, after the lease is finalized, you can move in."

"I-I can't thank you enough."

"There is no need to pay for the accommodations either, Mr. Murphy. You will do us a favor by looking after the place," Uncle Bram added, sending Oscar speechless once more.

He left ten minutes later, still gushing his gratitude.

Leo donned his coat and hat and then went outside with the rest of his family. Three carriages stood there, and several horses. He mounted one of them, more than happy to be out of the carriage where his siblings would chat incessantly.

"Do not lean out the window, Anna," Leo said as the carriage started moving. He pulled alongside her window. "You could hurt yourself."

She gave him a wide, mischievous smile, which had taken them months to coax out of her.

"Leo?"

"Yes, Anna."

"I love you and all my family. Thank you for saving me." She then blew him a kiss and returned to her seat.

Leo rubbed his chest. Anna had been timid and terrified when she'd come to live with them, but now she said exactly what was inside her head, and often that was telling them how much she loved them. He'd never tire of hearing it. He crooked his finger at her, and she leaned out again.

"I love you too. Now get inside and stay there, you horrid child."

She giggled and did as he asked.

"Hello!"

"Hello, Miss Varney," Gray said. "Don't you think Lord Seddon looks wonderfully handsome today?"

Leo hissed something foul beneath his breath.

"He is surely the most handsome of us all, but then that is expected with the title he holds," Alex added soberly.

"Desist," Leo hissed. Tabitha Varney had been hunting a husband for some time now, and her attentions had moved from Alex when he wed Harriet to Leo once more. The woman was terrifying.

Tabitha stood on her front step dressed in cream, and the dress gaped in the bodice, exposing her breasts.

"Get on with you, Tabitha Varney," Mavis Johns said. She was walking by the Varney house at a clip. "Put those away before you catch a chill."

"I swear that woman walks everywhere at that speed," Alex said as they rolled out of Crabbett Close, leaving a disappointed Tabitha Varney behind.

"So, is this the way it's going to be from now on?" Leo snapped. "You lot throwing Tabitha Varney at me?"

"It's fair, considering you did the same to me," Alex said, riding beside him.

They bickered as they rode, as they usually did. Those in the carriages hurled comments out the windows, and it was the mayhem of a Nightingale adventure. Once, this would never have been allowed. Their father was a stickler for propriety.

Mind you, he wouldn't be with them at all, if Leo was honest. He rarely, if ever, had gone out in public with his family unless it was a society event.

I will never be like that man.

CHAPTER THIRTEEN

"I like the Mulhollands, Mother."

"Yes, they are very nice men," Cyn said to her son as they walked in the sun behind people no doubt heading in the same direction.

A fair always drew crowds, as did a new tea shop. Her children loved both, so today they were indulging in a day of eating and fun.

"Large men," Meg said, swinging Cyn's hand. "But very nice."

Of course, she'd known they'd be curious why another two footmen were suddenly escorting them everywhere. The truth was, she'd employed Tobias and Montague Mulholland, at Mrs. Varney's recommendation, to watch over them after what Leona had said that day at the agency.

"You need more protection for your wee ones, my lady," Mrs. Varney had said after Lewis told her the story four days ago. "Big burly men who'll stand no nonsense," Mrs. Varney had continued.

Cyn had replied with "Do I?"

The story that followed was that the Mulholland twins

were her sister-in-law's husband's cousins and good boys, or so Mrs. Varney had said. They needed employment after the family they were working for had just up and left for France. What had followed had been a subtle manipulation about two young men in desperate need of work, and seeing as how Cyn needed two new footmen, it was perfect timing.

"Why do we need two large footmen with us when we leave the house, seeing as we have Prue and Mr. Dildersdale?" Simon asked.

How did she answer that?

"Mother?" Simon said.

"Right, sorry, I was thinking about another matter. You know that I have the Phoenix Agency and several other of your father's business interests to oversee?"

Her children nodded.

"Sometimes I am away from home for longer periods, and I wanted to ensure you have people watching over you."

"I am more than capable of looking after us," Prue said from beside Simon.

"I know you are, but you are often with me, Prue. The Mulhollands will be there solely for Meg and Simon should they need anything."

"Very well, my lady."

"And now we are going to take tea and eat cake, then wander through some stalls and buy useless things," Cyn said before anyone could question her further.

"I'm hoping they have one of those stalls that you have to knock over the wood. I have dreadfully good aim," Meg bragged.

While her brother took her to task for being a braggart, Cyn thought again about Leona's ominous words. In fact, besides Leo, she'd thought of little else.

Should she take her children from London? Tell them it was time to visit with their cousins for a while? Just long enough for things to die down and for her to ensure that, in fact, she had not caught the eye of the notorious Wolf. Things would run smoothly with Lewis and Mary at the helm at the agency, and she could deal with all the other business with the help of Kenneth's efficient man of affairs from the estate.

She was still mulling things over when they reached the Pickersons' tea shop, a single-story building that stood alone just before the opening to a park. Cyn could see the fair only a minute's walk away. Crowds of people were milling about, and Meg clapped her hands in excitement.

"Tea first," Cyn said.

Pickersons' was a white-painted brick facade and had a swinging sign that hung on two chains with a hat, teacup, and plate of cakes on it. Two large front windows showed her the place was full of patrons.

"Come, let us enter," Cyn said, nodding to one of the large Mulhollands who were accompanying them today as he opened the door. "Thank you... ah—"

"Toby, my lady."

"Toby, right? I promise I will learn which one of you is which shortly."

"Hello, Toby."

"Miss Meg." Toby bowed as her daughter walked by him.

"How is it you know which one is which," Cyn whispered.

"Toby's hair stands upright at the peak, and Monty's doesn't."

Cyn looked over her shoulder at the brothers who were still outside. Squinting, she noted that, in fact, Meg was right.

"You could have told me that sooner," Cyn muttered.

"It's not my fault you are unobservant, Mother," her daughter said in a snooty tone.

"You will fit right into society," Cyn said with a laugh. "Come along, Prue, Toby, and Monty."

"We will wait outside, my lady," they said at the same time.

Cyn waved them inside, and they reluctantly joined her.

"Do you not wish for tea?" she asked.

"We cannot take tea with you here, my lady," one twin said.

"If I say you can, then you can," Cyn added.

"It looks busy. I hope we get a table," Simon said from behind them.

"Well, we can always wander and go back for tea," Cyn said.

Her eyes swept the room briefly. There appeared to be two tables to the left that were free.

"Look, Simon," Meg said, sounding excited. "Theo, Fred, Anna, and Matilda are here!"

Cyn's head swiveled so fast, she wasn't sure it wouldn't end up looking down at her spine. She knew those names. Her eyes locked on Leo's as she saw him seated at a large table. On his lap was a small girl.

"You know them?" Cyn said in a strangled voice, dragging her eyes from the disturbing viscount and back to her children.

"Yes. We meet at the library sometimes and then at the park at Crabbett Close where they live."

How was it she did not know this? She was often with her children when they went to the park, but clearly not when they'd visited Crabbett Close. Mrs. Varney lived there, but not once had she mentioned the name Nightingale.

Why now was she destined to see Leo constantly? What fates had aligned so this was happening? It was extremely unfair, considering she wanted to avoid him.

"Ah, perhaps we could—"

"Are you looking for a table?" A young woman approached.

"We are. There are six of us," Simon said.

"Good boy," she said to him. Some thought servants were not to be seen or heard; they were just there to serve. She'd never wanted to be one of those people.

"We could come back if you are busy," Cyn said quickly.

"Don't be silly, Mother, there are two tables right there." Simon jabbed a finger in the exact direction where the Nightingales all sat. *Anywhere but there.*

"Come along, Mother. You remember meeting Matilda the other day in the park, don't you?" Meg said. "She was with Mungo."

Mungo? She saw him then, the large Scotsman who had been standing with his huge arms folded watching the girls run around with their kite.

Cyn had been in the presence of Leo's younger siblings and not known it. Before she could stop them, her children had gone to greet their friends.

She wasn't exactly dragging her feet, but it was a near thing as she, Prue, and the Mulhollands followed.

"Lady Lowell!"

And that was all I needed to improve my day, she thought, looking at the woman who had called out to her.

"Good day to you, Mrs. Blakey." She raised a hand, hoping that was enough of a greeting. It turned out she was wrong, and the woman waggled her fingers, indicating she wished to speak with Cyn.

It was a double-edged sword, if she was honest. Cyn was happy to walk away from Leo and the Nightingales but not happy to talk to one of society's most sharp-tongued ladies.

"Go and find tables," she told her children and staff.

"What on earth are you doing with your servants accompanying you, Lady Lowell? They do not take tea with us!" Mrs. Blakey sat with two of her cronies and her long-suffering husband. He was the only person Cyn liked at the table.

"I'm not sure how you know what my staff look like, Mrs. Blakey, but be assured they are wonderful people who deserve my respect."

The woman made a *pft* sound and waved Cyn's words away before continuing.

"Of course, you will do as you see fit, but I must warn you about something else, Lady Lowell."

"Oh?" But Cyn knew what was coming next.

"The Nightingale family is here. Can you believe the audacity? I had not thought to be subjected to taking tea with them, considering..." She let her words fall away.

Her friends tittered, and her husband sighed.

"They are my friends," Cyn said in a cool voice. It didn't matter how she felt about seeing Leo again; she would not listen to someone maligning him and his family when they had suffered so much. "Their father was the one in the wrong. Not them. I've never believed in the children being punished for their father's sins."

"Well!" Mrs. Blakey gasped.

"Now, if you are quite finished with your assassination of my character and that of the Nightingale family, I will bid you a good day." Cyn turned, and her eyes locked with Leo's again. He'd risen from his seat and was watching her.

Had he overheard her words?

"How rude," she heard Mrs. Blakey whisper.

Cyn had always tried to be pleasant in society and never make enemies. It seemed she'd just done exactly that.

"No, what is rude is you speaking in the manner you are so everyone can hear," Cyn snapped. "Perhaps, considering your son's penchant for wandering hands and the rumors about his, shall we say, appetites, you should not be one to gossip, Mrs. Blakey."

THE FALLEN VISCOUNT

"My son is a paragon!"

"No, he's not," the woman two tables to her left said. Cyn noticed it was Lady Sinclair. "He's far too free with his hands."

Mrs. Blakey flushed to the roots of her gray hair. She then rose and hurried out.

"Thank you," Cyn said, acknowledging Lady Sinclair, who she had always liked because she was strong-willed and never took a step back when a forward one was on offer.

"Most welcome. That beastly woman had it coming."

Cyn's smile felt strained, and then she was moving to where her children and staff now sat.

"Mother!" Meg shrieked, drawing all eyes. "Come and sit here and meet the Nightingale family."

"Don't shriek, sister, we all have excellent hearing," Simon said.

"Lady Lowell." Leo rose with a small girl in his arms. "I had no idea my siblings knew your children." He then bowed, making the child giggle. "How wonderful to see you again." This time the smile reached his eyes, and standing there holding that sweet child, he presented a handsome picture. Not that Cyn felt anything, but she was sure some women in the tea shop did.

"My son, Simon, Lord Lowell, and my daughter—"

"Meg," one of the Nightingales said. "We know them as Meg and Simon from the park." She grinned.

"Yes, thank you, Fred," Leo said to the young girl who had spoken. "It is lovely to meet you both," he then added to Simon and Meg.

They bowed and curtsied perfectly, which made her proud.

"You've met my uncle, I'm sure."

"Of course," she said, acknowledging both him and his wife. "They paid me a call after my impromptu swim."

"Did they now?" Leo said, shooting his aunt and uncle a look. "And that is Mungo," he then said, waving a hand at the large Scotsman.

"Good day to you, Lady Lowell," he said in a deep burr.

"I think the only other people at the table you do not know are Harriet, Alex's wife, and Gray, Ellen's husband," Leo continued.

She acknowledged everyone and kept her eyes from the man holding the delightful little girl in his arms.

"Lottie, say hello to Lady Lowell," Leo said.

"Hello," Cyn said, making herself look at the child.

"She is our daughter," Bramstone said.

"It is lovely to see and meet you all," Cyn got out of her tight throat. "I won't keep you any further from your tea."

Unfortunately, the two tables her family and staff now sat at were close to the Nightingales. In fact, Leo's chair was a mere foot from hers.

She was an adult and did not fall about the place anymore when Leo was near, Cyn reminded herself. She concentrated on Meg and Simon, who were debating what they wanted to eat.

"They are your staff?" Leo's words had her looking at him. The little girl had now left him to sit with the large Scotsman.

"They are the Mulhollands, my footmen, and maid Miss Bromley," Cyn said, daring him to question her. "Do you have a problem with my staff being here with me?"

"Not at all. We are a family who no longer stand on ceremony and have staff that are our friends as well. I just wondered why you needed them all with you when you take tea."

"It was my late husband's wish that I always have plenty of staff with me when the children leave the house," she said, thinking quickly. It wasn't the truth, but she was not about to tell him the real reason. Lies were necessary sometimes.

"Your husband was a good man."

"He was."

"Thank you for speaking as you did in my family's defense when you arrived. I'm not sure exactly what transpired, but we knew we were being discussed by the looks cast our way." Cyn heard the sincerity in his words.

"I cannot abide snobbish fools. Unfortunately, the world is full of them."

"Very true," he agreed. "Thankfully, we are both no longer counted among them."

"Indeed," Cyn said, turning away from him. She wondered how soon she could leave without it being obvious.

CHAPTER FOURTEEN

*H*yacinth had defended his family, and it was humbling she would do so when he had hurt her.

She wore a pale gray coat today, almost silver. It had small rose buttons down the front and rose embroidery on the collar and cuffs. Her bonnet was rose, as were her gloves. She looked exactly what she was—a wealthy member of London society.

"How is your injury?" Leo asked.

"Healing, thank you," she threw over her shoulder.

Leo studied her children, who, as it turned out, were his siblings' friends. The fact that all this time, Theo, Fred, Anna, and Matilda had been keeping company with Hyacinth's children was odd. But then, how would they know? His siblings were certainly old enough to wander there with no one accompanying them.

"Lashings of tea and cakes," Leo heard Alex say like an excited child. "Is there anything better?"

Food was very important to Nightingales, but none more so than Alex.

"My brother likes to eat," Leo said to Hyacinth when she glanced Alex's way. "Lots of it."

"I have a son like that," she surprised him by saying. "Simon can eat twice as much as me and Meg and still be hungry." Her daughter then drew her attention, and Leo's family drew his, but he was aware.

"Fred, you are not starving. Please do not stuff food into your mouth," Leo said.

His sister glared at him. "I feel like if I do not eat in haste, Alex or Theo will take it from my plate."

"They won't, because they have better manners than that," Leo said, giving both brothers a hard look. "In public, we do not behave like the heathens we are at home."

Leo heard a snort from behind him. He turned, but Hyacinth was not looking his way.

"I wish you will never contemplate leaving us, Leo. You and Uncle Bram are the only ones who can control Theo," Fred added.

"I will never be far away and at your house at least once a day, I promise," Leo said. "But as I have yet to find lodgings, you have no need to worry about it."

"We will miss you, Leo," Anna said.

"I have not moved anywhere. Your big brother will always be close."

Anna gave him a big smile and went back to her food and annoying Theo, which she excelled at.

He looked at Hyacinth again, because she was there and he couldn't seem to stop himself. She was studying Anna.

"She has not long lived with us," Leo said.

"And it was the best day of my life when they wanted me to join their family," his little sister said, listening to the conversation like everyone else around the table. Privacy was always in short supply being a Nightingale.

"It was also a special day for us," Leo said. "We are happy to have her as our sister."

"Leo is an excellent big brother," Anna said to Hyacinth.

"Excuse me, you have another big brother here, and I'm the one who brings you sweets," Alex said, outraged.

"I did not say you weren't an excellent big brother also, Alex."

"Well then, I am appeased."

The debate then started over who was the best Nightingale sibling and why, as it had many times before.

"How is your family, my lady?" Leo asked Hyacinth.

"Well, thank you. They no longer walk in society and live close to one another in the country." Her tone was polite but distant.

"Do you visit often?"

"When we can."

"You must miss them," he said.

"Of course. Now, when you are finished," she added to her children and staff, "we will inspect the stalls outside."

Leo looked at the large Mulholland men again and Miss Bromley. Why did he have a feeling there was more to her having three staff with her today?

"Simon, are you off to boarding school soon?" Leo asked her son when there was a lull in conversation, which was not often with his family.

"I am, my lord. Eton," he said, looking at his mother. He was nervous, Leo thought, and that was completely understandable.

"You'll enjoy it. There are many wonderful things to learn there."

"He does not like learning," his sister said.

"I can speak for myself, thank you," Simon snapped.

"That will do," Hyacinth interrupted them with practiced ease, like he did when his younger siblings argued.

He spoke to Simon about what he'd find at Eton, and the boy asked him questions. Alex joined in, as did Gray. He seemed to relax as the discussion continued, and Leo was glad they could put his fears at ease.

"Thank you," Hyacinth said softly when they moved on to another topic. "He will be more comfortable having spoken to someone who has attended Eton. I have tried to allay his fears, but as I know little about it, I'm afraid it has not helped."

"He will do well there. He's also a big boy, so he will not be an easy target to bully."

As he was looking at her, Leo saw the anger at the thought of anyone bullying her son.

"He will be all right, my lady."

She nodded. "I promised him." The words were whispered, but he heard, as he was leaning in to speak with her.

"Who?"

"Their father."

"What did you promise him?"

She waved her hand about, now seeming to regret what she'd said. "It matters not."

"We are finished, Mother."

"Excellent. Let us head outside and walk through the stalls then. I'm sure there is some fudge somewhere to finish our day with more sugary goodness," Hyacinth said, rising. "Good day to you all."

She dropped into a curtsy and then was ushering her children, the Mulhollands, and Miss Bromley out the door. The Nightingale party soon followed, after making sure there was not a scrap of food left on any plate or drop of tea in a pot.

"She's a lovely woman, Leo," Aunt Ivy said, moving to his side as they strolled.

"You spoke a total of two sentences at the most with her. How can you know if she is lovely or not?"

His aunt smiled, that special smile she had for occasions when she wanted to soothe one of her nieces or nephews.

"I'm very sorry that your father's actions meant you could not marry her, Leo. She would have made you a fine wife. Did you love her?"

He felt his body stiffen at the question.

"I'm sorry if that opens old wounds." She patted his hand.

"No, it's all right." If anyone deserved honesty from him, it was this woman. "I don't think I had the depth to love back then, as I was the most important person in my life, but I think I cared about her."

"It's not too late, you know."

"For what?" He looked at his aunt, who had a hand in teaching him the true meaning of the word love alongside his uncle.

"To love her," she said softly. "You are both lost souls."

He snorted. "Have you been reading something romantic again?" Why did the thought of loving Hyacinth settle in his chest like a heavy weight?

They were walking between the rows of stalls that had been set up now. People were milling; children were excitedly weaving in and out. The scents and sights were a feast for his taste buds and eyes.

"Leo, my sweet boy, you locked your emotions away after what your father did. You love your family, and we see that daily, but everyone else sees the cold, aloof Lord Seddon. But you are a man made for great passion. A man who should love a woman and have his own family."

"Why are we having this very uncomfortable conversation while walking among people?"

"Because at home, if I spoke to you like this, you find an excuse and flee. You can't do that here, as we all came together. Plus, you would never make a spectacle of yourself."

"You're cunning," he said.

"I've learned to be with you lot. All I'm saying, my wonderful nephew, is don't shut everyone out because you worry they may hurt you. We would never find the one meant for us if we were not hurt occasionally by the ones not destined to be our soulmates."

He looked ahead of them at her uncomfortable words, and the two men before him parted, and there she was. Lady Hyacinth Lowell was laughing, and it was the first laugh he'd seen from her since the night he'd saved her. It lit her face and made his gut clench.

"All we want is your happiness, Leo."

"I know," he got out. "I just don't think love and marriage are for me any longer. One day I may wed, but I doubt it will be a grand passion." Someone stepped in front of him, and Hyacinth was suddenly gone, and he could breathe easily again.

"Then you will do yourself and whoever you wed a disservice, because you are destined for love, nephew, just like the others in your family." She rose to her toes and kissed his cheek.

"I love you, if that makes you feel better," Leo said.

"As I love you, but that is not what I mean, as you very well know."

"Mama!"

"Go," Leo said as Lottie shrieked at Aunt Ivy. "I will think about what you said."

"Good boy."

Leo wouldn't class himself as a coward, but in love, he was exactly that. Just the thought of giving his heart into a woman's care terrified him. Having another control his happiness and every waking thought made him shudder. He'd seen how his siblings suffered. No, he would not be venturing along that path and definitely not with the woman he had left once.

"Leo, come and heft the mallet to see if you are strong or weak," Theo called to him.

Pleased to have something else to think about, he joined his little brother.

"Uncle Bram made it reach the top, and the bell rang, as did Gray, but Alex didn't."

"I didn't get a good swing," Alex protested.

"Oh please," Leo said. "We all know who the strong Nightingales are."

"I have paid for you, Leo. Now show your brother you are stronger than him," Harriet said.

"Why are you on his side?" Alex demanded.

She giggled.

Leo lifted the mallet and slammed it down. To his relief, it made the bell ring. He then smirked at Alex.

"I'm doing it again," his brother muttered.

Leo spied his little sisters at a stall and went to investigate. He found them talking to Mrs. Varney and Mr. Peeky, who appeared to be manning the stall. Looking around, he couldn't see her daughter, thankfully.

"What has you both here?" Leo asked, inspecting the stall. There seemed to be flowers of every color made from all kinds of things. Some in paper, others wool, and some wood.

The residents of Crabbett Close were always popping up somewhere he did not expect them to be. They may be old, but they rarely acted it.

"I belong to the group, my lord," he said.

"As do I," Mrs. Varney added.

"Hello!" His sisters greeted them enthusiastically, like they did most things.

"Group?" Leo picked up a wool heart in blue and green.

"Blooming Lovely, my lord. We meet every Thursday and create flowers," Mr. Peeky said.

"Did you make this?" He pointed to the wool flower.

"Aye," Mr. Peeky said.

"Aren't they beautiful, Leo," Fred said. "So many colors."

"They are. You can pick two each," he said, pulling out some money. "I'm taking these two," he added, picking up the two wool ones closest to him.

"Mr. Greedy made that one, my lord," Mr. Peeky said, pointing to the yellow, blue, and red one he held.

"Is there nothing you lot can't do?"

"Nothing I know of." Mr. Peeky grinned. "The body needs to be busy, my lord, or it stops working."

"Very true, and the residents of Crabbett Close are certainly not at risk of that."

They purchased the flowers, and his sisters ran to show the others. Leo said good day to his neighbors and searched the people milling about for Hyacinth again. Before he could stop himself, he found her and her children flanked by her staff. Behind them, he saw two men.

They were both looking at the Lowell party, Leo was sure of it. Following a safe distance behind, he observed them for a while. When Hyacinth's party stopped, they did too, but they were far enough back to not be seen.

As if sensing him, they turned and met his eyes. Leo started forward, but the men walked away and were soon lost in the crowd.

Had I just imagined that?

"Oh, Lord Seddon!"

And that is just what my day needed, he thought, noting Tabitha Varney hurrying toward him.

"Psst!" Looking left, he found Matilda and Anna.

"Hurry, Leo, she is advancing," Anna said, waving him closer. He ran. The girls took a hand each and tugged him down beside a stall. "Crouch," Anna ordered. He did as he was told.

"Stay," Matilda said, rising. She then walked into Tabitha Varney's path. "Hello, Miss Varney," he heard her say.

"I was looking for your brother. He was here. I just saw him." Thankfully, Tabitha's chest was now covered by a brown shawl.

"He left, as he has a business appointment. However, Mungo went in that direction." She pointed left.

"And why would I be after that surly Scottish behemoth?" Tabitha Varney asked.

Leo's thighs were cramping, but he stayed where he was and hoped no one saw him. One of Anna's hands was in his, and her other was over her mouth to hide her giggling.

"Oh, but he is always speaking of you in glowing terms, Miss Varney," Matilda said, lying through her teeth, an ability she'd always had and her siblings were onto. Others, however, were not quite so lucky.

"She's terrifying," Leo whispered. "I've never known anyone who can lie like she can and with such ease."

Anna giggled again.

"He did?" Tabitha clutched her ample bosom.

Matilda nodded solemnly. "I would not lie to you about something so important, Miss Varney. He's very lonely too."

"Little witch." Leo snorted.

"Well then," Tabitha said. "I shall see if I can find him."

And just like that, they'd transferred her attentions from Leo to Mungo. It had started with him, and then they'd managed to shift them to Alex, and then when he married, it came back to him. It seemed that now Tabitha Varney had a new focus. Leo had to say he was not unhappy about that. The woman was always popping up wherever he was.

Matilda skipped back to them, looking happy with herself. Leo rose with Anna.

"What did Mungo do to incur your wrath, Matilda?"

"I have no idea what you mean, Leo." She gave him that

wide-eyed look she'd perfected. "He's lonely, so I thought it would be nice, as Miss Varney is lonely too, that they become friends."

Anyone looking at her would believe every word she spoke. He was not one of them.

"Thank you," Leo said. "Even if you are lying. It will be interesting to watch our surly Scotsman protect himself from her. Not that I condone that behavior, you understand."

"You're welcome." Matilda smirked. She then took his other hand, and she and Anna led him to the next stall.

Leo wandered behind his family with Anna and Matilda. They swung his hands and made him buy them things and chattered the entire time. He loved it, them, and the distraction they provided to stop him from thinking about Hyacinth and why he still had a niggling suspicion that those men had been following her.

"I want a word with you," a voice growled in Leo's ear twenty minutes later.

"Mungo!" Matilda cried. "I'm so pleased to see you. We missed you." She really was a brilliant actress.

The Scotsman made a low growling sound deep in his throat.

"What's wrong, Mungo?" Anna asked, eyes wide. Clearly, she'd been learning from her sister.

Mungo's eyes narrowed as they focused on her. "One of you lot did that." He jabbed a finger to where Tabitha Varney was heading his way. "Before today, she never knew I existed."

"Come now, Mungo, you are a fine figure of a man. Any woman would be happy to have you," Leo said, drawing his fire away from the girls. "Tabitha is likely just now realizing what a catch you are."

Mungo's look should have singed Leo's nasal hairs, it was so fierce.

"I have found you again," Tabitha Varney said, arriving breathless. "Come, there is no need to be shy with me, Mungo. Let's walk together."

"No," the burly Scotsman growled. "You get about your business now."

Tabitha giggled, fluttering her eyelashes, and Leo kept his face expressionless.

"Perhaps Lord Seddon could accompany you?" Mungo snapped.

"Oh no, I have Anna and Matilda. You go on, Mungo. Enjoy the lovely company of Miss Varney."

His eyes shot flames at Leo.

"There. You see, they do not need you," Tabitha said. "Come along with me, Mungo."

"No," the Scotsman said, stomping away from them.

"Go after him, Miss Varney. He's shy," Leo urged, shamelessly fanning the flames of interest his little sisters had lit. "That brusque facade hides a lonely soul beneath."

She did, picking up her skirts and running. They watched as she caught him and slipped her hand through his arm.

"I should feel bad about that," Leo said.

Matilda shrugged. "Let's win something by throwing that ball at the blocks, Leo. That will make you feel a great deal better."

"Heartless wretch," he said, looking for Hyacinth again. When he couldn't locate her, he wondered if she and her family had left, which he should be happy about. But what he was, was worried.

First, there was what Alex said Lord Lowell's spirit was showing him regarding the Baddon Boys and the bird of paradise. Then there was her agency, and him not knowing what was going on there, and now those two men he was sure had been following her.

The problem now was, what did he want to do about it?

CHAPTER FIFTEEN

"I'm seriously regretting agreeing to this," Ellen said as they stood outside the Duke and Duchess of Raven's residence.

"We could just leave and get pies, and no one would know," Harriet said, her American accent stronger when she was nervous.

"I like that idea, my love," Alex said, kissing her cheek.

"We are about to enter the Duke of Raven's residence, my sweet," Gray said to Ellen. "Sinclairs and Ravens are not what you would call normal or conformists. If we were to step a toe back into society, I could think of no better household. And if anyone upsets you, I will deal with them."

"And me," Leo and Alex said at the same time.

"If they don't annihilate the individual, I shall deal with what is left of them," Uncle Bram said.

"Why did I let you talk me into this?" Leo asked. His necktie felt too tight.

Ellen leaned into Gray when he wrapped an arm around her waist, comforting her.

Leo had told himself for years he did not want to be part

of a couple, and he almost believed it most of the time. But when he was constantly faced with the love this family had found, it was not easy to stand true to his belief. Plus, there was the loneliness, and also, lately there was Hyacinth.

He was lying to himself if he didn't acknowledge that. In some part, coming here was because he wanted to see her again. She intrigued him, and he was also worried about her. Something was not right, and perhaps tonight he could put his questions to her if he got her alone.

"I made it. All is well!"

They turned to look at Ram, who was hurrying toward them with his coattails flapping.

"Lord, the traffic, but you can all relax. I am here to help you navigate your first foray back into society." He punched Theo gently in the arm. "I say, young man, look at you all grown up."

Theo smiled, happy with the compliment.

"Now, you will all listen to me," Uncle Bram said. "We are the equal of any who we meet tonight, and I will not have you thinking otherwise," he said, making eye contact with every one of them.

"Except Gray. We all know we're far better than him," Ram said to his cousin, who rolled his eyes.

"Chins raised and take no insults from anyone. However, it is my belief there will be none of that. The mix of guests will be eclectic, as the duke's family are wed to those who do not walk in society, and they will all be present."

"Yes, Gray is right there. The Sinclair and Raven families are almost as odd as us," Alex added.

"Exactly. Thank you all for coming when I know this is hard for you, but it is time," Uncle Bram added. "I am extremely proud of every one of you."

"Then let's get it done," Leo said. He then fell in behind his aunt and uncle with Theo. This was his little brother's first foray into society, and he would make sure the experience was a good one, even if the thought of what they were about to do was making him want to relieve his stomach of its contents.

The Raven town house was as you would expect from one of the most powerful noblemen in society. Grand on every scale and yet also a welcoming place, Leo thought as he stepped inside.

Uniformed staff lined the walls. Light from lamps showed off huge vases of colorful flowers and gilt-framed pictures. They passed elegant furniture as the Nightingale family joined the line of guests waiting to greet their hosts.

Leo intercepted a few looks from those around them but ignored them. He had a title and was the equal of most that would attend tonight.

"I've never seen anything like the inside of this house, Leo," Theo whispered.

"The house we grew up in was grand like this, do you not remember?"

"Perhaps I did not appreciate it then, as usually all I wanted to do was slide down the banisters when no one was looking," Theo said.

"If you care to glance slightly to the right between those shoulders before you, brother, you will see someone you know," Alex whispered in Leo's ear.

Leo obliged and saw the back of a woman's head. She turned to smile at something the person beside her said, and the breath lodged in his throat. Hyacinth was here.

"I see that you have located who I mean." He could hear the smirk in Alex's voice.

"Who are you trying to locate?" Theo asked.

"An old friend" was all Leo said as they moved forward. But he kept his eyes on her as Theo chatted beside him about everything he saw.

Hyacinth's hair was pinned in place with tiny sparkling emeralds. She wore blue, and he could see the length of her pale neck above the line of her dress.

"I want you to speak with her this evening, Leo."

"What?" He shot Ellen a look. As usual, she was stunning in oyster silk, and the large proprietorial man at her side would ensure that she received only compliments this evening, even if there were those who remembered exactly why the Nightingales had been tossed out of society.

"Hyacinth. I fear she is lonely, Leo, and needs friends. We were once that before we treated her shabbily."

"Ellen, we had problems of our own to deal with," Leo said. "Our intention was never to hurt her."

"Even so, I'm sure Hyacinth is lonely," his sister hissed in his ear.

"There was no way you could tell that from a few conversations when we touched on nothing personal." Leo did not like to think of Hyacinth as lonely. It made his chest burn.

"It was her eyes. I could tell, looking at them, and the other thing."

"What other thing?" He shot Ellen a look.

"The vision I had of her weeping over a coffin with her two children huddled at her side."

"And the visit I had from her late husband." Alex was looking at him over Ellen's and Gray's shoulders now.

"We are in a receiving line about to enter a society gathering, which we have not done in years. Is now the time for this discussion?" Gray asked.

"Yes, listen to the man who is making sense." Leo glared at his siblings.

"Don't use that stuffy tone with me," Ellen said. "We are just concerned about Hyacinth and explaining why to you so it sinks into your thick head."

"I do not have a thick head."

"The thickest," Alex added. "But back to Hyacinth. If I get the chance this evening, I will have a quiet word with her about what her late husband is showing me. If she is receptive, of course."

He tried very hard never to lose control. It was something he'd worked on since leaving society. Staying calm in all situations. Some said he was too controlled, but Leo liked it that way. His siblings, however, and clearly any mention of Hyacinth, could test that.

"You will not do so here, Alex," Leo gritted out. "People will already be judging us. If they hear you talking, we'll be run out of London again!"

"That will do," Gray said. "I realize you are all nervous, as am I about reentering society, but perhaps we could save the verbal jousting match for another less public setting?"

"We are simply talking, husband, and there is no harm in that," Ellen said.

"About Hyacinth needing friends," Alex added, simply to annoy Leo. He ignored them.

The problem was, he agreed. He felt she was lonely too, plus there was that worry he had that something wasn't right with her.

"Good Lord!"

Leo looked to where the voice had come from and found they had reached the front of the receiving line, and the Duke of Raven was looking at them with delight on his face.

"Well now, this is wonderful," the beautiful woman at his side said. The Duchess of Raven was her usual stunning self, and beside her duke, they were a regal couple.

"You got them here, Bram." The duke shook Uncle Bram's hand. "Well done."

"They knew it was a worthy cause, Duke."

"Excellent. Well, go on in. The others in our family will be pleased to see you here," the duchess said.

They entered the huge ballroom full of light and color. The noise from music and guests chatting hit them on all sides. Leo stood for a second, adjusting. He then exhaled slowly when he felt the large hand of his uncle settle on his shoulder.

"We are here, all together, Leo."

He nodded, schooled his features into a blank expression, and entered. His eyes moved, taking in the people he had not seen in many years and searching for Hyacinth. Leo could not see her and told himself to stop looking.

They moved into the room and among the guests. He heard the gasps of surprise and whispers from some. People greeted them, and some even seemed genuinely pleased to see them.

"It's like walking down Crabbett Close with every local's face pressed to the window watching," Gray muttered from behind him.

It was an apt description, Leo thought. Except the Crabbett Close locals liked the Nightingales. It was fair to say some people in the duke's ballroom did not.

CHAPTER SIXTEEN

Cyn heard the whispers as she headed to her destination and knew they were because Leo and his family were here. She'd seen them in the receiving line, and it had given her a jolt because she'd never thought he would appear in society again.

Nodding, smiling, and acknowledging people, Cyn headed for the wall to her right, where she could stand and observe, which she liked to do most evenings. Then she would decide who she wanted to speak with, or those in society she could tolerate usually found her.

These events were draining. That was the only word she could use to describe how she felt dressing up and going out alone, night after night. Putting on a fake smile to honor Kenneth's wishes that she keep up appearances for Simon and Meg's sake.

"How dare they," Lady Gulliver said with a loud sniff two feet in front of her.

Following her eyes, Cyn saw Leo and his family. He was walking slowly through the crowds, who in turn were watching him and his family. His chin was raised, and his expression was the perfect blend of haughty disinterest.

"Why, it's just not right," Lady Gulliver continued. "That man died owing money to many."

"Agreed," Mrs. Brantley said.

"Surely you ladies are not speaking of the Nightingale family?" Cyn said, attempting to remain calm. This was the second time she'd heard someone speaking about them like this.

"It is a family's shame, Lady Lowell," Mr. Brantley said. "As such, they should not be here."

"As one of the most powerful peers of the realm invited them, perhaps you could take it up with him, as clearly he does not believe the sins of their father should taint a child," Hyacinth snapped.

Muttering, the Brantleys walked away from her.

"Good riddance," Cyn said, looking at Leo again. Their eyes locked. She was the first to pull away. Heart thumping, she did not look his way again.

"My God, Cyn, what a crush!" Letitia said, joining her. "If I did not adore the Duke and Duchess of Raven and their odd family, I would have forgone the evening and taken a young man to my bed."

"No, you wouldn't, because Charles will be back in one week, and you love him to distraction and would never do such a thing," Cyn said, refusing to let her eyes drift back to Leo even though they desperately wished to do so.

"Oh, very well," Letitia said. "If you must be so... so logical about everything and not allow me to have fantasies, then I agree. You look quite stunning, by the way. That is a far better look on you than that hideous shade of beige you wore last time." She shuddered. "Why you allowed your seamstress to convince you it did anything but wash out your complexion, I do not know."

THE FALLEN VISCOUNT

"Are you quite done?" Cyn asked her friend.

"For now," Letitia said. "Now, who can we gossip about?" She turned to face the guests, and Cyn tensed, knowing she'd see Leo and his family. "Well, well, well. Your hero is here."

"He is not my hero... well, what he did was heroic, but that does not make him my hero," she added.

Letitia knew all the grisly details of the Nightingales' fall from grace and how Leo's sudden departure had broken her heart.

"He was handsome dripping wet. However, he is a great deal more so tonight dressed like that. The man is divine now he's grown up and his soft edges are hardened."

She was used to Letitia's ways. Her friend always said exactly what she felt and usually made Cyn laugh with her descriptions of those around them at these often-tedious events. However, not tonight, and not when it came to Leo.

She'd spent the days since she'd seen him yet again shoring up her defenses, as clearly the man still unsettled her. But she hadn't counted on seeing him this evening.

Did his appearance tonight mean he was to attend more society events? Or just this one, as the duke was a friend? *Was the duke a friend?* She'd believed they'd severed all ties with society. Was she wrong there?

"I'm sorry, this must be hard on you, my darling Cyn." Letitia's arm slipped through hers, and she was pulled close. "Forgive me for my frivolous tongue."

Cyn exhaled slowly. "I have seen them twice since the night I fell into the Thames."

"You never told me that."

"It was nothing. He came into the agency, actually, because his family is looking at taking the lease next door. Then I saw them when I took Simon and Meg out."

Leo was now talking to the Earl and Countess of Raine and Mr. and Mrs. Deville. She could find him because he was

133

so tall. Tall and handsome; she couldn't deny that no matter how much she wished to.

"Was it hard seeing him again?" Letitia asked.

"I wish I'd been better prepared and maybe seen him coming." Cyn then went on to explain what had happened.

"Oh dear, but I'm sure Lewis was a pillar of strength," Letitia said.

"As you can imagine, he loved every moment, especially as he did not know the backstory between Leo and I."

"You can't avoid them all evening, you know," her friend said.

"I know, and actually, now we have seen each other again, I can deal with this. I was merely a child when I fell in love with him." She'd thought about this a lot. "I am no longer that and do not have those feelings. Exposure to him will make it become a common thing, and I will be able to forget the past completely if he continues to walk in society."

"If you say so, but I'll add he is a handsome man, and you are a beautiful woman—"

"Do not finish that sentence," Cyn said. "Now tell me, how was your visit with your mother?"

"Most of the time she tittered about my lack of restraint and forthright speech, but for all that, we muddled along. Now, are you to hide on this wall all evening, or can you come with me and see what is being auctioned off?"

"I am not hiding, but I will stay here, if you don't mind, as I have already looked at the items being auctioned. I will secure us two glasses of champagne while you decide what to spend your money on," Cyn said.

"Oh, very well, but I see right through you, you know," Letitia said. "You will skulk in corners for the remainder of the evening. At least ensure you seek that champagne, and I shall return shortly."

She waved her friend off and walked around the wall in

search of drinks. Weaving in and out of guests, she neared a waiter who held a tray of sparkling glass flutes.

"Cyn, how wonderful to see you this evening!"

"Somer, Dorrie," she said with a genuine smile. "The duke will be pleased there is a wonderful crowd this year," Cyn said.

The two lovely ladies before her were twins and born into the Sinclair family, of which there were many.

"Why are you walking around the walls of James and Eden's ballroom?" Dorrie asked.

"I'm not. It was just the quickest way to the champagne," Cyn said.

The twins had lovely soft pale skin, green eyes, and thick black hair. They were extremely beautiful women like their elder sisters.

"She's hiding, and I know why," Somer said.

"I'm not hiding," Cyn lied, because she was avoiding Leo and his family.

"Very well. If you wish to deny it, then we will also. Now, how is the Phoenix Agency going?" Dorset asked.

"Well, thank you. Busy. There are so many women in need of our support."

Somer made a noise in her throat that Cyn translated to disapproval. "There are many that are mistreated, and it's a disgrace. Should you need our detective work at any time, you have only to ask, and we will help."

And that was another odd thing about the Sinclair family. Not only were they wed to those that carried Raven blood, but the three youngest siblings ran a private detective agency. An unusual occupation for society members.

"Hello, Hyacinth."

She tried not to stiffen, but it happened. Ellen had arrived with her husband.

"Mrs. Fletcher," Cyn said, dropping into a curtsy.

"Hello, Ellen," the twins said as one.

"We are so very pleased to see you and Gray here this evening," Somer said.

Cyn then watched as the twins hugged Ellen and Gray. She remembered then they had once all been close friends.

"Lovely to meet you again, Lady Lowell," Mr. Fletcher said, bowing to Cyn.

"So, Gray, what are you working on?" Dorset asked him when the greetings were finished.

"I can't tell you that, Dorrie," he said.

The twins and the detective were soon chatting while they tried to get information out of him about the cases he was working on, which left her and Ellen facing each other.

"The thought of entering this room was terrifying," Ellen surprised her by saying. "But it was made easier being surrounded by those I love and knowing there were at least a few people in here that wanted to see us."

"And those that don't are fools, so you should just ignore them."

"I'm truly sorry for not telling you we were leaving London and why, Hyacinth. You deserved that from us," Ellen said softly.

Cyn sighed. "We have all moved on, and what you and your family went through had to be devastating. At the time, I thought only of myself, and I'm sorry for how you all suffered, Mrs. Fletcher."

"Ellen and thank you for that. It means a great deal to hear those words from you." Her smile was blinding, and she saw her old friend then. The young girl who she had shared confidences and dreams with.

"We have both changed a great deal," Ellen said, "as much has gone on in our lives, and perhaps one day soon we can take tea and talk about those changes, but for now, it would mean a lot if I can call you Hyacinth again."

"She goes by the name Cyn now," Somer said, clearly listening to their conversation.

"Cyn," Ellen said softly. "I like it."

"Hello, sister, I wondered where you and your large husband had gone," Alexander said, arriving.

"Mr. Nightingale." Cyn curtsied as Ellen's brother arrived at her side.

"May I have a word?"

"Really, Alex? Here?" Ellen whispered loudly.

"It must be here, or I will be driven mad with the noise he is making."

"Oh, very well." Ellen rose to her toes. "You two take the wall, and I shall stand in front chatting with the twins and Gray."

"Why are we creating a wall?" Dorrie asked.

"My brother needs to speak with Cyn about something. So, stand here with me and regale me with riveting conversation."

"Every word that spills from my mouth his riveting," Somer said.

"You are very much like Cam," Cyn heard Ellen say.

"Oh yes, and you should hear them debating," Dorrie added.

"Lady Lowell, may I call you Hyacinth?" Alexander said. She nodded, uncertain what he wanted to talk to her about. "And I am Alex."

He was like Leo but softer. His smile was genuine, and it reached all the way to his eyes. Her heartbeat did not increase when faced with him, however.

"What I am about to tell you is not easy for me to say and will be hard for you to hear, and I understand if you think I am quite sparse in the attic, but the words need to be spoken, or your late husband will be my constant companion."

"I beg your pardon?"

"Bear with me. After we fled society, the Nightingale siblings leaned into something we'd avoided. We are clairvoyants, Hyacinth."

"We?" Cyn said weakly.

"Ellen and I embrace what we are, but not Leo, Hyacinth."

"She's called Cyn now," Ellen said over her shoulder.

"Is she really?" Alexander smiled. "I like that."

"Ah, thank you," Cyn said, wondering if in fact what happened all those years ago had been harder on this Nightingale than his siblings, and he had lost his grip on sanity.

"I am quite sane, I assure you," he said as if he'd read her thoughts, which he'd just told her he could do...hadn't he? "I speak to the dead, Cyn. Now, before you run screaming from the room, which would not be easy with this crowd, I assure you, hear me out."

She gulped a mouthful of the champagne she held in a fierce grip.

"Listen to him, Cyn, as he speaks the truth," Ellen said.

"Our gifts are all different. Ellen has visions, and Leo finds things, like cuff links," he added, holding her eyes. "I speak to the dead. Your husband has been hurling thoughts at me since we met you that day at your agency."

His eyes looked clear, but surely he was quite addled?

"Lord Lowell is showing me a triquetra, Cyn. Do you know what that is?"

She shook her head to show she didn't and possibly to clear it.

"It's a symbol with many meanings, but more importantly it is a mark the Baddon Boys gang wears. A tattoo," he clarified.

A shiver of dread slithered down her spine.

"He is concerned for you, Cyn, and wants me to tell you to have a care. Is there a reason you are in danger?" His eyes were no longer smiling, and in fact, the look in them was exactly like the one his older brother often wore.

"I, ah—I don't think so."

"You don't think so?"

She exhaled slowly. Was this really happening?

"I see a bird also. A bird of paradise."

That had her spilling champagne over her hand. Alex pulled out a handkerchief and mopped it up.

"Is he... is my husband... I'm not sure how to ask this question."

"Is he happy?" She nodded, not sure why she believed every word this man was telling her, but she did. "His spirit feels light," Alex said with a gentle smile. "But he is clearly concerned about you, as he is constantly inside my head. My darling wife had a friend who passed, and she was persistent too."

"I'm sure I should be more shocked than I am."

"Your reaction is mild compared to some. I have had people faint when I speak to them this way, and not all of them were women. Now, can you tell me why he is showing me the bird and the symbol?"

Dare she tell him?

"Come, Cyn, I promise I am a friend and want to help you."

"If I tell you, please keep it to yourself, sir."

"Of course."

"As you know, I run the Phoenix Agency. Those that come there want a new start. We help them with that," she said so only he could hear. "We help ladies of the night, Alex."

"And do some of those women come from the Bird of Paradise, which is owned by the Baddon Boys?"

Before she could answer, Ellen spoke, "A lady is approaching. I suggest you continue this conversation at another time."

Alexander Nightingale squeezed Cyn's hand and said, "Be careful, as your husband has me believing trouble may be headed your way. Please call us if you find you need help."

"Thank you."

She watched him walk away with his family then. Kenneth's spirit had contacted him, and she wasn't sure what to do about that. But one thing she knew was that she needed to do something.

CHAPTER SEVENTEEN

Leo was slowly unclenching the muscles in his body. Ellen had left their ranks with Gray, and he'd watched her until she'd reached her destination, which had been Hyacinth. Alex had then followed, but not Leo. That woman disturbed him far more than the younger version of her had.

"Good Lord, fancy you lot crawling out of your burrows."

"Hello, Cam," Leo said.

"It's good to see you, Seddon, and out among your peers for the first time in a long while," Cambridge Sinclair said. "I was just telling your cousin it was time."

"Stephen," Leo said, shaking his cousin's hand. "Good to see you again."

Stephen Blackthorne was his mother's second cousin, and they had all been close as children but had drifted apart when he joined the Army and the Nightingales had stepped away from society.

"Wonderful to see you all here, Leo," Stephen said.

"Are there any weddings or celebrations imminent in Crabbett Close?" Cam asked. "I want some more of Mrs.

Douglas's treacle cake and Mr. Peeky's spiced rum." He smacked his lips together at the memory.

"I have just got the grass stains out of my carpet. My hope is there are at least six months before it is needed for the aisle again," Ram said.

Leo stood there watching the guests while trying not to search for Hyacinth and failing. Cam regaled them with hilarious stories about what had been happening at his newspaper.

"It was a sad day when Lord Lowell passed away. He was a good man," Stephen said, noting who Leo was looking at.

"You knew him?"

"I did. Kenneth was an astute businessman and a fair man despite his gruff exterior. We were, of course, surprised when he married Hyacinth, but for as many years apart they were in age, they seemed comfortable in each other's company."

Leo felt a twinge of jealousy that another man had made Hyacinth happy.

"We saw her the other day. Did you know she runs an agency helping women seek employment?" Stephen would not share what they discussed with anyone else, so Leo felt safe talking to him, and his cousin may have more insights about her.

"Does she really? Although I'm not surprised. Kenneth was not your average nobleman, and he had his fingers in many business pies. Perhaps he encouraged Hyacinth to do the same?"

"Perhaps."

"It is good to see you and the others here, cousin," Stephen said.

"I don't think I want to reenter society completely. This, I will admit, is all right, but I'm not sure I want more," Leo said.

"It is a start, cousin, but now I will leave you, as I need to dance with Miss Healy."

Leo watched Stephen walk to where a pretty auburn-haired woman was chatting with an older man.

"Seddon. Good to see you again," Mr. Hampton said, approaching him. Cam had now lured Ramsey away to the supper room.

Leo spent the next few hours talking, and for the most part, it was comfortable. There were still a few looks and whispered words, but he was an adult, as was his family, and words no longer hurt them.

When the Duke of Raven stepped on the raised platform to begin the proceedings, Leo moved to stand with his family.

"First to perform tonight," the duke said after his speech about those in need and why he did this each year, "is my beautiful duchess and the lovely Lady Lowell."

Leo couldn't believe what he was seeing. Hyacinth was taking the seat that had been placed beside the piano, where the duchess now sat, and in her hands was a violin.

"I didn't know she played that," Alex said under his breath.

"I didn't know either." Was this something she'd learned later in life, or was it something Hyacinth had never told him about, as she'd thought he wouldn't be interested?

"She really is a stunning woman," Harriet said.

"She is," Leo said before he could stop the words leaving his mouth.

"I remember she used to look at you like the sun rose and set when you did," Alex said softly. "It was nauseating."

"But now, because you look at me like that, you completely understand," Harriet added.

"Exactly."

"Nice recovery," Leo whispered to his brother. But he

remembered the look Alex spoke of, because it had sometimes annoyed him that she was so besotted with him. The small-minded bastard he'd been had wanted her because she would have been a docile wife who took orders. He couldn't discount that back then. He'd even thought that taking a mistress would have been acceptable after he'd married Hyacinth.

"Why did you not tell me I was a small-minded imbecile?" Leo asked his brother.

"You were the heir and spoiled and indulged. I doubt you would have listened. Besides, I was not that different from you until I went away to war," Alex said. "Seeing oneself for what they were is never healthy. I suggest you put it from your mind."

"It's hard when we are faced with our past failures," Leo said.

"Ah, but we also get a chance to right the wrongs. Perhaps it's time you really talked to Cyn."

"Cyn?" Leo raised a brow.

"Apparently, she goes by that name now. She gave me leave to use it. Has she not done so with you?"

The innocent look did not fool Leo. His brother knew very well that he and Hyacinth were not on first-name terms again yet.

The music started, and he forgot about everything but her. The duchess was clearly talented also, but it was Hyacinth he could not take his eyes from. Her dress was cut low across her breasts, so when she leaned forward, he and everyone else in the room were rewarded with a glimpse of the curves beneath. Leo fought the urge to stomp up there and throw his jacket over her.

"That's a fierce expression, brother," Alex said. Leo ignored him.

Small emeralds in her hair twinkled as they caught the

light from the chandelier above. She was exquisite and totally engrossed in the music.

"She's very good," Alex whispered. "A woman of hidden talents it seems."

"When did she give you leave to call her Cyn, Alex?"

"I just told her that her husband's spirit has been visiting me."

"I thought we discussed you not doing that here tonight."

"Lowell would have given me no peace until I did. We talked, and I told her about the triquetra and the bird of paradise. I then told her she needed to take care, as clearly her late husband was trying to tell me that there was danger around her."

"What did she say?" Leo asked, his eyes still locked on Hyacinth. The music she played was hauntingly beautiful.

"She told me that the women she helps at the Phoenix Agency are ladies of the night. I asked her if any of them come from the Bird of Paradise, but as someone was approaching, she didn't get a chance to answer. But she listened to me, at least, and did not run screaming from the room."

"That's something then," Leo said, applauding loudly along with the rest of the guests when Hyacinth and the duchess had finished.

"I told her if she needed help to send us word." Alex nodded.

"Thank you." He watched her walk from the stage.

"And now we will watch the auction and see if our bids are accepted," Alex said.

They watched the rest of the proceedings, and Leo's bid on the complete collection of the Captain Broadbent and Lady Nauticus books signed by the author was successful. Both Cam and Lord Raine raised a fist at him, as clearly they'd wanted them. Leo waved back.

He then stood with Alex and Harriet watching the dancers when the quartet started the next set, and he wondered if he would remember the steps if he took to the floor. Leo had once enjoyed dancing, perhaps because it was the only real chance to hold a woman and it not be deemed scandalous.

"Ask her to dance," Alex said, nudging Leo in the ribs.

"Who?"

"Don't play the fool with me, brother. Cyn is over there talking to that woman who keeps shooting glares our way."

"Why is she glaring at us?" Harriet asked.

"Not us, darling," Alex said. "Leo."

Dressed in peach satin, Harriet looked lovely. She and Alex made a handsome couple.

"That is Lady Bancroft. She was there the night I rescued Hyacinth from drowning."

"Then she should not be glaring at you after such heroic behavior," Harriet said, outraged on his behalf.

"Dance with Cyn. It will make you feel better," Alex said.

"How would dancing with a woman I was once to marry and walked away from make me feel better?"

"Champagne?"

Leo took a glass from the tray the young footman held out to him.

Alex did the same, his eyes on the man. "Do I know you?"

The footman smiled. "I'm a Greedy, sir. I know you are the Nightingales from Crabbett Close."

"Good Lord," Alex said. "How wonderful. Which side are you related to?"

"I'm their grandson on my father's side."

"Wonderful people, the Greedys," Alex said, doing what he did best—talking.

"We shall be sure to tell them what an excellent job you're doing," Harriet said.

He looked happy with that and wandered off to distribute more champagne.

"Crabbett Close residents are everywhere," Leo muttered.

"Amen. Now dance with Cyn."

"Why does he need to dance with Lady Lowell?" Warwick Sinclair said from behind Leo. Clearly he'd been standing there listening, and the Nightingales had not realized it.

"Because they were once to marry and are now acquaintances," Alex said.

"Oh, that's right," Warwick said. "I'd forgotten."

"Is it stuffy in here? I feel like it is. Should I get doors thrown open?" the Duchess of Raven said, stopping in front of Leo.

He bowed, as did Alex, and Harriet dropped into a curtsy.

"All this bowing and curtsying is exhausting." The duchess wrinkled her nose. "It is not necessary to do so again."

"I shall endeavor to ignore you then, Duchess," Leo said.

"I'd be most grateful. Now back to the doors."

"We've discussed this, Eden. Opening the doors will make the older guests moan they may get a chill, and then you'll have to close them again," Warwick said.

"True." She sighed. Eden then turned her green eyes on Leo. "Cyn is a wonderful person and a favorite of our family because of the wonderful work she does. You should dance with her."

"I... ah—"

"Leave the past behind, Leo. It's best there." She then slid her arm through his. "Come along."

"To where?"

"Just a walk," the Duchess of Raven said.

Leo knew she was a powerful woman. She was a duchess, after all, but as he no longer walked in society, he did not have to play by the rules. However, he was a gentleman and liked her family, so he found his feet moving.

"I have no wish to dance, Duchess, if your intention is to find me a partner."

"I remember when you disappeared from society," she said softly so he had to bend to hear her words. "I thought at the time it was so sad that you and Cyn would not wed, as clearly that was intended."

"Duchess, I really—"

"But then I also knew that the love was one-sided, and your heart was not hers."

"I was young," Leo said, his tone stiff.

"You both were. She suffered, you know. In fact, many in society made sure of it."

"Pardon?" His eyes searched for her again. Hyacinth was standing surrounded by a small party of both men and women.

"Cyn was ridiculed and teased by those who were pleased to see her downfall," the duchess continued. "Especially by the ones who thought you were too good for her."

"The ruin was mine, not hers," he said quickly. Her words had shocked him. Not once had he thought Hyacinth would suffer because he'd left her unmarried.

The duchess tsked. "The ruin was not yours or Hyacinth's. But society has some members whose intelligence would fill a thimble, Leo. Unfortunately, many of those have power. You of all people know exactly what they are capable of. Did you think she would not be made to suffer?"

He hadn't, to his shame.

"And now we can dance, as we have reached the floor. One hopes you have not forgotten," she said, waving him into the line opposite where she was now standing.

"Do I get a say?"

She smiled, and he heard at least two men sigh. "Do as you are told now, Lord Seddon."

He knew there was no way he could walk away from her,

but he wanted to. The Duchess of Raven had just made him extremely uncomfortable.

"Move into line, Seddon. Do you need a few pointers on moves before the music starts?"

"No, thank you, Zachariel, I am more than capable of dancing, thank you."

"Just Zach, which you called me two nights ago when you skewered me with your foil." The youngest Deville reminded Leo of Alex. They could both be excessively annoying upon occasion.

"Stop tormenting my nephew, Deville," Uncle Bram said, joining the line.

"Torment? Surely not."

"The arms should be held in a well-rounded form, Seddon."

"Yes, thank you, Cam," Leo snapped as Eden's brother joined the line.

"Cambridge, that will do," Dev said to his brother.

"I'm simply helping him out. After all, he has not danced in years." Cam's expression was innocent, but Leo knew better. There was absolutely nothing about him that was innocent.

As the music began, Hyacinth stepped into the line two down from the duchess. Leo checked out of the corner of his eye who she was partnering with and saw it was Baron Ellington. He glanced at his uncle, who gave Leo a steady look, which he interpreted to mean behave.

Bad blood lay between Ellington and the Nightingales, as was evidenced by the man's behavior the night he'd pulled Hyacinth from the water.

"He is not worthy of your anger, Leo," Zach said softly. "He is a brainless fool."

"I know." But he wanted to punch the man. In fact, his fist

clenched at the thought, especially now he was partnering with Hyacinth.

Her pretty face was once again expressionless. His eyes ran over the golden curls. He'd always wanted to see it released but had never had the chance, and he doubted he ever would. She did not look his way.

The music started, and Leo was forced to concentrate so he didn't end up face-first on the floor when he tripped over his feet.

"There, you see, it is not hard, and you are quite a natural," the duchess whispered as he took her hands and turned.

"You are too kind," he replied, his tone dripping with sarcasm.

Ellington was glaring at him when he chanced a look his way. Pure hatred radiated from his eyes. Leo smiled.

"Excellent response, Seddon," the Duke of Raven said, and when he'd appeared in the dance, Leo had no idea. "Don't stomp on my wife's feet," he then ordered before moving on.

After that he danced, talked, and ignored those he did not want to speak with. Leo kept an eye on his family too, making sure all were happy and didn't need him. They seemed comfortable, and of course, Uncle Bram, Alex, and Ellen all had spouses; they were never alone like him.

CHAPTER EIGHTEEN

What felt like hours later, Leo experienced a desperate need come over him for solitude. There were people in his life obviously, but not this many at once usually, and his clothes were suddenly feeling too tight. He made his way through the crowds to the door and walked through.

Leo wanted to breathe some cool night air, and he wanted it now.

"Up the stairs, take the hall, and at the end, you will find the room where Eden has hung artwork. Go and study it, Leo. There are also doors that lead to a small balcony in there should you wish to inhale smoky London air."

The words were spoken by Devonshire Sinclair from behind him.

"I will lie if anyone asks where you have gone." He smiled, his vibrant green eyes flaring. "I can see you are in need of solitude, my friend. Go and take a few minutes."

"Thank you, Dev, I will not be long."

"For what it is worth, Leo, we're glad to have you back

among us," Dev said before he turned to reenter the ballroom.

Humbled at the words, Leo climbed the stairs and then found the room at the end of the hall. Entering, he let the peace settle over him. Lamps lit the long room, and he saw that the walls were indeed lined with artwork, but right now, he did not want to study it; he wanted the smog-filled London air.

Opening the door, he stepped outside and found her there.

"I'm sorry, I did not know you were here, my lady. Lord Sinclair directed me this way."

She was standing with both hands gripping the railing, looking out to the gardens below. Moonlight showed him enough of her that he could see she was tense.

"I'm leaving. You can have the balcony, my lord."

"Please. Don't go."

"We cannot be alone out here. You have been away from society too long if you believe otherwise. Even a widow like me cannot flaunt the rules in such a way."

"I wish you no harm, my lady." He moved closer but stopped a few feet from where she stood. "I want to apologize."

"You have no need to do so," she said stiffly.

"But I wish that you would at least hear me out while I endeavor to try."

"It's a night for it," she said softly. "Your sister just did the same, but there is no need for you to do so. I understand why you did what you did."

"That's typical of her, wanting to beat me to it," Leo said, which had Hyacinth snuffling out a laugh.

"I'm not asking you to forgive me, my lady, but I am apologizing for walking away from you without a word. I know that what I did hurt you. And I am also apologizing for the way you suffered at the hands of some of society."

"How do you know I suffered?" She was now facing him fully, her lovely topaz eyes on his.

Leo watched as she drew in a deep breath and then exhaled slowly, the actions forcing her breasts to rise above the neckline of her dress. He should not be noticing that, but she was an extremely beautiful woman; it was hard not to notice many things about Lady Hyacinth Lowell. *Cyn*.

"I was told," Leo said.

"I must admit to holding on to my anger toward you and your sister. It kept me sane in the months after you both disappeared from my life. I fueled it with indignation that you would treat me in such a callous way, and yes, there were those who were happy to tell me at every turn that I had been a fool to love one such as you."

"We did treat you callously," he said solemnly.

"No." She sighed. "Yes, I was hurt, but I was also a naïve girl who saw only her own pain when, in fact, yours was far greater. Your life had turned on its axis, and had I been thinking clearly, and of someone other than myself, I would have seen that too. Perhaps I have hung onto my anger too long." She held out her hand to him. "Shall we move on from that disastrous time in our lives, my lord?"

He closed the distance between them and took the hand. It was small and slender in his.

"Thank you. I am honored to have your forgiveness, my lady. Can I call you Cyn? Because my siblings will forever torment me with the knowledge that you said they could but not me."

"I doubt it's much of an honor," she said, which had him barking out a laugh. "But you have it just the same, and yes, please call me Cyn."

"And I am Leo, as you already know."

He didn't want to release her hand because it felt good to hold. She did not pull back either. Their eyes just stayed locked on each other, and the need to tug her close was powerful.

"You are beautiful," he whispered.

"And very different from the woman you once knew," she said.

"As I am different."

The sounds of London could be heard around them. The clop of hooves and voices reaching them from the streets below. Someone shouted, but it did not draw their eyes from each other.

He touched her cheek, running a finger slowly down to her jaw. Her skin was cool to the touch from the night air. He then ran his thumb along the soft pout of her bottom lip.

"So beautiful." The words came out a rasp, and then he was closing the distance between them and kissing her. Their hands were still clasped and trapped between them as he took her lush mouth into a deep kiss. The feel of her pressed to his body was heaven. Her soft scent wrapped around him as he devoured her mouth.

"No." She pushed back out of his arms. "That should not have happened."

"But it did," Leo said. His body was hard with the need to hold her again. The need to explore every inch of this woman's body he'd once believed he'd marry.

Her eyes closed briefly. "But it will not again. That—whatever it was—was a mistake."

"A very nice one," Leo felt compelled to say.

Her chin raised. "Because I am a widow, it does not therefore mean I am... I am free with my favors," she snapped.

Leo's temper twitched. "I did not suggest you were. That kiss was something we both wanted."

She exhaled loudly. "Yes, you are right." Her face told him

she was not happy to concede that point. "I don't know what came over me, but I assure you, I will not behave in such a rash manner again."

He didn't want anger between them, not now, when they'd just cleared the air.

"Then we shall put it down to a moment of insanity and not think of it again," he lied. He would be thinking about it a great deal. His body was still feeling the residual effects of that kiss and her lush form pressed to his.

"How are your children?"

Her shoulders lowered slowly at the question, and he saw some of the tension ease from her eyes.

"They are well, th-thank you, and badgering me to go to something called the Crabbett Close games." She sneezed loudly.

Clearly, she was still nervous. When they were younger, she'd sneezed a great deal, and it had annoyed him. Now he found it delightful.

He'd been wrong to give in to his need to kiss her. Leo knew there could never be anything between them, as there was too much water under the bridge for that.

No more impulsive urges, and definitely no more kisses.

"The Crabbett Close games are a lot of fun." He then went on to describe in colorful detail what took place, and by the time he'd finished, she was laughing, the kiss well and truly behind them.

Not that I'll forget the feel of her lips on mine.

"Are you reentering society, my lord?"

"I don't think so. I only attended, as the duke is a friend, and the cause an important one."

"And will you be taking the lease on the property next to my agency?"

"We will, so I'm sure we will be seeing each other again,"

Leo said, and he wasn't sure how she felt about that, as her expression gave nothing away.

"Now, if you will excuse me, I must return to the ballroom before someone notices I've gone. It has been... enlightening."

"Very much so," Leo added solemnly. "Before you go, can I ask you something, Cyn?" Her name felt odd after years of thinking she was Hyacinth, but seeing as she'd agreed to him using it, he would.

She nodded.

"Are you in danger?"

The open expression on her face changed in seconds. The shutters came down.

"I—why would you ask me that?"

"Your husband is showing my brother things that suggest you may be, like the bird of paradise and the symbol the Baddon Boys wear tattooed on their arms. You help ladies of the night, some likely coming from the Bird of Paradise, which is run by the Baddon Boys gang."

She frowned.

"Yes, I know it is hard to believe, but I assure you, Alex really does communicate with the spirits of those that have passed."

"Alex told me that you all are clairvoyants."

Leo exhaled slowly. "Yes, that is the truth."

"And the cuff link led you to the Thames that night where you saved me?" She did not scoff but simply watched him through her beautiful topaz eyes.

"Yes, I find things," he said in a rush. "Missing things, and often they lead me to a person like they did with you."

"I'm not sure if I need to sit down or run screaming from this house," she said.

"Definitely run screaming from the house. I would be grateful if you kept this to yourself, Cyn."

"I'm not sure anyone would believe me."

"Very likely. Now, back to my original question, are you in danger, and are the Baddon Boys gang involved?" She stiffened, and her eyes moved to his left ear, avoiding eye contact. She then sneezed. "I'm simply trying to help. If you—"

"I have no wish to continue this discussion here in case someone overhears or sees us together. I must return to the ballroom before I am missed. Good evening." She walked away from him before he could bow.

Leo studied the sway of her skirts and the two fat curls that fell down between her shoulder blades.

With a handful of words, her calm had fled, and she was nervous again, but not from his presence. No, it was due to his mention of the Baddon Boys.

CHAPTER NINETEEN

Cyn hadn't seen Leo again since the Raven ball, as she had come down with a stuffy head and sore throat, so that had been an excellent excuse not to leave the house.

Being housebound was a double-edged sword for her. She had time to read and be with the children, but on the other hand, there were her thoughts that kept circling back to Leo and the kiss they'd shared.

Both had brushed it off, but that kiss and the feel of being pressed to Leo's hard chest had been unlike anything she'd experienced before. It made her long for more. Long for something she'd never felt.

Kenneth had married her so his children would be cared for and happy when he died, which the doctors had told him was imminent due to his weak heart. He'd assured her it would be a marriage in name only, as he loved another—his mistress.

"Letitia has called, Mother," Meg said, running into the room where Cyn was reading on a sofa. Actually, there was very little reading happening; it was mostly thinking about Leo and that kiss and the Phoenix Agency.

Was Alex right? Was she really in danger? Leona had ominously claimed that the Baddon Boys and, more importantly, their leader, the Wolf, were suspicious of a lady that was interfering by helping the girls leave them. Kenneth had then shown Alex those symbols. It was all too close to the truth, and she had no idea what to do about it.

"Wonderful. I am ready for company. Do you wish to go to the park for a walk? I'm sure we can persuade Letitia and perhaps see what vendors we encounter along the way."

"Oooh, spiced cake!" Meg shot back out of the room.

"Off you get, Berry, you are turning my legs numb." She shooed the cat off her lap, and Berry glared at her, then stalked away to find somewhere else to sleep. "You have the best life, you lazy creature."

Brushing hair from her skirts, she went to meet her friend.

"In 1610, Galileo observed four 'stars' near Jupiter with his telescope, Letitia," Simon was saying when she tracked her friend down.

She and Simon were looking through the telescope that Kenneth had purchased. He'd passed his love of astronomy onto his son and daughter.

"Hello," Cyn said, drawing all eyes. "What has you here today, Letitia?"

"Charles and I are going to the country for a visit with his brother. As we took Simon and Meg with us last time, which our five nieces and nephews loved, I wondered if they wished to accompany us again?"

"Oh, well—"

"Yes!" her children shrieked.

Cyn hated when Meg and Simon were away from her but was not selfish enough to make them stay, especially with what was going on with the agency at the moment. It was perhaps a good time for them to leave for a while.

"I shall miss you all, but yes, of course. If you wish to accompany Letitia and Charles, I have no problem with that," Cyn said.

She was hugged by her children and then Letitia. Her friend's eyes then narrowed. "You look washed out, and when did you last have your hair styled?"

"I've been sick."

"You do look peaky, but we will take a walk in the lovely fresh London air, and then you shall rest when I take these two away for a few days."

Simon wrinkled his nose. "It smells of smoke outside, so it is hardly fresh air."

Letitia waved her hand, dismissing his words. "Now off you go to collect your things. We shall walk somewhere, and hopefully there will be some sweets in our future."

"As you wish, Your Majesty," Cyn said, dropping into a deep curtsy with a mocking smile on her face.

She tidied her hair, pulled on her long coat, and then left her room, only to find a Mulholland coming down the long hallway toward her. His face was serious, and he looked angry. His hair told her it was Monty.

"Good day to you, Monty. Is everything all right?"

"You'll pardon me for interrupting you, my lady, but there is a problem with a few of your household staff."

"What has happened?"

He looked uncomfortable now.

"Come, Monty, please speak plainly."

"Lilly, one of your maids, is not being fairly treated by your senior staff, Lady Lowell."

"That's a serious accusation, Monty, considering they have been in this household for many years, and I've never had another staff member complain before."

Color flushed his cheeks. "I understand I am new to your employ, my lady, and you have no reason to trust me."

"I did not say I don't trust you, Monty. Now please tell me what is going on," Cyn said, and then she sneezed, but not because she was nervous; this was the residue of her stuffy head.

"Lilly and Jeremiah, your footman, were found together in a compromising position. They are now being confronted by the other staff members."

"Oh dear, really?" Cyn whispered. "Where is this confrontation taking place? Please take me there at once."

They hurried down the stairs and found Letitia, Simon, and Meg awaiting her.

"You go on. I'll see you soon. I have a staff matter to deal with first, Letitia. You two, behave yourselves."

"Are you sure you don't need my assistance?" Letitia asked.

"Quite sure. Purchase me a wedge of spiced cake, and I will meet you at the park. Prue, you accompany them."

Cyn heard the raised voices as she descended the stairs into the kitchens. Reaching the small dining area where the staff took their meals, she found her butler, housekeeper, and cook on one side of the table, and on the other, Toby Mulholland, Jeremiah, her footman, and Lilly, the maid.

"She's to be turned out at once!" Hadleigh was saying in a tone she'd never heard him use before.

"Good day to you all," Cyn said, drawing their eyes and a few gasps.

"My lady!" her butler said.

"What is going on, Hadleigh?"

"A small staff matter, my lady. I have it in hand." His face was flushed red.

"I'm sure you do, but I wish to know what it is you have at hand, please?" Cyn said the words in the tone Kenneth had taught her to use when she wanted something done.

Be polite yet firm if you want respect.

Everyone started speaking at once. Cyn raised a hand.

"As Toby is the last to enter this household and likely has not formed allegiances to anyone but me and my children, he will speak." She nodded to the large Mulholland, who was currently wearing the same expression as his brother had earlier. "Speak plainly, Toby, and tell me the truth," Cyn added.

"Lilly and Jeremiah are in love." This was greeted by scoffs from her three senior staff members. Cyn sent them a quelling look that shut them up. "Lilly has found herself in a compromising situation." His face was now flushed red.

"She must go!" Mrs. Tipply, Cyn's housekeeper, said.

Lilly was pale but not weeping, and Jeremiah was at her side. Cyn noted they were holding hands. She wondered briefly what that would be like. To have a man who loved you so much, they would stand at your side and hold your hand while hell rained down all around you and your future was suddenly uncertain.

"And Jeremiah can stay?" Cyn asked her housekeeper. She was then rewarded with three nods from her senior staff. "Why?"

They frowned.

"When clearly it takes two people to make a baby. Why is it Lilly must be dismissed and not Jeremiah?"

"She's the one at fault," Mrs. Peel, the cook, said, folding her arms over her heaving chest. Indignant, her face was now flushed with color.

"It's her fault," Cyn said slowly.

"Exactly," Hadleigh said.

"I don't agree," Cyn added. "It is the fault of both parties, and unlike you three, I will not be tossing my staff out on the street because they made an error of judgement that is going to result in a child." The last word came out with a snap to it. "They will be staying, and we will be supporting them. If that is not the case," she said, raising a hand when her housekeeper opened her mouth, "it will not be Jeremiah and Lilly who are dismissed. I hope I've made myself clear?"

Shock was the only word for the expressions on her staff's faces.

Cyn turned to Lilly and Jeremiah. "Do you both wish to marry?"

"Yes, my lady," they said together.

"Excellent. Then we will see if we can expedite that. Both of you will come to my office tomorrow morning, please, to discuss this matter further. You may now go about your business, as I wish to speak to my butler, housekeeper, and cook. Toby, we are leaving the house shortly. Please wait for me by the front door."

"Very well, my lady." He bowed and then left. Jeremiah and Lilly did the same with haste.

The silence that followed was loud with disapproval from her staff.

"Out on the streets of London at this very moment there are women with babes who are living there, as they have no one else to care for and support them. Often it is men who have put them in that position." She made eye contact with each of them. "I have never believed a person should be punished for a moment of weakness, especially not because she is a woman and the one who suffers a far worse fate than a man when she is found to be with child."

"It's the way of things, my lady."

"Men have made it that way, Mrs. Peel, but that does not mean it is right," Cyn said. "You all like Jeremiah and Lilly, but because she is with child—something that was not her fault alone—you were willing to toss her out on the street in a heartbeat to an uncertain future and let him stay. That was heartless of all three of you and disappointing."

They met her words with silence.

"My beliefs do not follow those of others of my birth, and I will not have Lilly put on trial and found guilty for an act that two people partook in. Nor will I have her babe punished. Now, you three have until tomorrow to make your decisions."

"What decisions, my lady?" Hadleigh asked, clearly confused now.

"Whether you will accept Lilly and allow her to continue working here until she no longer can, or whether you wish to leave my employment. Because make no mistake," Cyn added, "I will be keeping a close eye on this situation, and if you do not treat her with respect, as I have already stated, it will not be her employment that is terminated."

Leaving behind her stunned senior staff members that had been a part of this household for far longer than her, Cyn walked from the room and headed for the stairs.

Reaching the front entrance, she pulled on her bonnet and then tugged the ribbons so hard, one snapped.

"Drat."

"Can I help, my lady?"

"I am merely angry, Monty. Let's go," she added, stalking out the front door.

Seconds later, she was walking down her street with Toby and Monty several paces behind. Stopping, she waited for them to reach her. "Walk at my side, will you, please? I have no wish to get a crick in my neck."

They did, flanking her on either side, keeping their strides small to match hers. Cyn felt suddenly tired. Too much emotion could do that to a person. Kenneth had once told her that, which was why he rarely showed any.

"Thank you for supporting Lilly and Jeremiah, Mulhollands."

They didn't speak for several minutes as they walked past the impressive facades of the homes that shared her street.

Cyn knew some of her neighbors but not many. If she was honest, she did not have a great many friends. Letitia and Charles. Lewis too, but most of the people in her life were acquaintances. She often felt lonely and was ashamed of the emotion, as she had so much.

"We had four sisters, my lady." Monty said. "One died in childbirth far from our home. She died alone, as our father would not let any of us be with her. She was unwed, you see."

"I am so sorry," Cyn said, touching each of their arms. "That must have been a terrible time for you all."

"It was, and it is why we were supportive of Lilly," Toby added. "Thank you for supporting her also, my lady."

Why those words made her want to weep, she had no idea, but they did. Or perhaps it was for the brothers who lost a sister in such terrible circumstances.

"I know you are men, so I'm of course excluding you from this next statement, but a great many men are fools."

"You will get no disagreement from us," Toby said.

CHAPTER TWENTY

"What?"

"What?" Leo replied, glaring at his brother. Alex was seated across from him at the desk in 11 Crabbett Close.

They were both working, as had been their uncle until he'd been called away to deal with a loud noise outside the door, which suggested someone was doing something they shouldn't be. Chester was under the desk, lying on Leo's feet and snoring.

"You keep raising your eyes from the paper and staring at the wall behind me before lowering them again. Then you make that irritating flicking sound with your fingers."

Leo stared at his brother. His hair stood up at the front because he'd been running his fingers through it while thinking, which he'd done since childhood.

"I beg your pardon, but I do not make an irritating flicking sound with my fingers."

"Oh please, you do it when you are distracted. But my point is, why are you distracted? Not that reading all these papers wouldn't drive anyone into an asylum, but still, you can usually be counted upon to stay on task. However, what you are is testy," Alex said.

"I am not testy." Leo sounded exactly that. In fact, he'd been testy since the Raven ball. He'd tried to tell himself it was not because of her and had avoided going anywhere Cyn may be. But it was not working.

Alex put down the paper in his hand and sat back in his chair, studying Leo.

"What's going on, Leo?"

He looked down at the papers before him, then back at Alex.

"Come on, vent your spleen, you know I'm the wisest of us all and my advice will be brilliant."

Leo scoffed.

A tap on the door was followed by Gray entering. Behind him was a shriek almost like a war cry. Ellen's husband stepped inside and closed the door swiftly.

"Theo is teaching Anna to slide down the banister. Mungo is at the bottom catching them, and Bram is at the top helping them climb on. Ramsey is standing below, in case anyone should fall, they will land on him."

"Your cousin is here again?" Alex asked. "I'm beginning to wonder if he can't live without Mungo's abuse."

"I'm more inclined to think it's Bud's cooking," Gray said.

"I will join them as soon as my brother has told me what is on his mind, as I have excellent form in banister sliding and can show them how it is done."

"I just did that," Gray said, looking smug.

The stuffy Detective Fletcher had changed a great deal since he'd entered the family. Once, he would never have contemplated sliding down a banister, but now he was game for most activities they got up to in the Nightingale household.

"What is on your mind, Leo?" Alex asked.

"Nothing."

Gray looked at him. "Now that's a lie."

"You have no psychic abilities, so how is it you think something is wrong with me?"

"Years of interviewing people who were determined not to speak the truth," Gray said.

"My money is on Cyn being the root of the problem," Alex added with deadly accuracy.

"Lady Lowell?"

"The very one," Alex said to Gray.

"Ellen told me all about her after the ball. I don't remember her or Lord Lowell, but then I did not walk in society for long."

"She and Leo were to marry," Alex said.

"He already knows that and likely everything else," Leo snapped.

Gray sat on the edge of his desk. "Come on, Leo, talk. It will make you feel better," he said.

Why not? He couldn't stop thinking about her, and his concern for Cyn was growing, especially after he'd ridden past the Phoenix Agency yesterday. Leo had told himself he was just checking the property they had taken the lease on next door. But what he'd seen was a large man skulking about in the shadows, clearly watching Cyn's agency. He'd stopped, but the man had left at a run.

"I believe she is in danger."

"Why?" Gray asked.

"This entire Baddon Boys connection that Alex said Lord Lowell was showing him, and the Bird of Paradise brothel. I'm sure it has something to do with her agency, especially as her clients are ladies of the night. I asked her if she was in danger."

"When did you ask her that?" Alex said.

"At the ball, but she did not give me an answer. I'm sure

she is being followed also." Leo went on to explain what he'd seen at the fair and at her agency again yesterday.

"Firstly, you should have told me what Lowell or his spirit was telling you." Gray jabbed a finger at Alex. "Secondly, you need to come to me if you have concerns."

"I thought Ellen would have told you about Lord Lowell's messages," Alex said.

"I'll be having words with her about that. But you two, come to me with anything going forward."

The Nightingale brothers nodded solemnly.

"Those looks don't fool me," Gray added. "But back to Lady Lowell. If she has drawn attention from the Baddon Boys, then there is cause to be concerned. They are growing in numbers and wealth each year, no matter how hard we try to crack down on them. They are linked to many crimes in London, and not just in the area they used to frequent," Gray said. "After their leader died two years ago, the new one who stepped in is the worst kind of criminal. He's intelligent, hungry, and cunning."

"A bad combination in someone with nefarious intentions," Alex said.

"Exactly. His goals are power and wealth, and he has been taking on other gangs to dominate their territories. There have been some bloody fights, and many have lost their lives," Gray said. "It's my hope that your Lady Lowell is not caught up with them, as it will not go well for her."

A shiver of unease traversed Leo's spine.

"What is this man's name?" Leo asked.

"We only know him as the Wolf."

"Does Cyn like butterscotch?" Alex said with a faraway look in his eyes.

There is not much I would sell my soul for, but butterscotch is one thing. The memory slid into Leo's head. He remembered when Cyn had told him that, because it was two days before he'd walked away from her.

"Yes."

"Which would explain why the taste is in my mouth, and now I want some," Alex said.

"I want you and Ellen to help me out with a few of the cases that we are struggling to resolve at Scotland Yard," Gray said.

"Really?" Alex looked excited. "I say, I've always wanted to be a detective."

"You will not be a detective but an adviser," Gray said.

"I'm going for a ride," Leo said as they launched into a discussion about cases and what Alex would call himself.

"Excellent day for a ride," Alex said, cutting Gray off midsentence and rising also.

"Fresh air is always good for the constitution," Gray added.

"I do not need any of you accompanying me. I wish for time alone with my thoughts."

Alex laughed. "As if that's ever going to happen in this family."

Gray smiled in that way he did when he wasn't sure how to take Nightingale carry-ons, as he called them.

A particularly loud shriek and a muffled oof had them all heading to the door. Opening it, they moved to the banister and saw Ram lying on his back below, with Anna on top of him.

"Thank you, Ram," she said, bending to kiss his cheek. "You have the makings of an excellent big brother."

He wheezed out a reply as she got off him and then staggered to his feet.

"I'm beginning to wonder if he's been tossed out of his home, he's here so much," Mungo snarled from his position in the front entrance watching over proceedings.

THE FALLEN VISCOUNT

Leo moved quietly around his family, who all began to debate the merits of Mungo's words. He wanted some peace to think about what to do with Hyacinth, and he'd not get it inside these walls.

Grabbing his hat and coat, he picked up his cane last and slipped out of the door. He'd made it ten steps down the street on the cool London morning when the sound of running footsteps reached him. Turning, he found Ellen hurrying toward him with her umbrella.

Sighing, Leo stopped. "What?" he demanded.

"I'm coming with you. We took a silent vote, and I won. But we decided that you didn't need too many of us, as clearly you have something weighty you are dealing with, and I'm the least likely to chatter constantly."

Leo blinked at the rush of words. "Is this you not chattering?"

She smiled.

"You all came to that conclusion in the two minutes since I left the house?"

"We are fast thinkers." She grabbed his arm. "Now where is it we are going?"

"Where is your protective husband?"

"He trusts you."

They walked on in silence, and he enjoyed having Ellen close even though you'd need an oxen to pull that statement from him. Reaching the end of the street, he looked at Nicholson's bookshop.

"I still expect to find George in there," Ellen said.

George Nicholson had been murdered in his store, and it had been Gray who found the murderer. It was now run by his sister and her husband, who was outside sweeping the front steps.

"Good day to you, Mr. Smith," Ellen said as he nodded to them.

"Good day," he replied. "Lovely day for a walk."

"It is indeed," Ellen said.

They walked on past Nitpicks Trinkets and Treasures, which the younger members of his family loved, and Appleblossoms Bakery, which had the best apricotines according to Ram.

"Ellen, I think you should return to the house. I have something I need to do."

"I have time. I will go with you."

He huffed out a breath. "I don't want to tell you where I am going."

"As it likely has something to do with Cyn, then I wish to come."

"How do you know it has something to do with her?"

"The Baddon Boys connection, and what Gray told you about them has unsettled you. So, my conclusion is you are going to see her."

"Were you listening at the door?"

"Of course." She squeezed his arm.

"I have an urge to find her," he muttered.

"Well then, find her we must. As I'm here with you, we have the perfect reason to call at her house." Ellen then moved away from him and stepped into the street. Raising a hand to the approaching hackney, she flagged it down. "Hurry it along, brother."

"I'm the eldest," he muttered. "Don't order me about."

"But clearly not the most intelligent among us."

He helped her inside and followed after giving the address he wanted to reach.

"And what will you say when you get there?" Ellen was fussing with her skirts in that way women did when they were settling on a seat.

"I have no idea," Leo said, "but seeing as you are with me, I will say you wanted to visit with her."

"There, you see, it is a good thing I followed you and not Alex."

"Not just because you love me and wish to spend time in my company then?"

"That as well." She flicked gloved fingers at him.

He found a smile, even though the tension inside him was climbing again, as it had the night he'd needed to find his cuff link.

"I still cannot believe you told her you wanted your cuff link back after you'd saved her that night."

"I wasn't myself," Leo said, slipping his hand into his pocket to grip the round disk that had not left his person since Cyn returned it.

"Who else could you be if not the insufferable Lord Seddon, but we digress."

"From what? I thought we were discussing that night and my cuff link?"

She glared at him. "It's a figure of speech, brother."

"Is it? I hadn't realized." Needling his siblings was a wonderful way to focus on something other than his own problems, and right now, Cyn was presenting herself as one.

"I wonder why she carried it with her for so long," Ellen said, ignoring his attempts to get a rise out of her. "One could surmise she wanted your memory with her at all times. Or she never forgot you."

"Or, as she stated, to remind her that she will never be something for a man to discard with ease ever again," Leo added.

"No." Ellen's nose wrinkled.

"You look like a rabbit scenting something when you do that."

"It's my belief that I am right, and she wanted it to remember you by," she added, ignoring him.

"You cannot romanticize everything, sister."

"Of course I can, especially if I'm right." She gave him a haughty look.

Family, Leo thought. They could annoy you more than anyone else. The carriage slowed and stopped, and Leo opened the door.

"You will behave yourself in there and not make a fool of me."

Ellen climbed out and patted his cheek. "You can do that all by yourself. You don't need me, brother."

Shaking his head, he followed her up to the front door of the impressive and large three-storied white town house that had been in the Lowell family for many years.

Leo knocked. The door was opened by her butler seconds later.

"Good day, we have called to see Lady Lowell." Leo handed over his card.

"I'm afraid she is not at home, my lord."

"Is she expected back soon?" Leo asked.

"As to that, I cannot say, my lord, but I will of course tell her you called."

"Did she say where she was going?" Ellen asked.

"She did not."

"Thank you," Ellen said as she and Leo turned to leave.

When they were back out on the street, Leo wondered what he was supposed to do now.

"We could try her agency," Ellen said. "Unless you no longer have a hankering to find her."

"One has hankerings for food, not to find people, Ellen."

"I stand corrected."

"Come on." He took her arm and went to wave down another hackney.

They knocked on the Phoenix Agency front door twenty minutes later. It was answered by the man Leo knew as

Lewis. One look at his face, and Leo could tell something wasn't right.

"Hello. We have called to see Lady Lowell," Ellen said.

"She is not here."

"Are you wanting tea, Mr. Lewis?" a voice called from somewhere inside.

"Is that Mrs. Varney?" Ellen asked.

The man nodded, still clearly uncomfortable.

"She lives on the same street as us," Ellen said. Leo had not spoken as yet, and his eyes were still on the man. Sweat was glistening on his forehead. Something was very wrong; he could feel it.

"Tell whoever is out there to come in. I've enough tea in the pot for more. It'll help us wait upon their return!" Mrs. Varney called.

"What's going on?" Leo asked, trying to keep the demand out of his voice.

"I-I, nothing," Lewis said quickly.

"Something," Leo said, taking action by nudging the man back inside. "We are friends of Lady Lowell and can help."

"Well now, this is a nice surprise," Mrs. Varney said, beaming. "I'll see to that tea, as I know just how Lord Seddon and Mrs. Fletcher take it." She then bustled through a door.

"We wish her no harm," Leo said. "Tell us where Lady Lowell is, as we want to offer her our help if it is needed."

They watched as the man battled with his loyalty to Cyn and his worry for her.

"Miss Coulter, she lives here at the Phoenix Agency, left a note for me. I had popped out and just returned, so I did not see her and Lady Lowell leave. It said there had been an incident with a woman and they had gone to assist her."

"Incident?" Ellen asked.

Lewis remained silent.

"Your loyalty is admirable, but if you think Lady Lowell is

in danger, then we can help," Leo said, battling down his need to roar at the man. "Do you believe she is in danger?" But he knew the answer to that, just as Ellen did.

He steadied her as he felt her go into one of her trances. She was getting a vision, and he knew it was to do with Cyn.

He saw the ring then. It had rubies and diamonds, and he knew without a doubt that it was owned by her, and that he needed to find it.

"We have to go. I just saw Cyn surrounded by men, and she was scared," Ellen whispered.

"Show me the note," Leo demanded.

Something in his expression made Lewis grab it. Reading the words, he felt his blood run cold.

A boy has called to tell us that a woman needs our assistance. We are to accompany him, and when we have her, we will bring her back to the agency. Please ensure all is ready in case she needs our care, Lewis.

"We need to find her. She is in danger," Ellen said, the urgency clear in her voice.

"Are there others here at the moment?" Lewis nodded. "Then stay and watch over them. We will find Lady Lowell."

"And Miss Coulter. She has already suffered so much," Lewis said, and the look on the man's face told Leo he cared for Miss Coulter very much.

"I will bring them back safe," Leo vowed. Seconds later, he and Ellen were heading back out the door to find Cyn.

Stay safe until I arrive.

CHAPTER TWENTY-ONE

"How do you know this boy, Mary?" Cyn asked as they followed the lad down a narrow road in the East End of London. It was winding around the buildings that climbed on either side. Doors opened onto the street, and they could not see much inside, as the windows were small or nonexistent.

"Lionel lives at the Bird of Paradise brothel. He does all the odd jobs needed, and they look after him. He comes to the Phoenix Agency for food and if it's cold out sometimes."

"There are so many in need," Cyn sighed. "But can you trust him, Mary?"

"No more than many, but in this, I think he is telling the truth."

She had called at the agency after Simon and Meg had left for their trip with Charles and Letitia. Mary had been talking to the boy in the entrance when she arrived with Monty.

"And he said that a woman is in desperate need of help?"

"Lionel said they hid her here so he couldn't find her. Isn't that right, Lionel?"

WENDY VELLA

The boy nodded at Mary's question. He had not said a great deal, just led them to where Cyn hoped Clara was.

"I'm pleased Leona was able to leave yesterday. She will be safe with the others now," Mary said.

Cyn had purchased a house out of London where some of the girls could go to heal and learn the skills needed to start a new life.

"Yes, it was best for her to go as soon as possible," Cyn agreed. "If anyone came looking for her, it would mean trouble for all of us."

"Yes," Mary said.

"There is a building up there. It has a lion on the roof," Lionel said suddenly. He then ran away before they could stop him.

"I don't like this, my lady," Monty said from behind her. "You shouldn't be here. I've heard about these Baddon Boys and the danger they represent to you from Lewis, and why did the lad flee if he's not going to alert people that we're here?"

"We will find the woman and leave as fast as we can, Monty. All will go well," Cyn said with more conviction than she actually felt.

She thought he muttered, "I'm not so sure about that."

Mary nodded again. "Stay alert, my lady. Monty is right. I should have insisted you stay at the agency."

"It's daylight, Mary. Surely not too much harm can come to me with the sun high in the sky? And Monty is with us."

"They don't live by the same rules you do, my lady," Monty said. "There are many who are unscrupulous and would take advantage of the opportunity seeing you presents them."

Cyn shivered. Had she been wrong to come here? Had her need to aid the woman blinded her to her safety?

"Make haste then. We will find her and leave as fast as we can."

"That building there," Mary said, pointing. The outside was a brick facade, and one side was blackened from smog. On the roof was a large statue of a lion, which seemed odd in such a setting.

"We must be quiet," Mary said. "In and out, hopefully with Clara, before anyone notices."

"I'll go first, my lady," Monty said.

"Very well."

Monty knocked on the door. Mary and Cyn stood at his back. No one answered the knock. Monty then tried the door, and it swung open. The stench hit Cyn first as they entered. Fetid air had her breathing shallowly.

Moving through the single room on the lower level, they found little except for rat droppings and sacks.

"Hello!" Mary called. A scratching sound from the floor above had them all hurrying to the stairs. Monty reached them first and started to climb.

"Stay back," he ordered as they reached the top. A single door was closed. Monty opened it and stepped into the room. Light filtered in through the narrow grimy window. Stepping to Monty's side, Cyn saw the body huddled on the floor under a thin blanket.

"Dear Lord," Cyn whispered, hurrying closer. She dropped to her knees beside the person. Mary did the same opposite. Monty remained standing, watching over them.

"Is she…? I can barely ask," Mary whispered.

"Alive? Yes, she is," Cyn said. "There now, we have you," she bent to whisper into the woman's ear.

She rolled onto her back, and swollen eyes looked up at Cyn.

"Help me."

"We are going to do that for you now. Are you Clara?" The woman nodded. "Can you walk?"

"Move back, my lady. Let me help her," Monty said. "I'll pick her up, and we'll get her out of here. No point in staying and courting trouble. There's little we can do for her here anyway."

Cyn and Mary moved and then helped steady the woman as Monty got her upright. She was unsteady. He then gently lifted her into his arms and made his way to the stairs.

It was slow going, and all Cyn could think about was getting out of this place. The stench was horrid, and the pall of desperation nearly choked her. That anyone should stay here, even for an hour, was horrifying. But to do so alone in Clara's condition must have been terrifying.

She knew there were both bad and good men in the world, just as there was the same for women. But that someone could inflict such pain on a person willingly was beyond her belief.

They made it down the stairs and out onto the street. The woman was panting with the effort it took and clearly weak and in pain.

"Now, we must walk a few steps farther, Clara, to reach my carriage," Cyn said. "Are you all right, Monty?"

"Aye," he said. One look at his face, and she could see his anger matched her own.

The thudding of rapidly approaching feet had fear sluicing through Cyn.

"Hide!" Two boys appeared. "Hurry!" one of them called, running past. "It's the Baddon Boys!"

She looked to where they'd come from but saw no one.

"They're coming if the boys say they are," Monty said. "That little blighter snitched on us," he snarled. "I'm going to lower the woman to her feet, and you steady her between you," he added.

"Monty—"

"I need to have my fists free, my lady," he said, his voice a low growl.

"Oh dear, do you?"

He didn't reply and simply lowered Clara, and Mary and Cyn rushed to her sides. Looking around, she saw the boys were watching them now from a narrow opening between two buildings. "Come, Mary, let us move Clara that way."

"We can't leave Monty alone," Mary whispered.

"We are not. We are putting her there out of sight before the men arrive, in case our fists are also needed. Plus, then she will at least be safe."

"You can't fight, my lady!" Mary said, scandalized.

"I doubt I'll be much help, but surely I must try if they set upon Monty," Cyn said with far more calm than she was actually feeling. In fact, she was terrified. A terror so strong, her knees felt weak, and she was struggling to draw air into her throat, as it felt too tight. The last time she had felt such fear was the day her mother told her Leo had left London with his family in disgrace.

"You run, my lady. It is the way it should be," Mary hissed.

"No, it is not," Cyn said. "I brought you here, and I will stay until we can leave together."

They reached the boys, who were now watching wide-eyed. Cyn opened the small bag she carried around her wrist and handed over coins to each of them. "If you look after this woman until we return, there will be more of those for you. If we are not able to return to you, then take her to the Phoenix Agency on Lenton Street and ask for Lewis. Will you do that for me?"

"Aye," one of them said solemnly.

"Please run, my lady," Mary begged her.

"She's right," one of the boys said. He was helping Clara to a narrow opening between two buildings. "You need to run if you're a nob."

"Every life is worthy of saving," Cyn snapped, enjoying the flush of heat the boy's words had produced. That he believed her more worthy of survival than him, as did Mary, made her angry. "Now please care for Clara, and remember what I told you about the Phoenix Agency," she added.

"I see them now," Monty called. "Four men approaching. Flee, my lady! You also, Mary!"

"I am not leaving you to face four men, Monty."

"They will care little about your title, my lady. Leave at once." She could hear the desperation in his voice.

Her eyes went to the four men approaching. They wore dark hats pulled low and long black coats. They looked menacing.

"I will not allow Toby or the rest of your family to lose another sibling."

"Please go," he begged her.

"No." Cyn slipped her hand into her pocket, wrapping her fingers around the handle of her pistol, which she always carried with her now.

"Catch!" Cyn watched as Mary caught the piece of wood the boy threw her, and then he and the others disappeared into the shadows.

Clara was safe, at least, for now.

"You're meddling in business that doesn't concern you, Lady Lowell," one of the men said as he reached her. "These women belong to us, and we don't like anyone taking them away. The Wolf is not happy."

"I beg your pardon?" Cyn said in her haughtiest tone. "No woman is owned by a man, especially not one who mistreats her." Eyeing the four men before her, Cyn wondered how she was going to get out of here with everyone safe. She could feel eyes on them but knew no one would come to their aid.

Most just wanted to live their lives without trouble. To go against a gang like this would challenge that.

"Our women are," another of them snarled. "Where is Clara?"

"I have powerful friends that can make your life extremely difficult. I suggest you step aside and let us pass," Cyn said.

All four of the men laughed.

"My lady, when I say run, please do," Monty said.

"I will not be leaving you," Cyn said, pulling out her pistol. "Move, gentlemen, if you please, as I will not hesitate to shoot you."

"You'll only hit one of us, and even then, it's not likely seeing as you're a woman."

Her fingers itched to slap the sneer off the face of the man who had spoken.

"At least one of you will suffer then," Cyn said.

"More than one," Monty added.

There was no way out of here. Panic gripped her. What had she done bringing Monty and Mary here? At least her Simon and Meg were far from London. Charles and Letitia would care for them if something happened to her. Dear Lord, she didn't want to die here in this filthy street.

"This is your last warning. If you do not let us leave, I will fire my pistol, and contrary to what you believe, I'm an excellent shot," Cyn said with more courage than she felt.

The men advanced; she took aim and fired. The man on the right yelped, and Cyn watched him grip his arm. Relief that she hadn't killed him was replaced with the knowledge that she would now have to use some other means to escape and fight.

Monty charged.

"Kick, punch, do whatever you can, my lady!" Mary cried.

It could never be a fair fight. One strong man and two

women against four men who were no doubt used to fighting.

If you ever need to subdue a man, you go for his nose or groin.

It had been Charles who taught her that after Kenneth died. He said he never wanted her or Letitia to be helpless.

Forming a fist, she struck out as one of the men approached her and missed. *Bothering hell.* He grabbed her arm and forced it up her back painfully. She raised her knee and managed to connect with some of his groin as he twisted.

"Bitch!" His hand swung toward her, and before she could duck it, he slapped her hard enough across the cheek to make her see stars. But she didn't fall. Stumbling backward, she bumped into someone. His grunt told her it was the man.

She then heard him grunt again after a solid thwacking sound.

"Take that!" Mary cried from behind her.

Righting herself, Cyn faced the angry man heading her way again.

"Make fists with your hands!" Monty roared.

Her face burned, but that was nothing like the rage consuming her. These men thought they owned women. She wanted to reeducate them, which was laughable, but it was how she felt.

Rage gives you strength, Charles had told her that day.

"Move your feet!" Monty instructed, and then she heard another thwack, which she hoped was him punching someone and not the reverse. Cyn started bouncing on her feet like Simon did when he wanted to annoy Meg, jabbing out with her fists at the man before her. He swung a large dinner plate–sized fist at her; Cyn ducked this time, and it sailed over her head.

"We've been watching you, Lady Lowell, but until now, you've not interfered with our business overmuch. That's changed. Now the Wolf wants you stopped," the man growled.

"You'll end up hanging from a noose if you touch her," Monty yelled.

"No one will catch me," the man said, his expression smug. He advanced on her again, and Cyn jabbed, putting as much force as she could behind it. It was more luck than skill that had her connecting, and the man grabbed his nose.

"Bitch!" He lunged at her and forced her to her knees.

"My lady!" Mary cried.

"And now I'm going to teach you to mind your business," the man hissed as he bent over her.

Simon and Meg flashed through her head again then, and Leo. Would she ever see them again?

CHAPTER TWENTY-TWO

"Tell me everything you saw," Leo demanded as he looked at Ellen. She was seated across from him in the hackney. Her face was tight with worry.

"A man was bent over Hyacinth, and his hand was around her neck, Leo." She reached out a hand toward him, and he took it.

"It will be all right, Ellen." He moved to her side. "I promise we will get to her, sister."

She leaned into him, gripping his fingers hard.

He soothed her when inside, he was ice-cold with fear. When he knew with a certainty, even if Ellen hadn't told him, that Hyacinth was in danger.

"How do you know what direction we must go in, Leo?"

"I had an urge to find her ring." He wouldn't lie about that. For years, he had denied what he saw or felt, unlike his siblings, who had embraced what they could do. But no longer. His gift had saved Hyacinth from drowning, and now, when she was in danger, it was directing him to her again.

"The urgency inside me is growing," Ellen said. "I also saw

THE FALLEN VISCOUNT

a lion, Leo. It was sitting on top of a building. Ask the driver if he knows of one nearby."

"There are lions everywhere in London."

"Do not use that mocking tone with me," Ellen said.

"Sorry."

"Why Hyacinth?" Ellen asked. "Why are we now charged with finding her, Leo? Why is she the one you must seek again?"

Leo had a feeling he didn't want to know the answer to that, so he pushed it aside.

"I don't know, but I do know that if anything happens to you, your husband will likely kill me with his bare hands."

Ellen sighed. "I carry a pistol at his insistence, as well as my umbrella, but only because he taught me to fire it."

"If I tell you to go and get him and Alex, will you do that for me, Ellen?"

"No, I won't leave you."

"I didn't think so. Well then, sister, have a care, and protect yourself if the need arises for us to fight. I find I would not like anything to happen to you."

"I love you, Leo, and I promise."

"I love you too, but I am also terrified of your husband. So don't give him any reason to maim me."

She forced out a snicker. "He is a wonderful man, but you don't fool me. Nothing scares you."

In fact, he was scared by a great many things. His family in any pain or danger, the darkness inside him, and lastly, that he would be alone for the rest of his days.

Rising, he pushed open the hatch above him. He'd already told the driver to head toward the East End of London.

"Do you know of a building that has a large lion, possibly made of stone, perched on a roof nearby?" Leo called to the driver, feeling like a fool. There was silence, and then he spoke.

"Cinder Lane, sir. It's about five minutes from here. There's a large stone lion on the roof of an empty building. No one lives there now, but once it had been a stonemason's house."

"Really? Well, please take us there." Leo shut the door and sat.

"Perhaps you could apologize for mocking me now?"

"I could, but seeing as you constantly mock me, I feel it is a form of retribution."

The teasing was as natural as speaking between them, and he hoped it helped calm Ellen. It didn't calm him. All he could think about was getting to Hyacinth. She was in trouble, but would she stay safe until he reached her?

When the carriage stopped, he got out, and Ellen followed.

"There is where you need to go," the driver said after he'd paid him.

The sun was still high, but here, it felt darker. The buildings rose on both sides and blocked out any light.

"Be alert," Leo said, gripping his cane.

"And you," Ellen said, doing the same with her umbrella.

They walked down the street toward the direction the driver had said. He heard the scream. It was loud and filled the air with panic. Leo ran, his long strides leaving his sister behind. But he knew she followed, as he heard the thud of her feet.

He saw the group of people ahead of him. Men and two women, and they were fighting. Leo ran at the group. Grabbing the shoulder of a man a woman was struggling to hold at bay, he turned him and struck out with his cane in the stomach. Leo then brought it up under the man's chin, and he dropped like a stone.

He saw her then. On the ground with a man over her. His hand was around her throat like in Ellen's vision, and Cyn was struggling for release. With a roar, he grabbed him, dragging him off her. He tried to punch Leo, but he blocked it and then swung his cane hard. The man howled in pain as it connected with his jaw. Leo then swept his legs, and he, too, fell to the ground.

Ellen let loose an angry shriek, and Leo watched as she wielded her umbrella deftly at one of the remaining two men. The other man, who he recognized as one of Cyn's staff, was weaving and jabbing at his opponent. Soon, both were subdued and on their knees.

"Can you rise?" Leo asked Cyn, who was still on the ground.

"Yes," she rasped.

Holding out a hand, she took it, and he pulled her to her feet.

"Are you hurt?" She shook her head.

"Then we must leave here before these men want to continue what we finished."

"My lady, are you all right?"

"I am well, Monty, thank you," Cyn said, sounding anything but well. Her voice was weak and wobbly. He doubted she'd ever experienced anything like she just had before.

Monty Mulholland bore marks, and bruises were forming on his face. He had fought like the devil to keep his mistress safe. "I've never known another noble as brave as you, my lady. Are you well also, Mary?"

"Aye, a few bruises, but I've had worse," the other woman said, moving to where they stood.

"Ellen?" Leo said, his eyes on Cyn. She was pale and unsteady on her feet but trying not to show it.

"I am well, but we need to make haste to leave at once. If these are Baddon Boys, more could be on the way."

"Yes," Leo said, trying to tamp down his rage. "You are

foolish to have come here without more people to protect you," he said with remarkable restraint considering the red haze around the edges of his gaze.

She turned back to look at her staff, and he saw the mark on her face. Leo touched her chin. "Did that man with his hand around your throat do this?" he demanded.

She pushed his hand aside. "It matters not."

"It does matter," Leo gritted out, rage coursing through his body. "Just as it matters why you would do something so reckless that it could have cost you your life."

Her eyes narrowed at his hard tone, but he saw the flash of guilt.

"I didn't know they would come. W-we were—"

"Retrieving a woman who needed your help. I know, Lewis showed me the note," Leo snapped.

"We must leave," Ellen said again.

"Come, Monty, let us collect Clara," Cyn said, moving away from Leo.

He wanted to pick her up, take her home, and lock her in a room where he could watch over her, which told him many things—all of which he was going to ignore for now.

Leo followed as she hurried to a building and into the shadows. He then stood back as she talked to the boys that were there.

"Here is the money I promised you, and thank you for looking after Clara," Cyn said, handing out some coins to the boys. They then ran off and soon disappeared.

Monty moved deeper into the narrow opening, and when he reappeared, he was holding a woman. Presumably Clara, and the woman from the note he'd read earlier.

She was pale and battered.

"Who did this to her?" Leo asked.

"I don't know, but one of the Baddon Boys," Cyn said.

"Let's go," Leo said.

THE FALLEN VISCOUNT

Ellen, he noted, held Cyn's hand now, and that she let her was telling. He worried that she was not being truthful about her injuries, but soon he'd check her over. For now, getting everyone to safety was paramount.

They walked until they reached a street with more traffic and people. They were an odd procession, and many whispered and stared, but he cared little for that. Only that he got Cyn, Ellen, and the others to safety.

"Where is the carriage, Monty?" Cyn asked.

They all looked around them.

"There," Mary said, waving her hands.

"Thank you," Cyn said to him as the clop of hooves drew the Lowell carriage closer. "You saved us this evening. You and Ellen."

"We will ride with you to the agency and then, if need be, collect Mr. Greedy, who is a healer, to see to the girl," Leo said.

"I will take a seat with the driver," Monty said as the carriage stopped before them.

Leo opened the door, and Monty placed the woman, Clara, on the seat inside.

"We can—"

"Arguing is not helping her, Cyn," Leo said. "Get in the carriage at once before more trouble arrives. Ellen and I are accompanying you to the agency in case trouble follows."

"There is no need—"

"There is every need." Leo picked her up and deposited her inside. "Sister." He waved Ellen in next, then Mary. Leo was last, and he closed the door behind him after telling the driver to make haste.

Clara moaned softly as the carriage started moving.

"'Tis all right," Cyn said after shooting Leo a glare. She had taken the seat next to Clara and was now holding one of her hands.

"My name is Lord Seddon, and this is my sister, Mrs. Fletcher," Leo said as Clara looked around the carriage.

"We are taking you somewhere safe to be cared for, Clara. You have no need to fear anymore," Mary said.

He watched Cyn care for the injured woman. She wasn't getting away from him until he had answers as to why she had felt the need to plunge recklessly into danger. The actions could have cost her her life.

"You could have died," Leo snapped. Ellen shot him a look, then shook her head, as if to warn him not to continue this conversation now, with others in the carriage. *To hell with that.* "What of your children, Cyn? Are you happy for them to see their mother with bruises on her face and now a target for the Baddon Boys?"

"I did what needed to be done." She spoke the words quietly.

He could see the mark the man had left on her cheek and the bruising now darkening the slender line of her neck. He felt it again, the need to strike at who had hurt her. Her bonnet had gone, and her hair was half up, half down. Tangled curls rested on a slender shoulder. Her dress was the color of moss, and she wore a deep gray long jacket, which had lost its buttons and hung open. She looked rumpled and bruised. Scared, he added to that when her eyes flicked to his and away again.

The protectiveness he felt toward this woman was seconded only by what he felt for those he loved. His family for years had been his first and last priority, and yet since Cyn had come back into his life, she was there too, and Leo had a feeling she wasn't going anywhere.

CHAPTER TWENTY-THREE

Cyn hurt, but she had far more pressing concerns than her physical discomfort. She was currently seated in her carriage with Leo, Ellen, Mary, and Clara.

"There really is no need for you to come with us. I will of course have someone fetch a doctor," Cyn said, attempting to regain control. "We have no wish to disrupt your day any further."

"You are not serious?" Leo said, glaring at her. "You were just set upon by men, and had Ellen and I not arrived, things would have gone a great deal worse for you."

He spoke the words calmly, but she'd seen the rage in those dark eyes. Leo was furious at the risks she'd taken. He had no need to be, as she was angry with herself. Her ignorance of what could have happened nearly resulted in two of her staff being injured or worse. Cyn should have listened to Monty. Instead, she'd taken action without thought and had plunged them all into danger. Damn that Lionel, as surely he had double-crossed them.

"How would your children have fared had you not

returned home tonight, my lady?" Leo snapped at her. His use of her title told her how angry he was. "If you had died?"

Both Mary and Ellen were silently listening to the conversation between Cyn and Leo, their eyes going from one to the other.

"My children are away from London with friends," Cyn said. Now the immediate danger had gone, she could feel the tremors starting. While she'd been fighting for herself and her staff, she'd kept them at bay, but now her body ached, and she felt weak. She clenched her hands into fists so no one could see them trembling. Kenneth had taught her to hide overt displays of emotion, as they made a person weak. Right then, she was grateful for those lessons.

"That is not the point," Leo gritted out. "But as we are turning into the agency's street now, we will suspend further conversation."

Suspend it indefinitely, Cyn added silently.

"That, what you just experienced, does not simply happen without a reason. There is a great deal more to this, Cyn," Ellen said. "We know your agency is for ladies of the night, just as we know that you have raised the ire of the Baddon Boys."

"Let us help you," Leo said.

"I can't talk of this now," Cyn said. She needed to get Clara to the agency and then herself home before she fell apart.

When the carriage was stopped, Leo then lifted Clara into his arms as his sister opened the door.

"Monty can carry her," Cyn protested.

"As can I. Open the front door to the agency, Cyn."

There was little she could do but what he asked. Opening the door, she stepped inside and held it wide.

"Cyn!" Lewis came at a run, with Mrs. Varney not far behind.

"Lawks, what's amiss?" the woman shrieked.

"Upstairs," Cyn said to Leo. "Second door on the left. Mary, go with him and settle Clara on the bed."

"At once, my lady." Mary led the way, and Leo followed with Clara in his arms and Lewis behind them. Mary would be hurting too, but Clara needed tending before they tended themselves.

"Mrs. Varney, hot water to wash Clara, please, and any medical supplies. Bring tea or anything that you think will help her, as she has been badly hurt. As yet, I'm not sure how extensively," Cyn added. "We will go for help if it is required."

"We need Mr. Greedy," Mrs. Varney said.

"Tell me where I find him, and I will go and fetch him," Monty said. His face was bruised and one eye nearly shut.

"You need tending, Monty," Cyn said.

"We all need tending and will get it, but later. Now I will fetch this Mr. Greedy, my lady. The carriage is still outside."

"I'll fetch him, as my husband and family will be worried that we have not returned," Ellen said.

They all moved at once, and lifting her skirts, Cyn took the stairs up, ignoring the twinges and aches in her muscles. Reaching the room she directed Leo to take Clara to, she found him and Lewis standing beside the bed. Both looked at her as she walked in, but it was Lewis that Cyn focused on.

"Take Lord Seddon downstairs now. Mary and I will make Clara comfortable. Monty has gone to collect Mr. Greedy in the carriage with Mrs. Fletcher."

"What can I do?" Leo asked her.

"You have done enough, my lord, thank you." Silence greeted her words, so she added, "Good day to you, my lord, and thank you again for your assistance."

She didn't look at him but could feel his displeasure at her dismissal. Cyn only exhaled when she heard his footsteps on the stairs. She couldn't deal with him now, as she wanted desperately to stay in control, and seeing him was weakening that.

"Let's get Clara cleaned up and see how badly hurt she is," Mary said.

Between them they stripped off her filthy clothes until she was resting in her chemise.

"Get a clean one, Mary from the spare clothes we keep here," Cyn said.

Lewis arrived with water for washing, and behind him came Mrs. Varney with other supplies and tea.

"Off with you now." Mrs. Varney shooed Lewis out of the room. "The poor wee lassie," she added, looking at Clara. "We'll set her to rights."

Between them, they washed her, dressed her in a clean chemise, and slathered her bruises in something Mrs. Varney insisted they keep stocks of here at the agency.

"Let's get this tea down you now, Clara," Mary said, and Cyn could hear the tiredness in her voice. Like her, she was drooping after the day they'd endured.

"Not long now, Mary, and we can take care of our needs," Cyn said.

After Clara had taken some nourishment, she was soon slumbering. They all left the room quietly.

"She's bruised, but I don't believe anything is broken," Mary said.

"I agree," Mrs. Varney said. "But Mr. Greedy will know for sure. Now it's you two who need tending."

"I would love some tea, Mrs. Varney, and then, after I know Clara is well, I shall return to my house," Cyn said with a loud yawn.

"I have it brewing and some treacle cake for you both. Go on now and change, Mary, and then come into the parlor, and you can tell Lewis everything. He was terribly afeared for you both, pacing the floors till I thought he'd wear right through."

Mrs. Varney went to the kitchen, and Cyn, into the parlor. Stopping in the doorway, she looked at the only occupant.

"I thought you would have left?"

"As you see, I did not." Leo rose after lowering the mug he held. Before him on the table was a plate with cake. Cyn's stomach growled.

"Come and sit," Leo said, coming to where she stood. "Now, Cyn, before you fall."

"I'm all right."

"No, you're exhausted, terrified, and what happened has finally caught up with you, hasn't it?" His hands cupped her cheeks, and he looked into her eyes. "It's all right now. You are safe, as are the others, Cyn."

"I was so scared," she whispered, closing her eyes as the first tear fell.

She didn't fight him as he pulled her close, so close that she was soon pressed to his body. One large hand cupped the back of her neck, easing her head into his chest as she began to weep.

Cyn felt surrounded by him. His warmth, his scent. It all helped to settle the terror and fear that still gripped her. Never had she experienced what she had today, and she never wanted to again.

The hand at her back stroked her through her clothes, running up and down her spine in soothing gestures. It felt wonderful.

"The first time I had to fight someone who called my family something foul because of what my father had done was three days after he'd killed himself." He spoke the words slowly, as if recounting them wasn't easy. "I had left the house because my little siblings were scared, and I thought to comfort them by purchasing them some éclairs, which are a particular favorite."

She listened to the rumble of his voice with her ear pressed to his chest. Cyn knew she should move but had no strength in that moment to do so. Right now, she felt safe and wanted to hold on to that feeling as long as she could. Reality would soon return, she knew, but not yet. It had been so long since she'd been held like this; in fact, she could not remember a time she had been.

"I had nearly reached the bakery, and I saw three men who had been acquaintances. They walked up to me and explained to me in great detail what they thought of me and my family and the shameful act my father had done. I was filled with rage anyway, so the words just pushed me over, and soon I was fighting all three of them."

"Oh, Leo, I'm so sorry."

"It was a lesson," he said, kissing the top of her head. "I knew from that moment on that I never wanted to be vulnerable again. My uncle taught us how to fight. But my point is, when I returned to the house, I had weak knees and was shaking, as you are now."

"Did you get the éclairs?"

He snorted. "Yes, my siblings got their éclairs."

Easing off his body reluctantly, Cyn looked up at the man who she'd once loved and feared still did. They stared at each other for long moments. He leaned in and kissed her, and she let him, because right then, she needed that too. It was soft, achingly sweet, and she wanted more... so much more.

"Come, sit, and drink some tea. It will help," he said, taking her hand. She was led to a seat, and as her legs had no strength, she simply fell into it. He handed her a mug and a wedge of cake, and she took a large bite, sighing at the deliciousness.

"Now, I want to talk about this agency and, more importantly, who is angry with you for running it and helping the women who work as prostitutes to change professions and start new lives."

"Leo—"

"It is a wonderful thing you do here, Cyn, but it has put you at risk, and now you are in the sights of the Baddon Boys, and that scares me. So, I want to help you and have the means and people to do so."

She studied him sitting there across from her. He was so very different from the man she'd once known. There were depths to Leo that had not been there before, Cyn thought. Did she dare put her trust in him again?

CHAPTER TWENTY-FOUR

He'd spent the night rolling from side to side in his bed instead of actually sleeping after he'd dropped Cyn home.

She'd been silent, her eyelids drooping with exhaustion when finally they'd reached her town house. He'd escorted her to the door and then kissed her cheek, telling her he would return to discuss the situation further. What Leo had wanted to do was take her to her room, bathe her, and put her to bed… with him.

Lady Hyacinth Lowell was becoming a problem for Leo. He wanted her with a ferocity he'd never experienced before, and he wasn't sure what to do about it.

She had her life with her children, and he… what did he have? His family and the businesses they ran, but little else. But he could not think about anything that involved a future, if there was one, until he had helped her out of the mess she was in.

Leo now knew her life was at risk, as were the others at the Phoenix Agency. The thought of anything happening to her made his veins fill with ice. He had to keep her safe.

Rising, he walked to the window. It was still early, and the sun had yet to rise fully, if it did at all. Leo detested gray days, but as he lived in London, it was something he had grown used to.

Knowing there would be no more sleep in his future, he washed and dressed. The house was silent as he left his room. Unlike the days his younger siblings woke early, they tended to lie in bed these days until someone dragged them out.

Taking the stairs down, Leo decided on a walk. It was the best time of day because he wouldn't have to converse with anyone. Solitude gave him time to think, which he knew would be focused on Cyn. The beautiful woman who had crept into his head while he wasn't looking.

He reached the front entrance. Tugging his overcoat off the hook, he slid his arms into it and began doing up the buttons.

"Going somewhere?"

He wasn't proud of the unmanly yelp that came out of his mouth, but it happened all the same. Turning, he found Mungo standing behind him, looking as he always did. Large and intimidating, but as Leo was likely the same, he did not fear the man and, if he was honest, never had.

Mungo loved the Nightingales, even if his way of showing it was to growl at them.

"I have on my coat, which would suggest I am," Leo said pleasantly.

Mungo never looked uneasy or unsettled. He was a man comfortable in his own skin, even when he was scowling.

"What's wrong, my lord?" Mungo asked.

"Leo," he sighed. "You have picked me off the floor in a drunken stupor, watched me bemoan my life while a fever made me ramble, and then watched as I attempted to pick up the shattered pieces of said life for me and my siblings. Call me Leo, for pity's sake, Mungo."

"And succeeded," Mungo added.

"What?" Leo blinked, his hands stilling on the final button of his coat.

"You succeed at picking up the pieces of your shattered life for yourself and your siblings," he said.

Leo actually blinked. "Was that a compliment?"

Mungo frowned.

"Maybe I'm still dreaming?" Leo put his hand to his forehead to check for a fever.

"You're a good man… now," the large Scotsman said. "A leader and intelligent enough."

"No, stop." Leo raised a hand. "It's far too early to hear such exuberant compliments, especially from your mouth."

Mungo made a sound that sounded remarkably like Chester when he was annoyed.

"What happened yesterday? Miss Ellen said there was trouble."

"There was, but as yet, I'm not sure what to do about it. I'm going for a walk to think. But what I do know is the Baddon Boys have made a reappearance and their target is Lady Lowell."

Mungo was not one for large gestures, but the curl of his lips was enough of an indication that he was displeased with Leo's words.

"And what's to be done?"

"I've just said I'm not sure."

"Well, think on it, and when you have a plan, we will implement it," the Scotsman snapped.

"How do you know I will come up with a plan?"

"Because while you may act like there is a wide chasm between your ears, I know different."

"No, please, I don't think I can take any more of your exuberant compliments."

"Be gone with you, and don't fall into trouble. I'll be fleecing you of your savings tonight," Mungo said.

They often sat down with whoever wanted to play and lost money to Mungo. He was skilled at cards and seemed to know what was in everyone's hands when no one had shown him.

"I'm quite sure I've lined your coffers enough by now."

The small tilt of Mungo's lips told Leo he was pleased with his words.

"Aye, I'm happy to take your money from you, my lord."

Leo didn't sigh, but it was close. The man would never call him just Leo.

"Well, I'm going for a walk to clear my head. I will return for a large breakfast. Please tell Bud."

"Are you having trouble sleeping, my lord?"

"No," Leo said, having no wish to get into his sleeping habits, or lack thereof, because there would be a tonic from Mr. Greedy that tasted of something vile by nightfall.

"The sun has not yet risen fully. Perhaps some food before you leave?" Mungo said.

"Do you believe I can't function without it because I'm weak or because I'm an Englishman?" Leo asked.

"I hadn't realized there was a distinction," Mungo said, moving slightly to the right. He leaned his large bulk on the wall and folded his arms. His eyes were now locked on Leo as if he was ready for a nice long chat, which he wouldn't be, as he disliked talking and only spoke the bare minimum when required. In fact, this was likely the longest conversation they'd shared in some time.

"What's amiss, my lord?"

"I've told you about the Baddon Boys."

"There's more."

"It's nothing," Leo said.

"If a'thing's true, that's nae lee."

"Which means what?" Leo demanded.

"I don't believe you."

They had been deciphering Scottish proverbs and quotes for years with very little success. Leo was sure it was a game to Mungo.

"I'm going out," Leo said firmly.

"You'll take your cane."

Leo raised it.

"Hat."

He took it off the hook by the door and slapped it on his head.

"And you'll not get into a fight because you're looking for one. I'll have your word or follow you the entire distance."

Leo, who had turned to face the door, spun back. "You say that like fighting is a favorite pastime of mine."

"In your current mood, it very well could be," Mungo said calmly.

"I thought you just said I was a good man who had succeeded in getting his life back on track?" Leo said. "You are bloody exhausting."

Mungo merely raised a brow.

"Fine, I promise," he snapped.

"Have a good walk, my lord."

"Just out of curiosity, why won't you call me Leo?"

"Because you may not see yourself as a lord, however, I do."

They stared at each other for long seconds, and then Leo turned and let himself out the door, closing it softly behind him.

He then walked down the stairs and out the gate, wondering what the hell that had meant. Mungo saw him as a lord, but what the hell did he expect him to do with that information? Deciding it was too early to find the answer, he moved his feet.

Crabbett Close was quiet; people were still slumbering, and some were enjoying their first cup of tea, no doubt. Cold air chilled his face, but it felt good. Digging in his pockets, he found some gloves and tugged them on.

"My lord, what has you out at such an hour?"

Mr. and Mrs. Greedy were standing in their small front garden, both stoop shouldered and wrapped in layers. It was always a wonder to the Nightingales they were constantly active and involved in a great many things.

"Good morning to you. I'm out for a walk," he said.

"Well now, it's a mite chilly and early for that," Mr. Greedy said. "I'll be heading back to see Clara in a few hours. Nothing is broken on the outside, my lord, but I fear there is much healing to do in her head and heart."

"I'd like to go a few rounds with who hurt her," Leo said darkly.

"Aye, as would I, were I younger. But she's in good hands," Mr. Greedy said. "Mrs. Varney will be heading over there soon. She'll check on her before I get there."

"What has you out here at such an hour after the rigors of your day yesterday, Lord Seddon?" Mrs. Greedy asked.

"I couldn't sleep," Leo said, giving in to the inquisition that was likely to follow. After all, if he didn't tell them, Mungo would.

"Did you hear that, Mrs. Greedy? He can't sleep."

"Aya, heard it clear as anything, Mr. Greedy. Lord Seddon can't sleep," Mrs. Greedy said.

The people in this street did a lot of reiterating, always using their spouse's full names and then repeating every sentence before adding on to it. It was like a continual word game that sometimes drove Leo to the point where he demanded they speak plainly.

"That's it, Mrs. Greedy," Mr. Greedy now said. "He's not sleeping."

"Well then, you all have a nice—"

"You'll wait there, my lord. Fetch him one of those fresh-baked scones, Mrs. Greedy," Mr. Greedy said. "If a body hasn't had enough sleep, there's even more of a need for nourishment."

"Oh, no—"

"She'll not be a trice."

Leo watched Mrs. Greedy turn and walk back to the house slower than his younger siblings did when they had to go to bed. Silently swallowing his moan, he waited for what came out of Mr. Greedy's mouth next, as surely it would be something.

"I've sent some salve to Lady Lowell's for her bruises," Mr. Greedy said. "That's a woman with plenty of spirit, that one, my lord. Few of her standing would wade into a fight."

"It's not a moment I'm likely to ever forget," Leo muttered.

"She'd make someone a fine wife," Mr. Greedy said with no subtlety, as clearly he was alluding to him being the man who should be Cyn's husband. That thought didn't terrify him as much as he thought it would.

"Indeed, she would," Leo said, looking longingly down the street to his escape.

"She's hiding, my lord, as are you."

"Pardon?"

Mr. Greedy looked him in the eye. "Inner turmoil, my lord. It can make a soul tired and force us not to live the life we were meant to."

Leo stared at the elderly man dressed in a gray sweater and brown knitted scarf as if he'd never seen him before. How had he known Leo had inner turmoil? For that matter, how had he known Cyn was like him? *Was she?* He didn't like to think of her hurting, because it made his chest burn.

What had made her like him? What had forced her into hiding in plain sight as Leo did every day? And why was he desperate for the answers to those questions?

CHAPTER TWENTY-FIVE

"Our doubts are traitors, And make us lose the good we oft might win, By fearing to attempt," Mr. Greedy then said, still standing in his garden.

"I thought Mr. Alvin was the Crabbett Close resident who liked to quote Shakespeare?" Leo rasped out of his tight throat.

"I dabble," Mr. Greedy said.

"Here are the seedlings, Mr. Greedy," another voice said from behind Leo.

"Well now, young Lord Seddon was just asking after you, Mr. Alvin," Mr. Greedy said.

Leo sometimes thought he felt a great deal older than his actual years. However, when around the elderly Crabbett Close residents, he felt like a child in knee breeches.

"It's a mite early for the likes of you to be out of your bed, if you don't mind me saying so, my lord," Mr. Alvin said. He then stomped by Leo, who opened the gate for him, and headed up the path. Once he'd reached Mr. Greedy, he handed over the plants.

"The thing about seedlings, my lord," Mr. Alvin said, "is

they need tending. Lots of nourishment and nurturing to make a go of things."

Leo was fairly sure there was a deeper meaning in the words. He just wasn't sure he was up to hearing them today.

"Indeed," he said, looking to the open doorway and hoping that Mrs. Greedy appeared shortly.

"Then, as they grow, you still have to keep an eye on them," Mr. Greedy took up the lecture. "They still need guidance. Some even need a mate to make it in the world."

And they were back to Cyn again, Leo guessed.

"Aya, take beans and peas," Mr. Alvin said.

Leo wished he was one of those people who didn't get deeper meanings to things, like Plummy, the local constable. He was a man who had no depth and took everything as it appeared. For instance, he would think these two men were discussing vegetables. Leo knew different.

They'd moved on from nurturing oneself in order to grow into a halfway decent adult to needing someone in his life to love. Namely, one Lady Lowell.

"You've the right of it, Mr. Alvin. Some things just need another half to complete them. Makes them more rounded and better vegetables," Mr. Greedy said.

Leo only just refrained from rolling his eyes now he'd recovered from Mr. Greedy's comments about lost souls. He and his siblings had been on the receiving end of many such lectures in their time in Crabbett Close. The only problem was he felt like they had an uncanny knack of hitting close to the truth, like now.

He watched as they bent to put the seedlings in the ground and hoped the lecture was done with.

"The poetry of the earth is never dead," Mr. Alvin said.

"Which means what?" Leo asked. That one had him stumped.

"John Keats wrote that to mean whether it is summer or

cold winter, the music and the poetry of the nature is never dead," Mr. Greedy said.

"Well then," Leo added when nothing else came to mind. It was clearly a morning for people giving him advice.

"Here you go, my lord." Mrs. Greedy used her cane to come to him. Leo didn't move, because if he set foot inside the garden, he'd be digging holes before he knew it. Not that he minded, but this morning he was restless and needed movement.

He took the scone slathered in jam and said his thanks, tipping his hat and wishing them a good day.

"And you also, my lord. You mind our words now," Mr. Alvin said.

"Of course. I'll remember every one," Leo said. He then hurried toward the entrance to Crabbett Close, eyes down in case anyone else decided they wanted to chat with him when they should be tucked up in their beds.

"Who plants seedlings at such an hour?" he muttered before taking a large bite of scone. The floury delight made his mouth hum its appreciation. "Who gives out advice from their garden to viscounts, and why do I always stand there and take it?" Leo muttered.

He walked and ate, and when that was done, he walked some more, all the while thinking about Cyn and what he should do about her. One thing he had realized was he needed to discuss the entire situation with his family.

With no direction in mind, Leo was still restless enough to keep moving. The thing about London was that most roads led somewhere, and since he'd come to Crabbett Close, he'd spent a lot of time walking in areas he once would have never frequented.

Leo found he rather liked it.

"Good day to you, my lord."

THE FALLEN VISCOUNT

"Mavis," he said to the large woman overtaking him.

Leo was no slug. He walked at a swift pace and had long legs. Mavis Johns passed him as if he were standing still. Shaking his head, he took a left down a narrow lane and came out one road from the street that housed the Phoenix Agency. Beside it was the building they'd secured the lease on. Mr. Murphy would move there this week, and he would start acquainting himself with their business affairs.

Soon he was standing across the road, studying the building he would no doubt be spending many hours in over the years. His eyes then moved to the Phoenix Agency. There was no sign that anyone was awake, but of course they could be.

He knew that Lewis, who had let down his guard slightly now he knew that Leo and Ellen had helped save Lady Lowell and Miss Coulter last night, was sleeping downstairs. Leo would also suggest they hire another to watch over the house until this business with the Baddon Boys was sorted. Plus, he was going to tell Cyn she could not come here without at least two large Mulhollands accompanying her, which after yesterday, he didn't think she'd fight him on.

He saw the two men then, coming from the rear of the Phoenix Agency. He stayed where he was, undetected, watching until they'd reached the road. Once there, they stopped and spoke to each other, then walked off down the road.

Suspicious over why they'd been at the rear of the building, Leo hurried across the road and took the path down the side of the agency. Reaching the end, he descended the stairs onto the property that would take him to where he'd seen Cyn on the day she'd injured her hand. This was where Lewis was now sleeping. He smelled it then. Smoke.

Checking the entrance to the downstairs room, he saw

nothing, so he walked around the exterior. When that yielded nothing too, he ran up the stairs that led to the entrance for the upper levels.

A bundle of rags had been placed by the front door. They were soaked in some kind of accelerant, and the aroma was pungent. The flames weren't exactly roaring, but they had charred the wood of the base of the door.

Leo toed the bundle away and then stomped on it until they were no longer flaming. He then kicked it back down the stairs to the dew-dampened grass.

Knocking on Lewis's door, he heard a curse, which suggested the man had walked into something. Seconds later, he was looking at Leo through blurry eyes.

"Lord Seddon." Lewis blinked a few times. His nightshirt was dark blue and came to his knees. His feet were bare, and his hair stood off his head. He looked nothing like the man of business he usually was.

"Someone just tried to set fire to this place. I have put it out, but you need to wake up now and be alert until I return. I am going to tell Lady Lowell."

"Dear Lord, the women… they, we would have all burned," Lewis said, grappling with what Leo had said.

"But no one is harmed. I will go now and return as soon as I can."

Leaving the way he'd come, Leo retraced his steps to the street. Once there, he looked for a hackney.

"Where do you wish to go, sir?" the driver asked when he'd pulled to a halt before him.

He gave the address and got inside. He'd known the Baddon Boys were ruthless. Known what they were capable of after what happened to Gray, but to burn a house down with people inside was cold-blooded murder. Something had to be done, and he would take steps to make that happen, and she would listen.

He'd seen her last night, only a few hours ago, in fact, yet the thought of doing so again was filling him with a ridiculous amount of pleasure.

"I am in so much trouble," he muttered.

CHAPTER TWENTY-SIX

Cyn's body woke her. She was sure every muscle ached as she rolled onto her side, squinting at the curtains, attempting to gauge the time from the light slipping between them.

Leo had brought her home after she was sure everyone at the agency was well. He'd told her not to leave the house again until he returned and to ensure a Mulholland was always close.

Cyn had nearly begged him to hold her again, wanting to feel his strength, but she'd resisted. It had been a moment of weakness she could not afford. She was strong and could deal with this and whatever else came her way, as she had been doing since Kenneth's death.

The staff had been horrified at her appearance when she limped into the town house. A bath was quickly drawn, and whisky laced with lemon and honey made for Cyn to drink. She'd then been ushered to bed. Thankfully, she fell into a deep, dreamless slumber.

Getting out of bed, she pulled on her dressing gown and

slippers, then began the walk downstairs, shuffling like an eighty-year-old.

"Berry, do not dodge in front of me," she cautioned the cat. "I am not as nimble as I usually am." The feline stalked down the stairs in front of her.

Cyn reached her favorite room, which usually got the morning sun. A small parlor that was lined with books and had two large chairs before a fireplace. There was no morning sun today as she drew back the curtains.

They'd spent many long hours in here discussing literature when they first married. He'd been a good man for all. He was stern natured but more a father than friend or husband. It was in this parlor that he told her exactly why he'd married her and what his expectations were for his children when he died. Cyn had been forced to grow up quickly after that. She'd had to learn to be a mother and run a household. Her husband had been relentless in his lessons. She'd also given up on her dreams of being loved.

"My lady, would you like tea?" Her butler stood in the doorway, looking nervous.

"Yes, thank you, Hadleigh."

"I would like to apologize for my behavior, Lady Lowell," he then said, face serious. "I see now my actions were unacceptable. As were those of Mrs. Peel and Mrs. Tipply."

"Are they truly sorry like you, Hadleigh?"

His smile was small. "They will come about, and I have told them they will be respectful of Jeremiah and Lilly."

"I understand my views are not what many others' are on this matter, Hadleigh," Cyn said, "but in this, I will stand firm."

"I understand and will ensure things run smoothly in that direction, my lady."

"Excellent."

"Can I get you anything else, Lady Lowell? Some salve for that bruise you have on your chin, perhaps?"

"I am well, but thank you, Hadleigh, and for your apology."

She sat and stared out the window at the empty street below after he had left. At least the Jeremiah and Lilly situation had been resolved. Cyn would still need to discuss their marriage and circumstance, but at least there would be harmony in the household.

She watched a hackney roll down her street and then straightened as it stopped outside her house. Shock had her regaining her feet as Leo stepped down from the inside. He then paid the driver.

What is he doing at my house at this hour? She'd only seen him last night, after all. Yes, she'd expected him to return to discuss this entire situation, as he'd said he would help her in dealing with it, but the hour was still early, and she was dressed in her nightwear.

He walked up the path as she rose.

"Hadleigh!" Her butler reappeared at her shriek.

"Lord Seddon is about to knock on my door. Put him in the parlor I just left and tell him I will be down shortly."

"Of course, my lady."

"Perhaps bring him my tea and something to eat," Cyn added, shuffling to the stairs in an ungainly manner. "Nightingales seem to be hungry most of the time."

She dragged herself up the stairs and found her maid in her room.

"I need to get dressed quickly. Make haste, if you please."

Fifteen minutes later, she was walking back down the stairs, which seemed to have multiplied since yesterday. Anticipation was the only word for the bubbling of excitement inside her. She was seeing Leo again and felt ridiculously pleased about that. He'd held her last night as if she'd been made from spun glass, and that was after coming to her aid in that street.

Cyn had no wish to examine too closely the entire business with him; for now she would greet him and see why he was here.

"Leo, what has you here at such an hour?" Cyn said, entering the parlor she'd recently left.

"Good morning, Cyn." He'd been seated, drinking the tea, but rose to bow.

"What has happened?" she asked, seeing the worry on his face.

"I was out walking—"

"At this hour and in such weather?" She looked skyward. It was going to be a gray, bleak day, Cyn surmised. "Plus, surely after yesterday, like me, you were weary."

"I rise early, but that is not the point, Cyn."

"Then please get to it."

"I will if you will cease talking for two seconds," he said.

She opened her mouth, but he said, "Cyn, shut up." Her teeth snapped together.

"I passed the Phoenix Agency whilst on my morning walk and saw two men leaving via the side entrance and looking furtive about it."

"Oh dear, that can't be good," Cyn whispered.

"When they had left, I went to check all was well," he continued. "I found a bundle of rags burning on the doorstep at the rear of the property."

"Dear Lord." Cyn braced a hand on the doorframe. "Lewis, Mary, and Clara are there."

"They are safe," he said in his lovely deep voice that she was sure should reassure her but didn't. "I woke Lewis."

"I must go there. Now," she added, looking about her as if her carriage would magically appear.

"I have put the fire out, Hyacinth. There is no need to

rush over. Besides, you are hurting from what happened yesterday. The agency will be safe until you arrive."

"I need to go there, Leo." This was their doing... him, whoever the Wolf was. The Baddon Boys and their leader. This was a threat to pull her back into line after what she'd learned yesterday. Plus, they had bested four of his men. She'd angered them. They had angered them, she thought, looking at Leo.

"I have put you in danger," Cyn said.

"They don't know who I am. It is you that is in danger, as is evidenced by the fire and what took place yesterday.

"I will go over there now. I can call my carriage," Cyn said to Leo, who was still standing in front of her. "Thank you for alerting me. I will deal with it now."

"I believe I told you last night you are no longer dealing with this alone. I am involved. There will be no rushing anywhere without at least two footmen."

Cyn had been making her own decisions for quite some time now, and having those reins wrestled from her was not easy to take.

"I am not trying to be ungrateful, Leo, but I dislike being ordered about."

He smiled, and it transformed his face, lighting his lovely eyes and making him seem younger.

"Forgive me. With my siblings, I have to throw out orders, or they will ignore me."

"My children are like that," Cyn conceded.

He moved closer. She felt his fingers on her chin. "Does it hurt?"

"My entire body is one large ache, but I shall live."

"Stay here then, and I will go back to—"

"No. It is my agency. I will go." She turned to walk back out the door. He grabbed her arm and turned her to face him.

"It is not a weakness to let others do something for you,"

he gritted out. She could feel him back her slowly into the door and close it.

"And this is what you do? Let others take charge?" She scoffed. "You do not differ from me."

"You were hurt because thugs set upon you," he snapped. "Thugs who belong to a gang with a notorious and deadly reputation. That reason alone should be enough to have you staying here and locking the doors."

"And yet I would never turn my back on those that need me, as you would not. As you do not with your family," Cyn said. Her heart was thudding hard, being this close to him.

"I am a man."

She scoffed, but it came out more a squeak as he moved closer. So close that his chest now brushed her breasts.

"Who is stronger than you and has fought before. Therefore, I can take care of myself. However," he added as she opened her mouth, "I understand you are equally as intelligent as me and capable of much. But in this, you know I'm correct, Cyn."

She couldn't speak because her mouth was as dry as cinders.

He closed the inches between them and kissed her. It was slow and thorough, and her head was reeling in seconds. She felt it again, that surge of heat inside her when he was near. Last night it had been the heat of his big body comforting her, but this was different. Fire spread through her veins as his lips took hers.

"I woke thinking of you," he whispered, easing back a scant inch. "Woke needing to see you."

"Yes," Cyn whispered, unsure what she was agreeing to, because right then, thinking was beyond her.

His lips met hers again. This kiss was deeper, more desperate. Cyn reached for him, wrapping her arms around his neck to hold him close. She'd wanted this for so long but thought never to experience passion as others did.

"More," she whispered as his lips moved to her neck.

"So much more." His hot breath brushed the damp skin he'd just kissed.

The touch of his hands travelling up her sides was bliss. His fingers left a trail of heat wherever they landed. She'd never been this close to someone before, but she'd heard how Charles made Letitia feel, and Cyn had wanted that for herself.

No one knew Kenneth had not touched her. All believed they'd had a marriage in every way.

"You make me lose reason, but I need to stop because you are hurting, Cyn."

"Don't stop," she whispered. When he held her like this, she forgot everything but his touch and the feelings he aroused inside her. Everything that awaited her outside her front door could no longer touch her. "I want this, Leo."

"We are in your parlor." His voice was husky.

"No one will enter," Cyn vowed. "Or I will fire them."

His snort was muffled, as his lips were now on her chest. Leo's tongue swept a scorching line down to the rise of her breasts. She felt him raising the fabric of her skirt slowly up one thigh as his other hand moved to her breast, and with a few tugs, he had it bared. It was scandalous, but then Leo thought her a widow who knew what happened between a man and a woman. When his hand cupped the soft, rounded flesh, Cyn moaned. The heat of his palm was wonderful. And then he was stroking the taut nipple with a finger.

"Everything about you captivates me, Cyn." He had eased back slightly and was watching his fingers stroke her. "My God, what you do to me."

She couldn't speak, just held on to him. Her hand was in his hair, curling into the ends while she grappled with each

THE FALLEN VISCOUNT

new sensation. This was what Letitia talked about. The passion she and Charles shared was something Cyn had never understood until now.

"We can't do this here," Leo whispered. "I won't take you against a wall the first time." Before she could speak, his head lowered, and he was kissing her nipple. A sound between a gasp and a moan slipped from her mouth as a white-hot spike of pleasure shot through her.

His finger slid under the hem of her dress and stroked her thigh above her stockings.

Cyn's hands were now on his shoulders, digging into the muscles she found there. She wanted to feel his skin then. Touch him as he touched her.

"Christ." The word hissed from Leo, and then his hands and mouth fell from her body. Cyn stayed where she was, eyes closed, her back pressed to the door. She felt him fix her clothing, and then he was pulling her into his arms.

The hardness of the arousal between his thighs pressed into her belly. She may be innocent, but she knew exactly what happened between a man and a woman. Leo wanted her as she wanted him.

"Forgive me," he whispered. "I have no control where you are concerned, it seems."

"I—ah, it seems I am the same," Cyn said.

He looked down at her, one hand cupping her cheek, and she wanted to weep. The gesture was so sweet, as was the look in his eyes. She wanted his passion and tenderness. Needed it in her life.

"Were you happy with your husband?"

She nodded because it was not a lie, exactly. She had been happy in that she'd had Simon and Meg and every comfort she could need. But there had been nothing more of what a husband and wife could experience.

"Now, we need to go to the agency," Cyn said, placing her hands on his chest and pushing. He did not move.

"You're lying to me."

"No, I'm not. I want to go there now."

"You know that's not what I meant. You were not happy with your husband. Did he mistreat you? Is that why you do what you do at the Phoenix Agency?" Leo demanded.

"No! Kenneth was a good man, we... he was just a great deal older than me."

Leo frowned. "Which means what?"

"I won't discuss my marriage with you, and I wish to go to the agency at once."

His hands fell away, and she missed them on her instantly. Her world felt steadier when Leo was holding her, which was reason enough to put some distance between them at once.

"Very well, but I think your feet will get cold in that footwear."

Cyn looked down. She was still in her slippers. Stepping forward, she turned and opened the door. Leaving her parlor, she headed for the stairs once again, determined not to wince or limp.

"Do you need me to collect something for you, my lady?" Hadleigh appeared.

"No, thank you. I will soon leave the house, as there has been a small fire at the agency that needs my attention."

"Do you need me to alert someone to accompany you, my lady?"

"Please tell the Mulhollands to go to the Agency as soon as they are able. I will accompany Lord Seddon, Hadleigh."

Exhaling slowly, Cyn once again climbed the stairs. Once she'd reached her room, she refused to think about what she and Leo had just done in the parlor. *Dear Lord, he'd kissed her breast.*

Stop it, Cyn.

Taking off her slippers, she pulled on sturdy black leather ankle boots. Then her warm midnight-blue jacket and bonnet. Lastly, she grabbed gloves. It had only taken her five minutes, and soon she was heading back down the stairs.

Leo made her lose reason, and that rarely happened. With what was going on in her life and two impressionable children, she could not do so again. Therefore, it was important she was not alone with him going forward.

Leo had said he'd put the fire out. Nevertheless, it could be smoldering, and they were not there. She needed to move fast.

Grabbing her reticule, she checked her pistol and money were in there and then left her room once more. Hadleigh opened the front door when she reached it.

"Thank you. I am unsure when I will return."

"Very well, my lady."

Leo was standing beside the hackney he'd arrived in, conversing with the driver. Cyn missed the first step and had to jump the last two, which jarred her sore body.

"Christ, are you all right?" He reached for her, his hands gripping her shoulders.

"Yes," she rasped, breathless.

"From memory, you were constantly tripping over your feet."

"Yes, well, I was in a hurry today, and my body is not feeling as sprightly as it usually does," Cyn muttered as he led her to the hackney.

Leo lifted her inside before she could step up and then joined her, closing the door behind him. She sat back and tried to appear relaxed when, in fact, the truth was far from that. Cyn was in turmoil.

CHAPTER TWENTY-SEVEN

"So not everything has changed about you," Leo said. "You still sneeze when you are nervous and are clumsy."

"I am not nervous. There is a great deal of pollen about," she lied.

"Of course there is, silly me," Leo drawled. "You are still as beautiful as you always were, but there are other differences also."

He'd just put his hands on Cyn. He'd kissed her breasts and tasted the skin of her neck. Her scent was now lining his nostrils, and the feel of her body was imprinted on him.

Something about this older, wiser version of her got to him. Once he'd thought only that she would make him a pretty, dutiful wife; he now respected her, but there was more.

She was stronger and determined to help those women who needed it. She was intelligent, which she likely always had been but hid that side of herself from him.

Because you were a shallow-minded fool and saw only what you wished.

Cyn was raising her late husband's children, which could not have been easy. What had her life been like with the late Lord Lowell?

Looking at her seated across from him, hands clasped neatly in her lap, eyes out the window, Leo felt his chest tighten. She was bruised and sore from yesterday's attack but still determined to go to the agency and make sure all was well there.

She was natured like the women in his family, Leo realized.

What did he feel for her? And did he want to pursue it, knowing that she walked in society when he didn't? That any connection with her would mean he would have to, as he could not ask her to leave the life she'd always lived.

Could he step back into that? His eyes studied the side of her face, and he felt it again, the burn of heat in his chest. As the carriage had stopped, he pushed it aside, like everything else he had no wish to address in his life.

After helping her down, she paid the driver before he could. Leo swallowed his protest and followed her to the Phoenix Agency. He saw the flowers as she bent to pick them up. Someone had placed them on the steps along with a note.

"Who would have left these?" Cyn asked, opening the missive.

Leo read it over her shoulder.

These will be the flowers people place on your grave if you don't stop your meddling, Lady Lowell. The fire may have been extinguished, but you will not be so lucky next time.

Leo took the card from her now-trembling hands. "Come, let us go inside." He took her arm. The flowers he left there, and he crushed them under his heel as he guided Cyn up the stairs. She had yet to make a sound.

"Lewis, can you please remove the flowers from the

bottom step?" Leo said when they entered and saw him seated at the desk.

"Of course," he said, shooting Cyn a look.

"It's all right," Leo said, taking her arm. "I am here with you."

She spun to face him, pale eyes wide. It was anger he saw, not fear.

"A faceless bully who uses his men to intimidate and harm people will not intimidate me!"

"Good girl, and he shouldn't."

"But I don't know what to do now, Leo."

"I do. We are going to have a meeting with my family, and they will have ideas. Especially Gray."

She turned in a circle, taking in the building's interior. "I can't let anything happen to this."

"We won't."

The door opened again, and in walked Lewis with the Mulhollands on his heels. Monty's face bore bruises the color of a moldy peach today, and one eye was nearly closed. Toby looked angry.

"Oh, Monty." Cyn walked to him. "I am so sorry. You should be resting."

"'Tis not your fault," the man said, clearly uncomfortable with her apologies. "And I have no need of more sleep."

"Check on Clara," Leo urged her.

While Cyn went to Clara, Leo talked with Lewis, Miss Coulter, and the Mulhollands.

"You must all be vigilant now. The Baddon Boys see Lady Lowell as a threat, and the Phoenix Agency is where the women they believe are theirs have come."

The staff all showed signs of what had happened yesterday. Two bore bruises, and the third, Lewis, was grim faced. Toby was the only one unscathed.

"I will let no one into this house," Lewis vowed, his eyes

going to Miss Coulter, who gave him a shy smile. "But I fear they will keep trying, considering what has happened just today."

"Clara is not well enough to be moved," Monty said, looking a little mean with that black eye and anger in his eyes. Anger that all the people in the room felt.

"Could she be moved next door?" Leo asked.

"Pardon?" Toby frowned.

"My family has taken the lease there," Leo said. "If we can get you all in there with no one seeing, you will be safe."

Cyn walked into the room, looking so sweet and pale, he wanted to hold her.

"You have taken the lease on the property next door?" Lewis asked.

"For business purposes, but no one is using it as yet," Leo said.

"What are you discussing?" Cyn asked.

He told her what he'd suggested.

"Yes," she said instantly. "If we are being watched, I'm not sure how we can get you or what you need next door, but I would rather you all were moved for your safety."

After a thorough inspection of the fence between the properties, it was decided to make an opening. Monty began pulling boards free with Leo's help. Cyn, Lewis, and Miss Coulter began assembling what was needed for them all to live next door.

Two hours later, they had everyone, including Clara, who Toby had carried, next door. It would be easy to collect anything they needed, but for now, they were safe until the danger passed.

"And now we are going to speak with my family," Leo said to Cyn. She'd worked as hard as everyone, which was just another sign she wasn't the woman he'd once known. "Come, Cyn. We will leave via the agency."

She allowed him to lead her back through the fence and up the steps. Then they were walking out the front door and down onto the street. Leo looked around but could see no one watching, which did not mean they weren't, only that they were well hidden.

"Come, we will walk until a hackney approaches. For now, everyone is safe." Taking her hand, he slid it through his. Leo was tired, so he could only imagine how she was feeling.

"I was supposed to go to the Luton ball this evening. I'm pleased to say I am not well enough to do so."

"I think that bruise on your face would create a sensation."

They soon found transportation and were heading to Crabbett Close.

"But will Ellen and her husband be there?" Cyn said.

"They will," Leo said.

"But how do you know?"

"My family will be there, Cyn," he said. Because they would know he needed them, and that he had not returned from his morning walk. "If they are not there, they will be out walking the streets to find me. I left early and did not return."

She looked horrified. "You should have sent word."

"I have been a trifle busy."

"I should change. I look grubby," she said, studying her nails.

"You look beautiful, as you always do." His words had her looking at him, but she did not speak again, clearly nervous about the turn her life had taken and what lay between them.

"Welcome to the madness," Leo said, waving Cyn up the steps to 11 Crabbett Close fifteen minutes later. The front door was open, and he heard raised voices from within.

THE FALLEN VISCOUNT

"How the bloody hell do I know where your foolish brother is!" Mungo thundered.

"Oh dear, are you the brother they speak of?" Cyn asked him.

"Very likely. Come along. There is nothing for it but to enter the fray." Placing a hand on her back, he nudged Cyn in through the door.

"He's a bloody adult. He'll be fine!" That was Alex's voice. "He does not need to account for his every minute, surely. Leo could simply be seated in a warm tea shop consuming scones slathered with jam. It's what I'd do if I were him."

Cyn giggled and then clapped a hand over her mouth as the eyes of everyone in the entranceway turned to face them.

"Where the bloody hell have you been?" Mungo roared.

"If you'll calm down, I will tell you," Leo said. "Take off your outer clothing, Cyn."

"Tell Bud we will need a rather large tea tray, please, Mungo." The Scotsman was now a foot from Leo and still glaring. "I'm sorry you were worried, but I will explain the whole of it shortly," Leo said so only the angry Scotsman heard.

He turned and stomped away without another word.

"I want answers, nephew," Uncle Bram said, coming to greet him. Leo was then hugged hard. Cyn had her cheek kissed. "But we can wait. Come along, the others are in the parlor."

They all disappeared, leaving Leo and Cyn alone with Chester, who was sitting in front of them with his head to one side.

"Is it wonderful?" Cyn asked him, her voice sounding wistful.

"What?" He guided her forward.

"To be surrounded by so much love?"

"It is possibly the best part of what happened to us," Leo

said, wondering who loved Cyn other than her children. *Had her husband treated her fairly?*

"Chester, shake hands with Cyn," he said to the dog. He raised a paw, and Cyn took it and shook gently. "Good boy."

"I have an enormous cat called Berry," she said to the dog. "I think she would like you, as would my children."

"Then we must ensure they meet."

"Leo. Get in here now!" Alex roared.

Urging Cyn into the parlor, he found his family scattered around it, but it was Ellen he saw first. She was weeping.

"What's happened? What did you do to her?" He shot Gray a glare as he hurried to his sister's side.

"Leo, we have covered this before. I love your sister. Therefore, I would not 'do' anything to her," Gray said from his position at Ellen's side. He was mopping up her tears.

"Then why is she weeping?"

"Oh L-Leo," she sobbed, staggering to her feet. She then threw herself at him. "I was so worried about you."

"You're crying because I went for a walk and stayed out for a few hours?" Leo was confused. Ellen rarely wept.

"There is a bit more to it than that," Uncle Bram said. "Tell him, Gray, as Ellen is incapable."

"We are to have a child, Leo," Gray said.

"What?" Leo felt the smile tugging his lips up. "You are to have a child?"

She nodded.

He hugged her again, this time gently, then shook Gray's hand after nudging her back down onto the sofa.

"A niece or nephew," Leo said slowly. "I will spoil it atrociously as I do all the small people in our life."

"There was never a doubt," Gray drawled. "Now sit and tell us your story. You also, Lady Lowell."

Leo turned to find Cyn watching from the doorway.

Uncle Bram guided her to a chair, and Leo took the one beside it.

"I'm really not sure where to start with this story," Cyn said when the room fell silent. "You all likely know what happened yesterday, and how Ellen and Leo came to our aid when those men set upon us."

"Good God, you were with child." Leo felt the color drain from his face. "You could have been hurt."

"Which we have discussed extensively," Gray added in a hard voice.

"Yes, I know," Ellen said. "Tell us about today."

"First, I need to tell you about the Phoenix Agency," Cyn said, shooting Leo a look before continuing. "The house belonged to my late husband and was sitting empty. I went to view it and found a woman sleeping at the rear of the property. She was homeless and without funds to support herself, as many are. I took her inside, and she told me she had once been a lady of the night."

"Mary?" Leo asked, and Cyn nodded.

"I started the agency to help women like her who had nowhere to go if they wanted to escape their lives. Over the last few months, a few of the women who have come to us have had unpleasant experiences at the hands of the Baddon Boys gang. Women who are known to them through associates also."

Mungo arrived, hefting a tea tray and lowering it to the table. He then poured tea into a mug, added a large dollop of honey and a slug of whisky without asking her, and handed it over to Cyn. She quickly took it, shooting him a nervous look.

"His bark is a great deal worse than his bite, my lady," Harriet said.

"Please, you must all call me Cyn," she said.

"It'll steady ye nerves," Mungo grunted.

She sipped to please him and coughed but managed to keep it down.

"Carry on," he then said grandly, going to lean his large bulk on the wall.

"A young lady called Leona came to me last week, wanting to leave her life as a prostitute at the Bird of Paradise, which is a place gentlemen frequent for, ah—"

"We understand," Leo said.

"Yes, well, it is owned by the Baddon Boys."

"Which we also know," Alex said. "Also, as I told you, your husband keeps showing me the bird and that you are in danger."

"Is he still doing so?" Cyn asked. Alex nodded.

"Carry on with your story," Leo urged. He then intercepted a look from his uncle and Alex that he had no wish to interpret.

"Leona told me that the man they call the Wolf, who is the Baddon Boys' leader, is not happy that a lady he called a high-class nob was interfering with his women, and she may have to be stopped, which is clearly me after what happened yesterday and today," Cyn said.

"You went to find Clara knowing that?" Leo asked. She nodded, and he pushed down his anger. No good would come from voicing it now. The damage was done, and somehow, they needed to keep her safe and get the Baddon Boys to stop pursuing her.

Looking at her sitting with her back straight—every inch the lady she was—and surrounded by his family, Leo realized something. She fit here, and he didn't want her to leave. Which, of course, was not possible, as she had a life and two children, but it did not stop him from wanting it anyway.

CHAPTER TWENTY-EIGHT

"So, they are safe next door at our new property for now?" Bramstone asked.

"They are," Leo said.

"Well done. It was an excellent idea to move them there, nephew."

Cyn had told her story and then listened to them discussing the matter. Each one of them had a voice and the right to be heard. No one was more important than the other in this room. They'd also asked her opinion.

Kenneth had always been the loudest voice in their household, and his word was law.

"I will make enquiries tomorrow," Gray said. "This Wolf has been creating mayhem and needs to be stopped. So far, we have not been able to do that."

"Perhaps you need to try harder," Leo snapped.

"Now there's an idea," Gray drawled.

They teased, laughed, and angered one another, but there was no doubting the love in this room, Cyn thought.

The sound of running feet stopped all conversation, and then the three girls Cyn knew as Frederica, Matilda, and

Anna burst into the room. She'd met them at the tea shop, and Meg had talked about them later that day. Last through the door was the youngest Nightingale male, Theo.

"Mr. Douglas just arrived, and the games are tonight!" Anna said, clapping her hands.

All eyes turned to the window.

"It's gray and miserable out there," Alex protested.

"It's always like that." Theo dismissed his brother's words. "They have called them earlier, in case it rains again. Mr. Douglas said it is time, as we have not had them in a while, and everyone needs an uplifting of their spirits."

"He said that, did he?" Bramstone Nightingale asked with a smile for his children.

They'd gone to hell, these Nightingales, but they'd gotten through it and out the other side because of this man and his wife. Together, they'd loved the broken children of the late Lord Seddon and put them back together.

"What is that look for?" Leo asked her.

She wouldn't lie, not to him after everything they had been through over the last few days. He'd done so much for her; she owed him that. "I think you are all very lucky to have one another and this wonderful family."

While around them people rose and talked about the impending Crabbett Close games, which she'd heard much about, Leo kept his eyes steady on Cyn's face.

"More wonderful than I can say," he said. "My aunt and uncle saved us. They taught us the meaning of love and respect. They taught us that with the right people in your life, you can rise above just about anything." That he was speaking so openly to her was humbling.

"I'm so pleased you had them then."

He nodded. "Who do you have, Cyn?"

It was an odd and deep conversation to have surrounded

by so many people, and yet, in that moment, she felt alone with Leo.

"I have my family," she lied. Her family had loved her, but they did not understand her in any way because she'd differed from them. And perhaps that was the reason she'd clung so hard to Leo and Ellen. Had they presented a life she'd longed for? A life with two people that could care for her in the way Cyn had always longed for. "And, of course, Meg and Simon. Plus, my friends Charles and Letitia."

His eyes held hers steady, and she could do nothing to pull away.

"Did they hold you when you cried?" His voice was deep.

"No."

"I'm sorry, because it's my belief we all need someone who will do that."

"Come, it is time," Bramstone said, and Cyn tore her eyes from Leo's.

"I shall leave you to your games." Cyn rose.

"Do you have an engagement tonight?" Bramstone asked her.

Cyn shook her head. She had no wish for the small talk and fake smiling she'd get in society tonight. Not with so much turmoil going on in her life right now. The odd thing was, she didn't want solitude either, and she usually craved that when her head was not sitting straight on her shoulders.

"Then come with us, Cyn. Come and laugh and have fun. It will take your mind off your troubles for a while," Bramstone said. "We would be honored if you did so."

"I really don't think I'm good company."

"That's all right. You won't be able to get a word in with this lot," he said, looking at the people in the room, and she saw just how much they all meant to him.

"You have a wonderful family, Bramstone." Cyn felt the

need to say the words. "The love you feel for one another is clear for anyone to see."

"Ivy and I had not realized what we were missing until we brought my late brother's children into our family. Then we were complete. Believe me when I say it was no sacrifice. They are very special to us," he said.

"Oh dear." Cyn pressed her fingers to her mouth as she fought back the choking emotion. "That's so wonderful."

His smile was gentle as he patted her arm. "Finding someone to love is wonderful, Cyn. Now I would be honored if you came to our games."

She felt a hand on her back as everyone in the room seemed to move as one to the door, and she knew it was Leo's.

"You will enjoy it, I promise. Perhaps just drink nothing without asking me first," he said.

"What?"

"Come on, there is no way I can describe this. You really have to see it for yourself." He took her hand, and soon she had on her coat and hat again.

"Ooooh, I'm so excited!" Anna was doing a little dance. Leo grabbed her and hugged her close. Placing a loud kiss on her cheek, he let her go. "Well, lead the way then."

Retaking Cyn's hand in his, they then headed out the door behind his family.

"Don't think. Just enjoy," Leo said. "The rest will wait for us after this."

Us, she thought. Would he be in her life now? The thought made hope flutter inside her.

The weather was no better, still gray and miserable, but it did not seem to dampen spirits as they made their way to the middle of the close, where a group of people stood. She noted a trestle table being set up farther down the road.

"What's that for?"

"You'll see," Leo said, tugging her behind him.

"Can you give me a hint on what these games entail? All my children told me was that they were fun and involved activities. I'll be honest, Leo, I'm not entirely sure my body is up to that."

"You only have to do what you can manage."

Which told her precisely nothing.

"Eat nothing pickled or slimy. Leave that to those of us that like them. The alcohol also may taste nice, but it has a kick."

"No slimy or pickled food," Cyn muttered. "Do I want to do this?"

"Change is good, my sweet Cyn." He stopped and pulled her close, placing a soft kiss on her lips.

"Leo!" She looked around them, but only Ellen had seen, and she was smiling.

"What?" he said innocently.

"Your family and others will see."

"Let them. Did I tell you I am excited that I am about to be an uncle?"

"I saw how excited you were."

"Ellen and Gray's baby will be thoroughly spoiled."

"I have no doubt," Cyn said.

They joined the others on the grass.

"No running, no drinking or eating foods that look odd," Cyn overheard Detective Fletcher saying to Ellen.

"For pity's sake, I am with child, not sick," Ellen said with her hands on her hips. "Women have been giving birth in fields for years and then returning to their labors."

"However, not my wife," Gray said. Ellen rolled her eyes.

"Good day to you all, Nightingales and Lord Seddon!"

"Plummy," Leo said from her side.

The man before them was dressed in constable's clothes

of a blue tailcoat with armlets, white gloves, and a top hat. He had a thick moustache that twitched as he spoke.

"How is it you always know when the games are on, Plummy?" Gray asked.

"'Tis my job to know the goings on in the streets I protect, Detective Fletcher. Hello, dear Miss Bud," the man then said, a silly smile on his face.

"Bud is our housekeeper," Matilda whispered from Cyn's other side. "Plummy is in love with her."

"Where did you get that?" Alex demanded. Matilda was sucking on something.

"What, this?" Matilda waggled a plum coated in sugar at their brother. He lunged at her, and she leaped back.

"Nancy makes the best sugar plums," Leo said.

"If I can have your attention, please!" A man was standing on a large box, addressing them. It was Mr. Greedy.

"He has the loudest voice," Leo said. "As well as being a fine healer, he is the spokesperson when required for Crabbett Close."

"You live in an exceedingly odd street, Leo." He grinned at her, and it was a glimpse of the man he'd once been.

"It is odd but also wonderful."

"You're a lucky man, aren't you, Leo?"

"I am, and perhaps until now I hadn't realized just how lucky."

"What do you mean?" Cyn asked.

"I will tell you later, but right now, you must pay attention, as teams are about to be named.

"Teams?" Cyn said weakly. He simply squeezed her fingers.

"Are there any new people with us today?" Mr. Greedy asked.

"Aya, I've seen Lady Lowell," Mrs. Varney called from somewhere. Cyn recognized her voice.

"Welcome, my lady," Mr. Greedy called back, as if it were an everyday occurrence for nobility to frequent their games... which it was, as the Nightingales were exactly that.

"Mr. Douglas, Roberta Alvin, who is Mr. and Miss Alvin's second cousin on their father's side and is visiting with them for a spell," Mr. Greedy continued.

"I wonder if, in fact, I'm dreaming," Cyn whispered. A sting on her hand had her looking down. Leo had pinched her.

"How about now?" His eyes were full of laughter.

"I can't believe you pinched me."

"We liked to touch each other, a lot," he said, waggling his eyebrows at her.

"Where has the angry viscount gone?"

"He's in here, but having you and my family close calms me," he said. "For now, that is enough."

Was it enough for now? She missed her children, and they would have loved this, but perhaps Leo was right. In this moment, she could push everything aside and simply enjoy whatever this was. There would be enough time later to return to reality and the fact that the Wolf wanted her scared or worse.

CHAPTER TWENTY-NINE

Leo saw Cyn up ahead of him, talking to Harriet, who was likely explaining what would take place. It would be detailed, as was Harriet's way.

Cyn was on his team along with Fred and standing at the first table, looking confused and adorable. An unsettled Lady Lowell was vastly different to the controlled, aloof one she usually portrayed.

"Do you love that girl, Leo?"

"What?" He spun to face his uncle.

"Of course he does," Alex scoffed. "He can't keep his eyes off her."

"Yes, thank you, Alex, that will do," Leo said.

"Nephew, it is the first time I have felt a lightness in you since I walked into your father's town house many years ago. She is driving your demons away, Leo."

Is she?

"Control is important to you, Leo. Control means you don't have messy emotions. Those you only have when with us," Uncle Bram added. "But I can see you unraveling, and I like it. If Cyn is the reason, then you need to see that."

"Ellen unraveled me," Gray said, listening shamelessly along with Alex.

"Like the edge of your knee blanket, do you mean?" Alex needled him.

"'Come forth into the light of things,'" Mavis Johns said from the end of the line, where she always stood. "'Let love be your teacher,' my lord."

They all stared at her. Mavis never offered a comment and usually only managed a few words if she spoke. She was the only woman who ran with men on the first leg, as she could hold her liquor better than anyone.

"Was that Wordsworth?" Alex asked.

"She substituted love for nature," Mungo said.

"How do you know that?" Leo asked, and the Scotsman's cheeks tinged pink.

"You read Wordsworth?" Alex whistled. "You have hidden depths, Mungo."

"Shut up," he growled.

"Very well said, Mavis," Uncle Bram said. "And accurate."

"I do believe the ground just moved," Leo muttered. "Now Mavis is quoting poetry at me."

"Are we ready?" Mr. Greedy boomed. "Go!"

They ran to the first table, manned by the Alvins.

"Hand that drink to Lady Lowell, Pixie," Mr. Alvin said to his sister. Both looked like Egyptian mummies, as they were wrapped up in so many layers of clothing.

"I should drink that," Leo said.

"Give her the pickled whelk then," Mr. Alvin said.

"Watch Mavis doesn't drink on the run!" Alex roared. Mavis shot him a smug look, then threw back her drink and glared at the young Douglas on her team, who Leo thought was named Todd. The lad swallowed the pickled whelk and then retched.

"I'm not eating that." Cyn wrinkled her nose, and Leo fought the urge to kiss it.

"Fine, don't say I didn't warn you." He handed her the cup and picked up the plate. Exhaling slowly, he swallowed it whole and managed not to gag.

Cyn was still sniffing the contents when he'd finished choking it down.

"Drink and be quick about it. They are getting away from us," Leo said. "It's a race."

Closing her eyes, she threw it back. They shot open, and her face turned red.

"Swallow," Leo ordered.

She did, choking. He then took her hand, and they were running seconds later.

"Wh-what was in that?" she gasped.

"Gin, treacle, and the secret ingredient of mutton fat." She made a gagging sound. "You could have eaten the pickled whelk."

They weren't running fast, as Cyn was sore, but Leo didn't mind. She was here and, for a brief moment, could forget about the hell that had descended upon her.

Fred was waiting for them at the next table, which was manned by the Varneys.

"Hurry it up!" his sister roared. "We would be last were it not for Mungo tripping Gray and him ending up on the ground."

"I'm old enough to drink now," Theo said.

"Very well," Uncle Bram said. "But do not moan tomorrow when your head hurts."

Theo wisely handed the alcohol to Mungo, who threw it back like it was water.

"Cake for Lady Lowell, please, Miss Varney," Leo said to the woman who was baring far too much of her chest and fluttering her lashes at Mungo, who was scowling back at her.

"He's shy," Gray said, finally reaching them. "But lonely, Miss Varney. So do not give up on our favorite Scotsman. He is secretly yearning for love. Secretly yearning for you."

Mungo lunged at Gray, who ducked and hid behind Alex.

"Large bites, Cyn," Fred ordered with her mouth full of smelly kipper as Leo drank the alcohol. "Or we will be here until midnight."

Cyn shoved all the cake into her mouth.

"Nice work, my lady," Leo said. She couldn't reply, as she was attempting to swallow it.

"Let's go."

At the next table, they picked up Anna, who was tapping her foot.

"Now, Cyn, there is not enough to eat or drink, so there will be a task," Leo said.

"Oh dear, r-really?" Her eyes had a look in them that hadn't been there before she'd taken that drink.

"It's a deuced chilly day," Anna said.

"Here, Anna? Really?" Theo sighed.

"Here." The girl nodded.

The Nightingales all jumped in the air twice and then turned in two circles.

"What are you doing?" Cyn asked.

"Deuced is the word of the day," Theo said. "Whoever sets the word sets the actions."

"I have no idea what that means." She frowned.

"I'll tell you later. Right now, choose something off the table."

"You'll enjoy this, my lady," Mr. Douglas said, nudging a cup toward her.

"It's molasses whisky," Fred said. "Hurry it along, Cyn."

She took a sip and then smiled, making a sound in her

throat that he thought he'd like to hear from her when she was naked and beneath him, which he should not be thinking about right now.

She threw back the contents while he ate the cake and Fred recited the alphabet backward.

Gray stumbled into Alex, with Ellen attempting to right him.

"It's truly pathetic that a hard-nosed detective like you cannot hold his liquor," Leo said, righting his brother-in-law. "And yet at every games, you insist on drinking."

Gray just smiled, and Ellen rolled her eyes.

"Can you manage him, sister?"

"I can."

Chester was bounding along beside them, looking happy with himself as people lobbed food at him.

At the last table, Cyn was now considerably more talkative but not completely foxed. He'd stopped her from drinking by shoving food at her. Leo was used to the games, but even he got lightheaded by the end. But this was his favorite table.

Fred got the cinnamon biscuit, and Tabitha Varney, who had joined into their team so she could continue flirting with Mungo, took the cake. Anna was currently reciting the poem on the paper she held while skipping.

"What's that?" Cyn asked, pointing to a plate of food that was wobbling.

"Aspic jelly."

"Absolutely not," she said slowly. "I refuse to eat that."

Leo picked it up and held it before her face. She gagged.

"This or the alcohol?"

She shook her head. Leo looked around to see who had eyes on them, and no one did, so he lobbed the contents of the plate over his shoulder.

"Smack your lips and say yummy," he whispered.

She did loudly, and her yum was convincing.

"Good girl." Leo drank a mouthful of spiced rum. "Try this. It's very nice."

She sipped and then took another mouthful. "It's very good."

Leo threw the rest back. "And we are done."

Cyn frowned. "It's over?"

"We lost," Anna and Fred said, scowling.

"Well, you both need to try harder next time," Leo said. They rolled their eyes and ran off holding hands.

"I was enjoying myself. There is so much laughter here," Cyn said, turning in a circle.

"There is, but I think it's time I took you home," Leo said.

She sighed. "Yes, you are likely right. This is not my life." The words came out tinged with sadness.

But it could be. However, he kept that thought to himself.

After a long goodbye to his family and Mungo had collected the carriage, he put Cyn inside.

"Are you safe to drive, Mungo? You are not seeing two of everything, are you?" Leo said, taunting the Scotsman, as was expected of him.

"Get inside before I thrash you," Mungo replied.

Laughing, Leo did just that. He took the seat next to Cyn.

"I like your family very much, Leo."

"They like you too." He took the hand she had on her knee and laced it through his fingers.

"Can I ask you a favor, Leo?"

"Anything."

"Can I have my cuff link back?"

Rolling up his cuff, he removed the one he'd taken back from her that night he'd saved her from the water.

"Thank you." She closed her fingers around it on a sigh. "It has been through much with me." She then leaned on his shoulder. Minutes after the carriage had rolled out of Crabbett Close, she was asleep.

What did he do now? What did he want with this woman? He felt a slither of panic that he forced down. Before he could make any decision, he had to make sure she was safe. That had to be the priority.

He woke Cyn as they stopped. "We are here now," he said, easing her head off his shoulder. She opened her sleepy eyes, and he felt that weight heavy inside his chest.

"Come." He helped her from the carriage.

"Go home now, Mungo. I will take a hackney."

"You'll have a care with her?"

"I will."

"And yourself," Mungo said. He then clicked his tongue, and the carriage was rolling away.

Leo opened the door, as there was no sign of the butler. Cyn took off her things, and he placed his hat and coat beside them. She then staggered slightly.

"Where is your room? I will help you there," Leo said.

"I-I'm just weary."

"I know. Let me see you safely to your room, Cyn, and then I will leave. You are exhausted."

They both knew she could simply call her staff, but instead, they climbed the stairs and reached her room. Cyn opened the door and stepped inside.

"I will leave you now," he said, standing in the doorway.

She turned to face him and then leaned in to kiss him. "Will you hold me, Leo?"

"It is not right that I am even standing here in your doorway, Cyn. But to enter and—"

"I care little what people think. Right now, I want you to hold me, because then I feel safe. You make me believe everything is going to be all right."

"That's the alcohol talking," he said, reaching for her. Just a kiss, and then he'd leave.

"No, it's me talking." She grabbed his hand and pulled him inside.

Leo kicked the door shut and took her in his arms. Their lips met in a long, heated kiss.

"Cyn," he whispered.

"Don't leave me."

"Do you know what you are asking from me?"

She nodded. "Make me feel, Leo. No one has ever done that for me before."

Her husband was a fool if he had not cherished this beautiful woman.

"Be sure," he said, moving closer.

"I am," she whispered against his lips.

"Your staff?"

"Will not enter my room without permission. I am a widow, Leo."

"And therefore, the rules differ from other women?"

She nodded, and that was enough for him. He locked the door.

CHAPTER THIRTY

Cyn knew she was deceiving him by not clarifying that she was a widow, yes, but also a virgin. However, right then, she cared little for that, only that he stayed with her. He made her feel warm inside. Made her feel strong and safe, when lately she felt like she was constantly scared.

"Leo," she whispered, wrapping her arms around his neck. "I need you." She'd wanted this since their last kiss. Needed to feel his big body pressed to hers again.

The noise he made was a low growl, and then he was lowering his head to kiss her. It was slow and achingly sweet.

Today had been a revelation. A window into what true happiness and love could bring. She had her children and loved them, but to have an adult love you with no restrictions…. An all-encompassing love like the Nightingales shared awed Cyn.

"I love your scent," he whispered, his kisses moving to the neckline of her dress. Fire ignited wherever his mouth touched, and Cyn was soon wrapped in the sensual spell that Leo was weaving around her. She felt his fingers easing the hem of her dress higher. He stroked her, caressing every inch of skin he uncovered.

"Undo your buttons, Cyn."

She stepped back. Her fingers fumbled but finally managed what he asked, and then he was kissing the tops of her breasts. Heat pooled inside her. Pressure built, and she ached to have it released. He licked around her nipple as he had before. His hand reached the top of her thigh, hot strokes of his tongue driving her passion higher.

Cyn felt her dress fall to the ground, and then he was pulling her chemise over her head, and she was naked before him. He took a step back to study her.

"You are a siren," he whispered. He traced a finger down her neck. "Your skin is soft like silk." Cyn closed her eyes as he stroked down her breast and across one nipple.

She was then being lifted into Leo's arms, and he carried her to the bed, lowering her gently onto the mattress. He then shrugged out of his jacket and tugged off his boots. Lastly, he pulled off his necktie and shirt. His breeches he left on. *For now,* Cyn thought.

"Are you sure?" he asked her again, and she nodded when she could find no words.

There were nerves but no doubts. Cyn's need to be close to this man she had always loved was strong. But this love was a great deal different. This was raw and so real that she felt it deep inside.

He braced himself over her and then kissed her again. Stroking, touching, igniting yet more fire.

"Open your legs for me, my sweet."

She did as he asked, and then his fingers were there, stroking her in a place only she had touched before. His caresses were gentle as he found the taut bud between her thighs.

"Leo," she whispered, awed at the sensations.

His kiss was hard and possessive as he slid fingers between the damp folds below and inside her. She moaned softly, and then he was taking her nipple into his mouth, and she shattered beneath him.

"That's it, Cyn, let go for me," he whispered, continuing the sensual torment until she shuddered and then slumped onto the mattress.

"I've never... I didn't know," she whispered.

"Clearly your husband was an inept lover," Leo gritted out, climbing from the bed. He then removed his breeches, and she got her first real look at him. All the sleek hardness of his body and the jutting arousal between his thighs.

"You are beautiful," Cyn whispered.

"No, that title is for you," he said, bracing himself over her again. "Take me inside you, Cyn."

Tell him.

But she didn't, instead opening her legs again. He settled between them, their eyes meeting.

"Are you sure?" he whispered.

"I am."

He eased inside her, thrusting until he was fully seated. Cyn had tried to swallow the cry of pain and failed.

"No!" He looked down at her. "Dear God, you're a virgin."

It hurt, but the pain was nothing compared to the feeling of him deep inside. It was as if they were one.

"Damn you, you should have told me." He growled the words at her, his face inches from hers.

"How?" She moved.

"Don't move!"

She did so again, and he moaned. Easing out of her body, he slid back inside.

"Too good," he rasped. "You feel too good for me to stop."

"Then don't," she said into his neck, her arms holding him tight.

He thrust back into her slowly, again and again. Cyn felt the tension climb inside her once more, and then that wonderful rush of heat and pleasure. Above her, Leo arched and reached his own release. He rolled, landing on the bed beside her.

"You should have told me," he said long minutes later.

"They weren't easy words to say." Cyn rolled onto her side to look at him.

"I had a right to know. I could have hurt you." She heard the anger in his voice. Gone was the man who had just made love to her. The man who had shown her over the last few days what being protected felt like.

"Leo, my husband married me to be a mother for his children, but he did not want me for anything else, as he still loved his mistress," Cyn said. "How was I to tell you that humiliating piece of information?"

"You should have tried," he said, his voice hard. "I could have hurt you."

"You didn't, and I'm sorry I did not tell you I was a virgin, Leo."

"You deliberately misled me, Cyn."

She didn't know how to answer that, because she had. Cyn had never said outright she was experienced but never denied it either.

"I don't like people lying to me," he said, moving to the side of the bed, away from her.

"I lied to you because admitting the truth was humiliating," Cyn said, sitting up and wrapping the blanket around her.

He pulled on his breeches and then rose to grab his shirt.

"You are leaving because I didn't tell you?"

"No... yes," he said.

"Well, what is it?"

He spun to face her. His eyes shadowed.

"This... all of it, I don't know...." His words fell away. "We need to deal with the Baddon Boys before—"

"We think about what is between us?" she finished for him. "And now I have angered you, which has given you a reason to leave."

"No."

"Yes. God. I am a fool," Cyn whispered.

"You are not a fool," he gritted out.

"I am, because today I let myself believe that maybe we... no, it matters not. Just go, Leo."

"You have children—"

"Don't you dare use them to run from me again!"

Leo had broken through her resistance and slid into her heart. Him and his family, and she'd felt a kernel of hope start to grow that maybe a future could lie there for her, Simon, and Meg. But now he was putting distance between them because she'd not been truthful with him. Because he feared what lay between them.

This man had hurt her once, and he was about to do so again. But unlike last time, she would show no one her pain. If Kenneth had taught her anything, it was how to hide what she felt deep inside. Closing her eyes, she exhaled slowly. When she opened them, her expression was empty.

"Go home, Leo. I don't think there is anything further to say. Yes, I lied to you and that was wrong, but I don't believe that is the only reason you are reacting as you are. You are scared—"

"Don't believe you know my thoughts." He glared at her.

"Well, tell me what you are thinking then," she snapped. The wonderful lethargy she'd felt after their lovemaking had gone. Now every muscle ache and pain in her body hurt along with her heart.

He began buttoning up his shirt in silence.

"You kissed me and looked after me. I-I tried to keep a

distance between us, but you saved me twice, and then today helped my staff. You took me to be with your family and take part in those games. You pushed me to accept you," Cyn said coolly, when inside her heart was shattering again. But this time, she knew it would hurt more. "But now you are using my lie to put distance between us."

He opened his mouth to speak, but Cyn held up her hand. "I want you to go." She rose, taking the blanket with her. Wrapping it around her body, she then walked to the door and unlocked it. "Unlike you, I grew up, and I won't let you destroy me a second time. Please leave," she added, opening it.

"I didn't destroy you," he gritted out.

"Get out of my house and my life."

"No. That is not happening. We will work this out when you are safe."

"You have no wish to work anything out, my lord. Because I have children, and when you are with me, you feel emotion, and you don't want that in your life."

"Cyn—"

"Get out," she said slowly.

He walked by her, and she stepped back out of his reach when he stopped before her. They stared at each other, and then he left. Cyn closed the door softly behind him and turned the key in the lock once more.

Moving to the window, she watched him walk outside minutes later, now dressed in his coat and hat. He turned to look up at her window. She stepped back and went to her bed.

Lying there, Cyn gave in to the tears that wanted to fall. She let them slide down her cheeks until she was done. She would weep no more. Tomorrow she would then set about eradicating Leo from her heart a second time.

CHAPTER THIRTY-ONE

Panic had been the only word for what he'd felt after making love to Cyn in her bedroom. When he'd realized she was a virgin, the anger had given him something to hold on to when inside he was reeling. He'd never felt such fierce emotion before.

He was currently seated in a public house three days after he'd walked out on her, drinking ale, feeling sorry for himself, and, at the same time, loathing the gutless way he'd behaved. With distance from Cyn, reality had returned.

"Another, my lord?"

"Please," he said to the waitress.

Leo had rebuilt the walls around his emotions after what happened with his father and vowed no one would penetrate them. Since Cyn's return to his life, he felt cracks forming, and that scared him.

How could Lord Lowell not have loved her, when everything Leo knew about Cyn made him love her more? He could allow himself to acknowledge that silently.

Clearly, her late husband had been a dictator. He'd taken a young woman, reeling from the loss of the man she'd believed she would spend the rest of her life with, and molded her into the woman he wanted to raise his children and then controlled her. Cyn hadn't confirmed that, but he knew it for the truth.

Unlike you, I grew up, and I won't let you destroy me a second time.

She'd said those words to him, and he'd walked away from her because he feared the hold she had over him. The power he would give her if he acknowledged what lay in his heart.

Since the day Ellen had knocked on his bedroom door crying, he'd made himself change. Shut himself away from what could hurt him.

He could still picture every detail of the day his father had taken his life with clarity. Staggering out of bed with a sore head after overindulging the night before and angry that someone was disturbing his precious sleep, he'd wrenched his door open. One look at the white face of his sister had stopped the roar he'd wanted to let loose. Leo had grabbed her shoulders as she swayed into him.

"What?" he'd demanded.

"H-he's dead, Leo."

His first thought had been Alex. His brother, who had been wounded away fighting for his country. He'd managed to rasp out his name. Ellen had shaken her head, her eyes huge in her pale face as she'd looked up at him.

"F-father. I-I found him."

Things were a little less clear after that. Leo had taken her hand, and they'd run together down the stairs and into his father's office. The butler had thrown a blanket over their father, but he'd seen the blood. Pulling his sister close, he shielded her, but she'd seen it... all of it.

"I hate you, Father," he muttered. *Hate the gutless coward you were.*

"So here you are," Alex said, sliding into the booth opposite him. "I have been trudging around London since I woke from my midday nap, which I had taken, as Harriet is from home. I went to the house to find you because I was bored, and Matilda told me you had left, and, in fact, you had barely been seen since the day of the Crabbett Close games."

"I have been busy," Leo said.

"You look sullen and out of sorts."

"I am neither," Leo said after a large mouthful of beer.

"Now we both know that is not true. Gray said that he and some of his fellow law enforcement colleagues are bringing in Baddon Boys to interview them."

"Good," Leo said. "She won't be safe until something is done. That Wolf needs to be stopped."

"Hello, darling, could I have an ale and an apple and blackberry pie?" Alex said, smiling at the waitress. She smiled back. Leo rolled his eyes.

"Manners cost nothing," Alex said, catching his look.

"You are married."

"To the woman that holds my heart and soul. But I can still smile and be nice to others. It is hardly their fault I am married."

Leo just stared at his brother.

"What's wrong, Leo? I thought the night of the Crabbett Close games, you and Cyn were close and drawing closer. We had hoped that perhaps—"

"I argued with her and made a fool of myself," Leo found himself saying, much to his surprise.

"Why?" Alex now had a serious expression on his face.

Leo looked into his ale. "She could hurt me." He felt raw and exposed, but this was his brother, his best friend. If he was to talk to anyone about Cyn, it was him.

"Yes, she could, but I doubt the woman who looked at you the way Cyn did would ever want to."

"How did she look at me?" Leo stared at his brother.

"Like the sun rose when you did, and now I want you to listen to me, Leo."

He nodded.

"I have many strong, honorable men in my life, Leo, but I have always counted you as the strongest and most honorable. You have a huge heart and capacity for love, which we, your family, are lucky to be the recipients of. But there is enough room in you to love Cyn and her children also. Let her in, brother. She is the woman for you now. Before, it was a young love, but this, what I see lies between you, is different."

"I have never felt what I do for Cyn with anyone before, Alex. I love you… everyone, but this… it feels like a vise has been placed around my heart. My chest burns when she is near, and…"

"And?" Alex prompted.

"She makes me weak and vulnerable. I never wanted to be that again."

"She also strengthens you, Leo. Harriet has changed me on the inside. I may laugh and joke and enjoy food more than is possibly good for me, but inside my heart is now full. I am loved by the most wonderful woman, who understands me. Harriet loves me for me. She sees my weakness, and my strength, and she has completed me, Leo."

He did not stop the tear that rolled down his cheek at his brother's words. "It is all I have ever wanted for you… all of you."

"I know it is, but it is also all we've ever wanted for you, brother. You have walked around presenting a facade to the world that you are the strong Lord Seddon, but inside you had darkness and demons that we could never reach. But Cyn has. Don't turn from that, brother."

Leo lowered his forehead to the table and felt Alex's hand on his head, patting it gently.

"Now that we have bared our souls, I am ravenous, and just in time for this lovely lady to bring me pie. Two forks, I think, my dear. My brother is hungry also."

"I love you, brother," Leo said, lifting his head.

"As I love you. Now we eat, and then you find her."

"I am a fool," Leo said.

"It happens to us all before we capitulate. It's a last struggle to hold on to the life we know."

"Very likely." He took the fork the waitress handed him and ate a piece of pie.

"You'll need a grand gesture, you know," Alex said.

Leo sighed. He knew exactly what he would have to do.

...

Leo walked up the steps to the Abbott town house alone the following evening. He knew his family would follow shortly. But he had to do this alone for her.

He moved into the receiving line and attempted to ignore those around him and the shocked whispers that he was there. The Duke of Raven's ball had been another matter entirely that people in trade, industrialists, and nobles had frequented. Those that would step into this event would have blue blood like him. Although not quite as tainted.

"Good evening, Lord Seddon," the Duke of Abbott said as he reached him. "It is wonderful to see you again."

"You also, Duke." Leo bowed to him and his duchess. He then moved on to the door that would lead to the ballroom, which had stairs down, so everyone would have their eyes on him when he entered. *You can do this for her.*

"Lord Seddon," a servant announced loudly.

All eyes turned his way as he started down the stairs. Even those dancing, as if sensing something was happening, looked his way. He found her standing by a wall, which she had been doing at the Raven ball. Did she always do that? Have her back to something solid because that was how she protected herself?

He couldn't read her expression from here, but her eyes were on him. Reaching the last step, he headed in Cyn's direction. People greeted him, and he acknowledged them with a nod.

"Well past due, Seddon," the Duke of Raven said as he walked by him.

Cyn stood with her hands clenched at her sides, eyes wide as she watched him approach.

"Why are you here?" She held herself rigid, back pressed to the wall.

"Because I thought the only way to show you that I am truly sorry for the way I behaved and how much I love you was by stepping back into society."

There was no softening in her topaz eyes at his words.

"I won't have this discussion here, Leo."

"Will you dance with me?" he asked as a waltz started. Holding out a hand, Leo held her gaze. For the longest seconds, he thought she would refuse him, and then her small hand settled on his, and the muscles in his body eased.

Leading her to the dance floor, he nodded to his family, who were standing with the Duke and Duchess of Raven.

"Your family is here," Cyn whispered.

"To support me, and to show you they care."

"Th-that was kind of them."

"I'm not going anywhere, Cyn. I was scared and a fool. You were right, but I am no longer."

"And what has brought about this sudden change?" Her eyes were on his necktie.

"The realization that I don't want to spend my life without you."

"My children—"

"I will love them as if they were my own, as you do."

He heard the small sob and pulled her closer, and for now, it was enough that he had her in his arms. Tomorrow, they would talk, but not here, with people all around them.

"I say, Seddon, how wonderful to see you again," Lady Haverstock said as she danced by in the arms of a younger man Leo could not place.

"And you, my lady."

"Are you back with us for good?"

He looked Cyn in the eyes and said, "Yes."

CHAPTER THIRTY-TWO

He didn't know what had woken him, but something had. Sitting up in bed, Leo looked around, but no one had entered his room. Was one of his siblings having a nightmare? Pushing the covers aside, he went out to the hallway to listen, but all was silent.

Going back to bed, he let his mind wander to the night he'd just shared with Cyn.

It had been spent talking to people he hadn't conversed with in years and being attentive to her. She'd thawed and even smiled at him a few times, but Leo knew it would take more than the grand gesture of walking into a society ballroom—the stuff of nightmares for him—to make her understand he wanted a life with her and her children.

After he'd helped Cyn into her carriage when she was ready to leave, Leo had climbed in with her and kissed her gently. He'd then told her he loved her and would call on her tomorrow… today. She had simply said, "Very well," but the smile on her face had given him hope.

Leo had then ridden home with his aunt and uncle,

listening to them discuss the evening, and thankfully they had not pushed him to talk about Cyn.

Climbing out of bed again, Leo looked at his pocket watch. It was three in the morning. What had woken him? The vision of his cuff link slid into his head.

He was dressed and running down the stairs as quietly as he could in minutes. Pulling on his coat, he grabbed his cane and let himself out the door. Hurrying down the street, he knew there would be a few hackneys close. He needed to find a main thoroughfare.

Surely Cyn was safe? She'd promised him she would not leave her house with less than two Mulhollands on her heels. So why, then, was he running down the road in the early hours of the morning, searching yet again for his cuff link?

"Leo?"

"Ram?" He stopped, the breath wheezing in and out of his mouth. "What the hell are you doing riding about London at this time of night?"

"I have been to a club and got into a conversation with friends. Before I knew it, the next day had arrived." Ram looked as clearheaded as he would if it were morning.

"I need to get to Cyn's house."

"Oh, for the love of God, what do you have to find now?" Ram stuck out his foot and held out a hand. Leo took it and climbed on behind him.

"My cuff link."

"Surely not the same one?"

"Yes."

Ram clucked his tongue in disapproval. "Why the bloody hell did you give it back to her?"

"She asked."

"Love." Ram sighed. "Makes fools of sane men."

Ram galloped through London, weaving around any carriages and horses in his way, until he reached Cyn's street.

"Stop here," Leo said, pointing to the tall home farther down the street. "I will walk the rest of the way."

"I shall wait in case you need me."

Leo thanked Ram and then walked toward Cyn's house. *Was I foolish to have come?* As the thought left his head, he watched the front door open. Seconds later, a cloaked figure was running down the street in the opposite direction.

You little fool. Following, he stayed close as Cyn ran on, stopping only when she heard the clop of a hackney. She then spoke to the driver, giving the address of the agency. Opening the door, she climbed inside.

Leo ran beside it as the carriage started moving. Opening the door, he vaulted inside and closed it behind him.

"Get out!" Cyn screeched.

Leo faced her, and the next scream fell away. He took the seat across from her.

"I can't work out if you are incredibly stupid or incredibly brave to be walking about London alone at such an hour, knowing that men are already after you." His words came out with a definite snap to them. "Just hours ago, you were dancing with me at a ball. Not once did you mention you would be recklessly leaving the house in the early hours of the morning."

"I didn't know I would be," she snapped back.

"Why are you?"

She handed him the paper that was scrunched in her palm.

I will kill your staff if you do not come to the Phoenix Agency at once. You and I need to talk. Come alone, or I will start killing them.

"How the hell did you receive this?"

"It came through my window wrapped around a rock."

"You are not serious?"

"Well, they could hardly knock on the door, now, could they?"

"You should have sent for me immediately, or at the very least brought a Mulholland with you."

"They received word when I returned from the ball that their aunt is dying, so I sent them to visit with her for the evening. They made me promise I would not leave the house, which, of course, I gave them—"

"Well, that's a lie."

"You read that note, Leo."

"I'm sure you have another footman in that huge house of yours you could have brought with you."

She folded her arms. "My staff are in danger, and it said to come alone, so I am doing that."

"They always say come alone!" Leo roared.

"I will not be responsible for my staff being hurt."

"Damn you, Cyn, what part of *you are in danger* do you not understand? Why did you not send for me?"

"I know the danger this man presents and did not want you in his path."

"While that warms my heart, it also makes me bloody furious. You know I can look after you."

"And yet I will not take that risk." Her chin lifted. "I had hoped to find a constable on the way to assist me with the man who may, as we speak, be inside the Phoenix Agency."

Leo thought about Constable Plummy, who patrolled the streets of Crabbett Close. He was an idiot. A loud clap of thunder would scare him.

"You cannot simply run into danger," Leo said in what he thought was a reasonable tone, but her eyes narrowed, which suggested it hadn't been. He tried to force down his rage at the risk she had taken yet again.

"You are not responsible for me, Leo."

"I love you!" he roared. "I am now responsible for you, as you are for me."

She was silent for long seconds, thinking about what he said.

"As I love you," she said in a prim little voice.

"Excellent," he snapped back.

"Why were you outside my house, Leo?"

"Because I needed to find my bloody cuff link again."

She pulled it from her pocket and held it out, but he didn't take it.

"Keep it. At least I will always know when you need me."

"Thank you for coming to the ball, Leo," she whispered.

"You're welcome," he said, sounding anything but welcoming.

"I think that we may perhaps meet the Wolf tonight."

"So it would seem. Would you go to my family and tell them what is happening?"

"No."

"It was a faint hope at best." He sighed. "Do you have your pistol?"

"Yes, and I would have shot him had I come alone, if it was necessary for me to do so." She then sneezed loudly.

When the carriage stopped, they got out. There was a light on in the property next door. His property.

"I am going inside, and you are not."

"You are not going in there without me," Cyn said. She then pulled her pistol out of her pocket.

"I have no wish for you to misfire that thing until you have another target. Put it away at once," Leo said.

"Because I am a woman, I therefore cannot fire a pistol with accuracy?" she shot back at him.

Ignoring her, Leo said, "You will stay outside."

"I won't."

There was no time to argue, so he started down the side of the house. Taking the stairs down, he slipped through the opening in the fence, with Cyn on his heels. As they stepped inside the ground floor, they heard a scream.

CHAPTER THIRTY-THREE

Cyn's heart was beating hard inside her chest as she followed Leo. Clutching her pistol, she hoped all her staff were safe.

Leo kicked the door open and stepped into the room.

"Back away from the woman at once." His words were cold, voice hard.

"My woman," a voice said.

"You do not own her, as you do not own any of the women who are unfortunate enough to work for the Baddon Boys," Leo said. He stepped to the side, and Cyn could point her pistol at the man now.

Leo started circling him, taking the man's eyes with him and away from Mary and Clara, who were huddled together in a corner. *Where is Lewis?*

"Well now, that was easy," a voice said behind her, and then she felt the tip of a blade press to her neck. "Step away from my man, Lord Seddon."

Cyn couldn't see who was behind her.

"You've caused me a great deal of trouble, Lady Lowell, and bringing a lord here has made things difficult also. But I am a powerful man and not without the resources to clean up the mess we are going to have to make."

"Let her go, Wolf," Leo said.

"If you move one step, my lord, I will plunge this knife into your beloved's neck, and she will not survive."

Leo's face was a mask of rage and fear.

"Leave the women. We have plenty more. Lock the door. We must depart at once in case they alerted others. The boys are waiting outside, and as much as it would be easier to murder him, that would mean I'd have to move to another country."

"I won't let you hurt her," Leo said, his voice deadly.

"Shut the door and lock it."

The door was slammed before Leo could move, and then Cyn was thrown over a shoulder, and they were running up the steps.

Where is Lewis? Have they hurt my friend? How was she to get out of this? At least Leo, Mary, and Clara were safe. Thoughts tumbled through her head as they ran out the front door and down to the street.

The thunder of hooves greeted them. Cyn tried to see who rode those horses, but from her position upside down, it was difficult.

"Who the hell are they?" the Wolf demanded. "Hurry, we must leave. There are too many of them!" His voice sounded desperate now.

She was jostled as they ran, but the sound of breaking glass stopped them. Cyn was dropped to the ground at the loud roar. Looking up, she saw Leo climbing down the roof.

The thunder of hooves was getting closer. Someone was coming to save them; she was sure of it.

"Shoot him," the Wolf called.

Cyn leaped to her feet at the words and ran at the man with the gun now pointed toward Leo.

"No!" she screamed, launching herself at him.

The gun discharged, and she felt a burning feeling in her arm, and then she was falling.

"Cyn!" she heard Leo roar.

"I-I'm all right," she said, staggering back to her feet.

The horses arrived, and all hell broke loose. She saw Leo's uncle and Alex. Also Gray, his cousin, and Ellen. How had they all known to come?

She stayed upright even though her arm was throbbing with searing pain. Leo ran at the Wolf, swinging his cane. The fight was deadly, as the man still held his knife. Leo lashed out with his foot, and the knife flew free. He then launched himself at the man.

Easing around the fight, Cyn made it to the steps, as she would only be in the way and useless in her current state. She heard footsteps behind her.

"Dear Lord, you are bleeding, my lady," Mary said, crouching beside her.

"H-how did you get out?"

"Clara picked the lock." Cyn's arm was then raised, and she yelped at the pain. "I need to see," Mary said.

"Soon. Wh-what is happening?" She tried to focus, but her head felt light.

"Lord Seddon is punching the Wolf. Good shot, my lord!" Mary called.

"The others, who I don't know, are doing well too. The Baddon Boys are being subdued," Clara said, clapping.

Cyn heard thuds as fists met flesh.

"It's over," Clara said finally, what felt like a long time later. "We won." As that meant her side, Cyn knew relief. Leo was alive and safe, as were Mary and Clara.

"Lewis?" she whispered.

"I'll find him," Clara said.

"Cyn!" Leo appeared before her.

"I-I am all right," she whispered, looking up at him. His expression was savage. "It's just my arm."

He didn't acknowledge her, as he was busy taking off her coat and wrapping it around her. She then heard a ripping sound as he tore open her sleeve.

"Get me something to bind it," he ordered. "And any spirits also."

"Here." A flask appeared, and Cyn thought a mouthful of that would be most welcome about now.

"Has it gone through?" Alex asked.

"Yes," Leo gritted out.

"I am quite w-well." But that was a lie. She was feeling odd now. Almost detached.

"Be quiet. You are not quite well and are bleeding excessively," Leo snapped.

"Oh dear, am I?"

"Don't look."

"I'm not bothered by blood," Cyn said. Her voice sounded weak and distant.

"I am when it's yours."

"Let me look," Uncle Bram said.

"He shot her, Uncle." She heard the desperation in Leo's words.

"I am not b-bothered by blood," Cyn whispered again.

"I found Lewis. He is all right, just a bit groggy," Clara called.

"This will hurt, Cyn," Leo said.

"What?" She looked down at her arm and watched as he poured what was in the flask directly on the bullet wound. Cyn shrieked as fire raced down her arm.

"We need to stave off infection," Leo said.

She squeezed her eyes shut as he bandaged her arm, fighting back the tears that wanted to leak out of her eyes. The pain was terrible. "Flask," she rasped.

Bramstone held it up to her lips. "Just a little now, Cyn. Sips, that's it. Good girl."

"Thank you."

His smile was so gentle, it made her cry. "I would have liked an uncle like you."

"Well now, how handy that soon you will have one, sweetheart." Leo's uncle then leaned down and kissed her cheek softly. "It will be all right now, Cyn. We'll look after you and your children."

She sobbed then. Deep sobs coming from that place inside her that wanted to be loved.

"Stop making the woman I love weep, Uncle," Leo said. "It is done now, Cyn." And then he was there, kneeling in front of her. His worried brown eyes were inches from hers.

"You are hurt and sobbing, so I will save the yelling at your reckless actions until you are better," he said gently.

"I-I would be grateful," she whispered. "But my actions were not reckless. I was s-saving you," Cyn hiccupped.

"And got yourself shot by flying like Boudica at a large man with a gun!"

"I thought you weren't yelling at me," Cyn whispered.

"He could have killed you." His hands cupped her face. "Do you understand that? You could have died tonight, and I would have been destined to live a life in hell without you."

"Perhaps you can bare your souls later, as she needs attention, and we will be once again waking Mr. Greedy from his beauty sleep," Uncle Bram said.

Leo kissed her softly and then lifted her into his arms. Minutes later, she was on a horse before him. His arms held her close.

"I love you," he whispered.

"I love you too."

"But I'm still angry with you."

Her shoulder burned, and her children didn't know him.

In fact, there was a great deal of uncertainty in her life. But right now, she just wanted to close her eyes and enjoy being held by Leo, which was exactly what she did.

...

She woke when he carried her into the house. Not her house, but his uncle's. She was stripped to her chemise and placed on a soft bed, which felt wonderful.

Warm water was then brought, and she was washed, which was not wonderful, as it hurt her arm. Leo stayed at her side the entire time; it was no matter that his aunt had tried to get him out of the room.

He held her hand, and his eyes stayed on her face the entire time. When she winced in pain, he leaned over her and kissed her gently, telling her how brave she was, and when she was well, he would yell at her some more.

"I'm here," a jolly voice said. She knew that voice. It was Mr. Greedy. "Well now, what have you done to yourself, my lady?" he said, appearing above her. "Let me see that arm, but first, I'll give you something for the pain."

Foul-tasting liquid was held up to her nose, and she gagged. Leo held her nose until she opened her mouth, and Mr. Greedy poured it in.

"Was that n-necessary?" Cyn gasped as the liquid burned down her throat.

"I simply expedited matters," he said. "It works with my siblings, so I thought it would with you."

Leo held her arm still as Mr. Greedy poured something that felt like fire onto it, and then he stitched the bullet hole together. Finally, her torment was over. The old man then patted her cheek and said he would be back tomorrow.

Cyn closed her eyes and fell into an exhausted sleep. When she woke, the sun was filtering through the curtain.

"You're awake." Leo was in the doorway, looking tired and

rumpled, carrying a tray. He lowered it to the side table. "How do you feel?"

"Sore," she croaked. He helped her up and then gave her a drink, which she gulped down.

"I sent word to your household, alerting them to what happened," Leo said, sitting in the seat beside her bed. "The Wolf is in a cell, as are his henchmen. Everyone at the Phoenix Agency is in high spirits and, as we speak, moving back into it."

"Thank you."

"I nearly lost you," he said slowly. "And I realized that to ensure that doesn't happen again, I will need to live at your side, Cyn." He took the hand she held out to him in both of his and kissed her fingers.

"I'm all right, Leo."

"I know, but I want to say something."

She nodded.

"I didn't ask you properly last time. The young fool that I was left it until it was too late. Had I asked you to marry me sooner, perhaps I would have gone through what I did with you at my side."

"No." She touched his lips. "We needed to change and grow, no matter how much that has hurt us in different ways."

"Will you marry me, Cyn? Be my love and my life. I want to help you raise your children and be a family with them and you."

"You don't know my children," she said.

"I will get to know them and love them as you do. Marry me, Cyn."

"Yes," she whispered, reaching for happiness. "Yes, please."

CHAPTER THIRTY-FOUR

"Good Lord, Mrs. Greedy has a new dress."

Leo looked to where she was making her way into the pew slowly, with her husband behind her, also looking dapper in a deep maroon jacket.

"Is that Uncle Bram's old jacket?" Leo asked.

"He didn't want it anymore, and Aunt Ivy asked if Mr. Greedy would like it. I believe Mavis Johns took the sides in for him," Alex said.

"This place," Ram said from beside him. "There are no words."

Today, Leo was marrying Cyn, and to his mind, it was long past time that he woke with her in his arms each morning. He wanted them to be a family with Meg and Simon. His family, Leo thought.

In the months since he'd asked her to marry him, he'd spent most of his time with them. They hadn't told Simon and Meg immediately of their plans, but when they had, their reactions had been pleased.

"Good Lord, why is Mr. Peeky walking down my carpet

drinking that glass full of thick black liquid that will likely stain," Ram said from Leo's other side.

"We will have them cleaned," Alex said. "But to be fair, you offered again."

"Like I've ever had a choice. Mr. Alvin simply appeared at my door, stating there was another wedding, and my hall runner was required for the aisle," Ram said.

"And very generous it was of you," Leo added.

"Why are you not trembling with nerves like the other grooms who've come before you?" Ram demanded of Leo.

"I'm marrying the woman I love. What is there to be nervous about?"

"That your freedom is over," Ram replied. "From this day forth, all decisions are to be debated with another person."

"I have no issue with that," Leo said, looking at the guests. The Sinclair and Raven families took up many of the pews, all dressed in their finest. Cam was smiling, likely due to the feast he would shortly sit down to eat.

The Crabbett Close residents sat on the bride's side, and Tabitha Varney wore a hat with so many flowers and feathers, Mr. Greedy, who now sat behind her, was in danger of losing an eye. She was making eyes at Mungo, who was standing to keep an eye on things. Arms folded and wearing a kilt, he wore his usual grumpy expression.

"I asked Mr. Alvin where the pews came from, and he said that he has connections in high places. It was all very secretive, and he would not tell me more," Alex said.

"It's best not to question what the residents in this town do," Leo said.

"I had wondered if she would come today, seeing as she is due to have the babe any moment," Ram said as their eyes went to the aisle.

"It's her brother's wedding. Of course she's here," Leo protested.

Ellen was waddling down the aisle on the arm of her husband, who had declined being a groomsman because he wanted to support her today. She wore lemon and looked beautiful, even with that large belly holding his niece or nephew.

"I swear, this baby has no wish to be born," he heard her mutter.

"Would you, knowing what the family it's coming into is capable of?" Gray teased her. He then lowered her into the seat next to Harriet. She collapsed with a loud sigh and then smiled at Leo.

"Are you all right?" he mouthed to her. Ellen nodded, but Leo saw how tired she looked.

"Close your eyes, Leo," Alex said.

"What? Why?"

"Just do it, and don't ask why," his brother said.

Leo closed his eyes. Long seconds later, Alex told him to open them, and there she was. His beautiful bride, standing at the beginning of the aisle on the arm of her son.

"Step aside, Leo, I may just have to take your place," Ram said.

"I'll kill you first."

She was magnificent. Her dress was a soft blush pink with an overskirt of lace. Cyn's hair was a mass of curls, with rose-buds pinned through it. In her hands, she held long-stemmed roses.

Leo wanted to walk down the aisle to greet her, but Simon was walking her to him. He stayed where he was.

Cyn had told her family she was to marry again, but they had declined to attend, and Leo thought that was likely due to the fact she was marrying a disgraced Nightingale. But she hadn't minded, telling him she was more than happy with the new family she now had.

Meg, Anna, Fred, and Matilda, holding Lottie's hand, all

walked before her, dressed in cream and carrying pink roses too.

Cyn, like him, showed no sign of nerves. Her eyes were on him, as his were on her. That this beautiful, strong woman loved him was humbling.

She'd healed well, but the scar on her arm was still a reminder of how he'd nearly lost her.

Together, they had purchased a new house to help women who needed to escape their lives across London. This she had tasked Lewis and Mary to run.

They were here in the front row, holding hands. That night of terror had galvanized Lewis into declaring his feelings for Mary, and she'd reciprocated. Seated with them was Clara, who had decided she wanted to stay and take Mary's place at the Phoenix Agency. She was almost unrecognizable from the woman he'd met that day.

"Hello," Cyn whispered when she reached Leo and Simon had returned to his seat.

"You take my breath away, sweetheart."

"I'm so happy, Leo."

He kissed her softly. "As am I, my love."

The service began, and Leo spoke when he was told to speak, as did Cyn, both in loud, clear voices. They then turned to face their family and friends as husband and wife.

Aunt Ivy was weeping, and Uncle Bram was close. *Happiness*, Leo thought, *it was everywhere today.*

"Well, kiss her then!" Cambridge Sinclair roared. "It's time to eat."

He faced his wife. Leaning in, he whispered, "I love you," against her lips and then kissed her softly.

"Come along, Lady Seddon," Leo said, taking her hand. "Let's eat."

Large tables had been set up, and a long trestle was buckling under the weight of the food piled on it.

"Ah, Leo."

Turning, he looked at Alex.

"What?"

"Two things, actually," his brother said, considerably paler than he was just minutes before. "Ellen has gone into labor, and our cousin is here."

"Where is Ellen?"

Alex pointed to where his sister was being led toward 11 Crabbett Close by Essex Huntington and Gray. Aunt Ivy and Bud were following. Mr. Greedy was on the move also, heading to his house to no doubt collect his medical supplies.

"Shall I follow them?" Cyn asked, sounding worried.

"Gray told me he would send word if they needed anyone else but to carry on with the reception for now, as her labor could take hours," Alex added.

"Which cousin?" Leo then asked his brother.

"Aunt Elizabeth's daughter Abigail. She's over there with Harriet and Uncle Bram."

Leo felt Cyn's arm slide around his waist, and he did the same to her, pulling her closer. His wife, he thought, here at his side.

"Which daughter was she?"

"The youngest one with the squeaky voice who used to shoot her slingshot at us when Mother visited her sister."

"Well then," Cyn said. "She should fit right in."

Leo snorted and then kissed her again. "Right. Let's greet my long-lost cousin, then eat and drink, because I have a feeling we will need it. Trust Ellen to want her baby to share our wedding day."

...

Alice Ellen Fletcher was born four hours later. Mother and baby were doing well. Gray stumbled out of the house and straight for the table that held alcohol. After downing a dram of whisky, he was able to tell them all that his daughter was the loveliest child ever born and his wife was an angel.

"My first took twelve hours," Mrs. Douglas was heard to mutter. "It hardly seems fair Mrs. Fletcher's was only four."

After visiting Ellen and his perfect niece—Gray had been right—Leo took Cyn in his arms on the dance floor.

"Another excellent wedding, Seddon," Lord Nicholas Braithwaite said, dancing by with his wife, Alice. "I was just commenting again on how you lot are very similar to our family."

"Thank you, my lord. I believe that is a compliment," Leo said.

Cyn giggled.

"So, this is true happiness," Leo said. "I thought I knew what that was, but the truth was far from it."

She smiled up at him with so much love that his throat felt tight.

"And it has only just begun," she whispered.

...

Thank you for reading THE FALLEN VISCOUNT. I hope you enjoyed Leo and Cyn's story.

Book #4 in the Notorious Nightingales series THE REBELLIOUS RAKE will be available soon, read on for the blurb!

Can he out run the sins of his past?

. . .

With the death of his father, Ramsey Hellion returned to England to distance himself from the hell he'd left behind. The day he met Miss Flora Thomas, his life took another turn.

Haughty and beautiful, she was a strong-willed woman who disliked him at first glance. Ram had always enjoyed a challenge, even one who refuses to yield to his charms.

The day his father's sins came back to haunt him, Ram realized he needs a great deal more from Flora than just her love. He needs her to save him.

Can she trust him with her heart?

Flora loathed men born with tolerable looks who believed they should be adored because they exist. Ramsey Hellion was one such man, so why did he intrigue her so much? Perhaps it was because when his rakish facade slipped, she saw turmoil beneath.

She'd learned the hard way how difficult a woman's life can be when controlled by a man, but when danger steps back into Ramsey's life, she must act. Flora knows she'll do what it takes to keep him safe, because no matter how much she's denied it, life without Ramsey Hellion was not something she wished to contemplate.

ABOUT THE AUTHOR

Wendy Vella is a USA Today and Amazon bestselling author of historical romances filled with romance, intrigue, unconventional heroines, and dashing heroes.

An incurable romantic, Wendy found writing romance a natural fit. Born and raised in a rural area in the North Island of New Zealand, she shares her life with one adorable husband, two delightful adult children and their partners, four delicious grandchildren, and her pup Tilly.

Wendy also writes contemporary romances under the name Lani Blake.

You can also follow her here:
Website: wendyvella.com
Facebook: authorwendyvella
Instagram: wendy.vella_author
BookBub: bookbub.com/profile/wendy-vella
Readers Group:
facebook.com/groups/wendyvellareaders

Printed in Great Britain
by Amazon